THE ROOM IN THE ATTIC

LOUISE DOUGLAS

Boldwood

First published in Great Britain in 2021 by Boldwood Books Ltd.

Copyright © Louise Douglas, 2021

Cover Design by Alice Moore Design

Cover Imagery: Shutterstock and Alamy

A CIP catalogue record for this book is available from the British Library.

Paperback ISBN 978-1-80048-601-0

Large Print ISBN 978-1-80048-597-6

Hardback ISBN 978-1-80162-780-1/

Ebook ISBN 978-1-80048-595-2

Kindle ISBN 978-1-80048-596-9

Audio CD ISBN 978-1-80048-602-7

MP3 CD ISBN 978-1-80048-599-0

Digital audio download ISBN 978-1-80048-594-5

Boldwood Books Ltd
23 Bowerdean Street
London SW6 3TN
www.boldwoodbooks.com

For Amaia and Sofia.
With all my love xxx

1

The night before I returned to All Hallows I dreamed I was walking barefoot along the attic corridor. As I passed the fourth door, I became aware of little fires burning in that dark room: on the rug, in the curtains and a dozen other places. I began to run, but the further I ran, the further the corridor stretched ahead of me and the more the fires burned, and I knew that I would never reach the end. There was no escape.

My wife woke me; a hand on my shoulder. 'Lewis! Wake up! You're having one of your nightmares.'

It took me a moment to bring myself back to the present: to our warm, untidy bedroom, pillows, a duvet; a wine glass on the bedside table; the dog snoring on his rug in the window bay. The room was dark, the city beyond still sleeping.

'Sorry,' I whispered. 'Sorry to wake you,' and I kissed my wife's hand and slid out of bed and went downstairs to drink a glass of water in the kitchen.

It was 4 a.m. The dying hour. I sat at the table, moved aside our youngest son's homework, and picked up the auction house catalogue that I'd left lying face-down on the table next to the fruit bowl.

I turned it over. The cover headline read: 'Rare Redevelopment Opportunity'. Beneath it, the picture of a derelict building was captioned: 'All Hallows. Grade II listed Victorian asylum/boarding school, outbuildings, 50 acres of walled grounds. Prime countryside location.'

There it was, in full colour: the same long, forbidding building with the bell tower at its centre that I revisited in my nightmares. If I looked hard enough, I could almost see through the windows to the pupils sitting at their desks in the classrooms: those ranks of boys in their brown sweaters and trousers, with identical close-shaven haircuts. I could almost smell the dust burning in the elbows of the big old radiators, hear the relentless ticking of the clocks on the walls. And there, outside, were young boys with their bony knees and striped socks, shivering as they grouped on the rugby field; the padded bumpers used to practise tackles laid out on the grass; the swagger of the sports master with his great, muscly thighs. 'Three Rolls', we used to call him because he walked as if he was carrying three rolls of wallpaper under each arm.

The auction had taken place a fortnight earlier, the building sold to clients of the firm of architects for whom I worked. If they'd asked my advice before the sale, I'd have told them not to buy it, but by the time the catalogue reached my desk, the paperwork had been signed, the deal was done.

I dropped my head into my hands.

I did not want to have to return to All Hallows. What I wanted was to speak to Isak, to hear his voice, and be rallied out of my anxiety by his dry humour. I picked up my phone and was on the point of calling him, but then I heard my mother whisper in my ear: *Lewis, don't. It's not fair to disturb him, not at this hour!*

I put down the phone, grabbed my coat and went into the garden to wait for the sunrise.

The All Hallows site had been purchased by an American company that specialised in converting abandoned European country piles into luxury living accommodation. My employers, Redcliffe Architects, had already collaborated with them on a former tuberculosis sanatorium in Switzerland and a dilapidated château in the Loire Valley, both lucrative projects. Everyone at Redcliffe knew we'd be front runners for the design work at All Hallows if we submitted a half-decent proposal.

The chief partner, Mo Masud, asked me to go to Dartmoor to take some pictures and scope out the site. It wasn't an unusual request and normally I enjoyed nothing more than poking around historic edifices, imagining how they might be brought back to life. I was Mo's right-hand man. It was my job to go. Still, I put off the mission for as long as I could, hoping something might happen to prevent me from returning to my former school. Deep down, I knew the last-minute reprieve I prayed for wasn't going to come. No matter how I tried to put the name All Hallows and all that it represented out of my mind, like shame it clung to me. Day by day the sense of encroaching dread increased and none of the usual distractions worked. I drank on school nights. I got up stupidly early to run for miles. My wife kept asking what was wrong. I couldn't tell her. It wasn't that I didn't trust her, it was simply that I did not have the vocabulary to explain what it was that was eating at me.

I couldn't avoid All Hallows for ever. The name popped up in the headings of emails and messages at work. A file was opened in the Tenders Pending folder and draft graphics of marketing flags saying: 'Exclusive homes for sale' appeared on the printer. Mo told me the Americans had asked for a meeting the following week. We needed the information. We needed it now.

* * *

The day I drove to Dartmoor was a typical early autumn day: the sky moody; a sullen rain falling. As I passed the once-noble sculpture of the giant withy man at the side of the M5 in Somerset, I remembered how, as we drove this same motorway more than three decades earlier, Mum used to put on a Now That's What I Call Music! cassette to keep me and my sister, Isobel, entertained, and we'd all sing along. Mum had a friend who owned a static caravan on a site outside Newquay. We used to spend our summer holidays there, Isobel, Mum and I, bodyboarding, picnicking on the beach, sitting round campfires on chilly evenings, listening to the waves crashing onto the sand. Dad never came with us. Isobel and I used to feel sorry for him, all alone at home working while we were having fun, but Mum said he preferred it that way.

The reed beds that used to surround the withy man were gone now and he was dwarfed by development. A melancholy descended on me as I passed him, poor fading thing. I put some of Isak's music on, turned the volume up loud to try to drown out the memories of the boy I used to be.

The journey from Bristol that day was straightforward, but once on Dartmoor I struggled to find the route back to my old school amongst the tangle of lanes. The landmarks I thought I recognised – stone stacks, brooks and copses – turned out to be red herrings. Soon, I was disorientated and I felt the old anxiety lurking around me, a creeping, bony-fingered thing.

I bumped the VW along rutted old lanes that went nowhere and carried out harried, nine-point turns in muddy gateways, beady-eyed sheep staring at me while their jaws rotated like teenagers chewing gum. There was no signal for the maps app on my phone. If the developers decided to go ahead with this project, access would be a nightmare. These ancient country byways had not been designed to cope with flatbed lorries weighed down by materials. A steady rain fell now, dulling the colours and blurring the verges and the drystone walls. It felt as if hours had passed before, at last, I found the turning to All Hallows at the end of a narrow, unkempt road. I followed the track and the Gothic gates loomed over the entrance.

This was it. I was here.

I left the car by the gates, turned up the collar of my coat and stepped into the abandoned grounds of All Hallows, built in 1802 as a lunatic asylum and refashioned a hundred and fifty years later as a boarding school for boys.

What was left of the place was quietly falling down inside a thick wall originally built to keep the former asylum inmates inside. Large stretches of the wall were hidden behind the over-hanging branches of grand old beech trees and beneath swathes of brambles that had grown over and around it. I took some photographs, a small video; made some voice notes. There was a rustle in the undergrowth. A squirrel darted out and ran across the lawn. A crow cawed and I jumped.

Grow a backbone, Tyler, I told myself and I heard, back through the years, the voice of one of the masters barking at me, telling me to stand up straight, stop slouching, walk like a man! I recalled Isak's quiet grimace of camaraderie and I smiled to myself. He was the best friend I ever had.

The rain was relentless; puddling the ground; dripping through the trees.

I walked forward, taking photographs with my phone.

The main building still stood grand and bullish even though its disintegration was clear. The clock tower at the centre of the façade was intact, along with most of the buildings on either side, but both recumbent stone lions on the pedestals at the foot of the steps were damaged, there were holes in the steeply sloping roof and chunks missing from the walls. Lichen and weeds had taken hold and birds had nested in the cracks in the masonry. Guttering hung from beneath the roof edges, drawing sharp diagonal lines. The west wing, where the fire had caused most damage, had never been repaired and was slumped like an old drunk crouching on one knee. I walked around that part of the school, trying to see through cracked and smoke-darkened windows.

Random memories flashed into my mind: Isak running across the grounds, his legs mud-spattered, his trainers soaked, elbows poking out and his orange hair sticking to his head, one of a long line of boys doing cross-country in the rain; Isak in our bedroom, sitting on the sill with his legs dangling out of the window, blowing smoke rings into the sky. He taking my hand after I'd been hit with the ruler, putting his cold flannel on the palm to soothe the burning; the two of us bound in a friendship so intense that I never felt quite myself if Isak wasn't with me.

I was twitchy. Overtired, overcaffeinated, overwrought. I kept seeing things that weren't there. What looked like a body was an old piece of plastic sheeting with puddles forming in the dips of its creases. What I first saw as a gravestone planted in the court-yard turned out to be an abandoned fridge.

'Stupid,' I muttered to myself, 'don't be so stupid!'

But the anxieties were multiplying. Looking up, I saw some-thing that might have been a face staring from a cobwebbed window. There were movements in the shadows, footsteps behind me, the sound of a child's laughter, the smell of smoke. I pressed the camera button over and over, taking as many pictures as I could as quickly as I could. I paused to flick through those I'd taken. They all showed the main building and its surrounding architecture. But there were other structures: the old stables; the caretaker's cottage; the lodge; the chapel. There had been an outdoor swimming pool, the lake with the folly on its overgrown island. We'd need a record of these features too.

The rain was falling more heavily now.

I headed towards the chapel. I didn't want to get too close. When I was near enough to zoom in for a photograph, I did so. Then I walked to the approximate middle of the grounds and I set the camera to make a panoramic video, and slowly rotated through 360 degrees, holding the device at right angles to my body. I took one clockwise and one anticlockwise, then tucked the phone inside my coat so I could look at the screen without it getting soaked. There was something odd about the second panorama. A woman appeared three times in the image, once at a distance, as if she was standing waist-deep in the lake. Then again, closer. The third time she was almost right in front of me – right behind where I was standing now.

I turned sharply. Nobody was there.

I looked back to the screen but the phone had turned itself off. The battery must be dead. Only it couldn't be. I'd had it charging in the car all the way down. I shook the phone in frustration. Pressed the 'on' button. Nothing happened.

'Come on,' I muttered, '*come on!*' but the device would not respond.

I put it in my pocket, looked up. A woman, the same woman who was in the panorama, was standing amongst the trees at the edge of the lake, hands at her side. Her long, dark hair was dripping, her dress, pulled low by the weight of the stones in its pockets, was soaked and her eyes were fixed on me as if she recognised me.

I knew her too.

I turned and ran back around the building, stumbling over roots and fallen brickwork. I reached the car, climbed inside and locked the doors. For a few seconds I sat with my eyes tightly shut, trying to control my breathing and compose myself. I could not afford to faint. I took out my phone, fumbling as I tried to plug it in to the charger but my fingers were clumsy and I dropped it between the seat and the door.

'OK,' I told myself. 'OK, Lewis, stay calm. All you need to do is drive away. Start the car. *Start the bloody car!*'

My hands were trembling so badly that it took several attempts to slot the key into the ignition. I glimpsed a movement through the window at my side and saw the woman walking between the gates and heading towards me.

'Oh God, no!'

I jiggled the steering wheel and the lock at last disengaged, the car juddered into life and I drove down the track, skidding and skittering, going too fast, desperate to be away. I was back on the A38 before I'd calmed down enough to try to rationalise what I'd experienced and to chastise myself for letting my nerves so completely get the better of me.

I stopped at the services.

I looked at the photographs on my phone, scrolling through them, searching for signs of the woman. I couldn't find her. And although the first panorama video I'd made had worked well, the second was gone. I looked everywhere, even in the deleted folder, but it had vanished. I had no proof that the woman was ever there.

But I knew. I knew who she was and why she lingered. It was because of Isak and me, and everything that happened in those last months of 1993 when I was thirteen and Isak was fourteen and we shared the same bedroom at All Hallows. The time that began at the very point when my whole world had fallen apart.

3

Nurse Emma Everdeen only knew what she'd been told, which was that around lunchtime on the previous day, the crew of a local fishing vessel, the *March Winds*, had spotted a lugger bobbing, apparently empty, amongst the waves about a mile off the Devon coast. When they went to investigate, leaning over the side of the trawler, they saw a woman and a child lying together in the bottom of the smaller boat, seawater swilling over and around them and both apparently lifeless; most likely drowned. The fishermen hooked the lugger and drew it close, tied it to their own craft and towed it into Dartmouth harbour. There, they climbed down the harbour steps where the lugger was being bumped against the wall by the incoming tide, and lifted the woman and the child clear. They were found to be alive, but barely: cold as ice, their clothes drenched. The woman, who was wearing a fine day dress made of muslin and rose-coloured twill, had a deep cut to her upper arm and it appeared she had attempted to tie her own tourniquet from a strip of fabric torn from the skirt of her dress and bound over the sleeve. She was still wearing her jewellery. The fishermen had made much of the fact that they were honest man who had not removed so much as a ring from her finger.

The pair were taken to the local doctor's house. A fire was lit and they were laid beside it, their wet clothes removed and replacements found. The jewellery was dried, a list made, and it was placed in a small velvet bag. The woman's wound was attended to and dressed and she and the child, assumed to be her daughter, were warmed by the flames and a tot of warm brandy poured into their mouths. The child woke and was so distressed that the doctor immediately treated her with a sedative. The woman remained asleep. When she failed to rouse, the doctor telephoned All Hallows, reasoning that the staff at the asylum, with their resources, would be in a better position to help the unfortunate pair. All Hallows superintendent, Mr Francis Pincher, discussed the matter with the general manager, Mr Stanford Uxbridge, and they agreed that the patients should be brought there, it being undoubtedly the best place for them.

Mr Pincher wasn't acting from altruism. He was a businessman whose priority was money and, having been made aware of the quality of the woman's clothing and jewellery, it was evident that money was connected to these patients. All Hallows' buildings were more than a hundred years old, large, chilly and costly in terms of maintenance. The asylum was overcrowded, there being more patients in need than available accommodation for them. Food and fuel and constant stocks of bedding, furniture and other materials had to be purchased. And there were staff wages to pay; not only the nursing and medical staff but also cooks, domestics, gardeners and caretakers, the groom, the coachman, the chaplain's stipend, the gravedigger when called for, the mole-trapper, the deliverymen and so on. Finally, on top of all this expenditure, the shareholders expected All Hallows to make a profit.

It was no secret that standards had begun to slip at the asylum. Staff were hard to come by in such a remote area. When there were not enough staff to supervise the patients, the patients had to be locked up, or restrained, for their own safety. Hardly a day went by without a nurse blowing the emergency whistle hung round her neck after one of the charges, frustrated at being confined, went berserk, necessitating the attention of the orderlies, who, if necessary, would beat him or her with their truncheons until the patient was quiet again.

The sale of just one or two pieces of the woman's fine jewellery would more than cover any costs incurred in the treatment of her and the child, leaving extra for the employment of additional staff, or to upgrade the facilities, or to provide a shareholders' bonus. And also, the superintendent reasoned, the mystery attached to the pair, and the solving of that mystery would give him a fine story to tell and could only benefit the reputation of All Hallows and spread the institution's name far and wide.

For now the imperative was to send the horse-drawn ambulance to bring the patients from Dartmouth to All Hallows. Mr Pincher sent his longest-serving nurse to collect them and accompany them on the return journey. Her name was Emma Everdeen and she was almost seventy years old. This would be the first time she had left the hospital boundaries for more than a year.

4

I was thirteen and three-quarters when my father and step-mother sent me to All Hallows boarding school on Dartmoor.

My mother had died eighteen months earlier and I was angry and unhappy and difficult. My stepmother said I was a delinquent but I wasn't: I was a Goth. I had no idea why she couldn't tell the difference.

I had been a Goth since soon after I started secondary school, a modern comprehensive in Bristol where, to begin with, everyone, even the teachers, called me 'Wingnut' which had been my nickname since primary school because of my sticking-out ears. The Goth thing started because my best friend, Jesse, grew his hair to impress a Goth girl and I grew mine to keep him company. As soon as my hair was long enough to cover my ears, miraculously everyone stopped calling me Wingnut, which was when I decided I'd be a Goth too. Added bonuses were that the make-up Jesse, I and a growing band of friends wore, hid my spots, and the ripped jeans, boots and baggy coat that were my out-of-school uniform disguised the fact that I was small and skinny and at the same time made me look less so.

The Goths at school looked sullen but were a friendly group. The bigger kids looked out for the littler ones. It was like becoming part of a ready-made family.

Mum never discouraged me. She liked my friends and they liked her. After school and in the holidays, when Dad wasn't around, everyone used to congregate at our house. We'd spill out into the back garden, which was long and thin, and we'd take off our vampire coats and Dr Martens boots and play Swingball barefoot on the scrubby old lawn and drink chocolate milk. Our lovely old dog, Polly, would limp out to join us and my friends would compete for her affection, she being the best Labrador-cross in the world. Also, one of the oldest. She was three months older than me – Mum and Dad had bought my older sister, Isobel, the puppy to stop her being jealous when I was born – and she only had three legs. Polly, I mean, only had three legs. She lost the other one after she was hit by a car when she ran out into the road chasing a motorbike when she was young.

Polly died in her sleep in her basket in the corner of my bedroom the week before Mum had her accident. I was nowhere near coming to terms with the loss of Polly when Mum went too. It was like being hit in the face with a sledgehammer twice. I couldn't understand how it was that my wonderful life could have changed so completely, so quickly, without me having changed at all. It made me realise I had no control over anything. I was like the homeless man who sat on the pavement outside the green-grocer's, wrapped in his old sleeping bag even in summer. Mum used to buy him a sandwich and coffee and suggest ways in which he could 'move forward' with his life and he always said: 'The universes are aligned against me, so what's the point?' Mum told me universes were inanimate and could therefore neither be 'for' nor 'against' anyone but this was a bit hypocritical because she also believed very strongly in the stars.

My friends stuck by me after Mum's death. They knew I couldn't talk about what I was going through, so they simply hung around with me, drinking Coca-Cola and listening to music. The teachers at school tolerated our little gang mooching about on our own, away from the hurly-burly of everyone else. If I froze, or had a meltdown, or fainted, Jesse and the others were allowed to take me aside, out of lessons. They might have looked like a bunch of misfits, but those teenagers instinctively knew what I needed.

Losing Polly and then Mum was like having my anchors cut. I felt as if there was so little of me left that a puff of wind might blow me away. Sometimes, in the mornings, when I woke up wearing Mum's horse-shaped pendant and her riding sweatshirt and hugging Polly's blanket, I couldn't remember who I was. At school, I often became disorientated, wandering away from lessons instead of towards them. Out of school, I'd find myself in the streets of St Werburgh's when I was supposed to be in St Andrew's. My mind wasn't working properly. But my friends held on to me. They stopped me floating away.

While this was all going on in my life, my sister, Isobel, who was eighteen, had become much closer to her best friend, Bini. Our father, who seemed incapable of talking to either of us, was being supported by a colleague, a manager at his workplace, which was a cardboard packaging company. This woman started managing Dad's life outside work as well as in it. At first this seemed a good thing. She cooked traybakes for Dad to bring home for our dinners and she did the supermarket shopping for us at the weekend.

Then she became more involved, coming to our house and passing opinions about matters that Isobel and I thought were no business of hers.

The woman told Dad that he needed to be more engaged with

me. She said I would never be 'normal' while I was involved with the Goths. Dad tried to stop me seeing my friends but he couldn't because I was with them every day at school, and after school I simply stayed out late.

Then the woman came round to our house one day while Isobel and I were at school and had a sort-out: throwing away Polly's toys, bed and blankets; taking Mum's clothes to the charity shop. She deep-cleaned my bedroom and tidied away all my personal things.

When I came home, I was devastated. I flew into a rage, called the woman all the ugly names under the sun. Mum would have been ashamed of me but I didn't care. As I crawled around my bedroom carpet trying to rescue any of Polly's hairs still left among the fibres, I heard the woman say to my father: 'Does that look like normal behaviour to you?'

That was the first time that Mum came to talk to me. She tried to make me feel better about the situation, but it was hopeless. If she wanted me to feel better, she shouldn't have bloody well gone and died.

She came again later, when I had calmed down a bit, and I was throwing a tennis ball against the wall at the end of the back garden, practising my bowling, with the twenty-four of Polly's black hairs that I'd managed to salvage folded in a tissue in my pocket. I was throwing the ball as hard as I could, thumping it against the wall, and I heard Mum whisper in my ear: *You'll be all right, Lewis.*

I heard her so clearly this time that I let the ball fly past me as I spun round to see where the voice was coming from.

Mum said, *You can't see me, you doughnut, but I'm always here for you. Hang on in there, kiddo. You'll be OK.*

* * *

The woman told my father that what we all needed was a new start.

Isobel's new start was going to Durham University with Bini.

Dad's new start was marrying the woman, who became my stepmother.

My new start was moving with Dad and my stepmother to Worthing. This was a town on the literal other side of the country, where the cardboard packaging company's headquarters were based.

Until then, I'd lived my whole life in Bristol. My school was there, the skateboard park, the rock slide at the Clifton side of the Downs, the allotments, the tree where Polly always rested when we were out walking and where Mum and I had scattered her ashes in the rain on the morning of the day when Mum died.

Bristol, Mum used to say, was her 'heart city'. It was where she belonged.

It was where I belonged too.

On the day we left, I stared out of the back of the car and watched as everything I knew and loved became smaller and smaller, and further and further away until it disappeared altogether.

Poof.

Gone.

* * *

I did not settle in Worthing. I hated my new school, where I didn't know anybody, and where people treated me like a freak. I spoke to Jesse on the phone, but the phone was in the hallway of our new house and whenever I was using it, my stepmother would lurk nearby, hoping she'd hear me say something derogatory about her so she could complain to my father later.

Every evening, when Dad came home from work, the two of them would disappear into his study for a muted conflab. Sometimes I would creep to the door and I'd hear snippets from a litany of grievances about me. Every time I walked into a room where they were present, my stepmother stiffened and my father's face became a little more tense. I had no privacy; my stepmother sought out my hiding places and found my secret treasures: the 'filthy' collar that was all I'd managed to salvage of dear Polly's things, the Valentine's cards that used to arrive for me every 14 February from a 'secret admirer' – i.e., Mum – my collection of Pogs.

Worst of all, she found the letters I'd written to Mum detailing my stepmother's pettiness and her little cruelties; letters that had been hidden beneath the piece of loose carpet in the bottom of my wardrobe. My stepmother must either have been spying on me or she'd gone through the room with a fine toothcomb, sensing that if she searched hard enough, she'd eventually find some evidence of my disloyalty.

I don't know how she found the letters. But one evening, after work, my father called me into his study 'for a word' and I saw them fanned out on the green leather surface of his desk. My fingers went to my throat, to Mum's horse pendant that I wore on a cord around my neck just as she used to. I closed my eyes and summoned her and she came.

It's OK, she whispered. *Keep your chin up.*

'What,' my father asked, sweeping his hand over the letters, 'is the meaning of this?'

I have always been inclined to blush. I felt the skin on my throat and cheeks begin to burn. I was recalling what I'd written, the foul language I'd used; praying he hadn't read the letters; praying *she* – my stepmother – hadn't.

I kept my head low to hide the blushing and shrugged as if I didn't care. My fingers rubbed the smooth surface of the little metal horse.

'Do you have any idea how hurt your stepmother is by the things you've written about her?' my father continued. 'Don't you appreciate anything she does for you? The sacrifices she's made?'

'I never asked her to.'

'Don't be so bloody selfish! She does it because she *cares* about you, Lewis. She wants the best for you.'

I was silent, staring at a spot on the carpet, hating my father, hating my stepmother, knowing that what he said wasn't true. The only reason my stepmother took any interest at all was because she wanted Dad to think she cared.

'We can't carry on like this, Lewis,' said my father. 'Up until now we've mollycoddled you. Not any longer. You need to change.'

I looked up then. 'Why do I need to change? What's wrong with me?'

'What's wrong with you? What *isn't* wrong? You're a mess, you look like a freak, your attitude stinks, your schoolwork's appalling, you're a disgrace, Lewis Tyler. I'm ashamed to call you my son.'

He doesn't mean it, Mum whispered. *He's lashing out because he doesn't know what else to do. You're perfectly fine as you are. All you need is to believe in yourself.*

It was the kind of thing she used to say to the homeless man. But no matter what she said, my father's words stayed with me. It was like they'd been branded onto the inside of my brain.

Two weeks later, I was packed off to boarding school.

My father and stepmother chose All Hallows, it being marketed as having a no-nonsense, no-frills approach to 'character education'. They thought it was exactly what I needed.

5

The child from the boat did not have a name at the beginning. Nurse Everdeen only found out she was called Harriet later, but the story of her arrival at All Hallows, when the nurse told it, always began with: 'Harriet March arrived at the hospital in the back of the ambulance carriage.'

'And you were there too,' Harriet would prompt.

'Yes, I was there too.'

The horse-drawn ambulance in which the unconscious woman and the drugged child were transported from Dartmouth town to the asylum in the wilds of Dartmoor had been purchased second-hand from London County Council, and had been overpainted in the asylum livery of oxblood and bronze. Inside were rests for two stretchers with a seat between them for the person attending to the patients. The ambulance had originally been designed to carry those who were sick in the medical sense, but had been adapted to cater for people driven insane by grief or hardship or syphilis; people who heard multiple voices inside their own heads and men injured in overseas battles who had returned home mentally insufficient or

prone to unpredictable violence. Inside were belts and mana-
cles for the restraint of such patients and a red flag that could
be waved from the window to alert the driver in case of
emergency.

It was already raining when the doctor's manservant helped
the ambulance driver load Mrs March – as the adult patient
already was known – on her stretcher into the back of the ambulance, the housemaid doing her best to hold an umbrella over the
unfortunate woman. The doctor held the nurse's arm to support
her as she mounted the narrow steps into the back of the carriage
and lifted up the child, who crawled into the corner at the far end
of the empty stretcher rest. Nurse Everdeen pulled the blankets
around Mrs March and secured her with belts, so she would not
fall when the track became bumpy. She offered a blanket to the
child, but the child scowled and shook her head.

Oh dear, thought Nurse Everdeen. It was not in her nature to
complain, but she wondered privately why she had been
burdened with the task of bringing the comatose woman and her
surly infant to All Hallows. In fact, she knew the answer to that
question perfectly well. It was because she was not so strong as
the younger nurses. It was because she could no longer bear the
weight of a basket of soiled laundry, or help lift a patient from a
stretcher to a bed. She could not so much as push a Bath chair.
She could be spared from her usual duties at very little inconvenience to the asylum.

They set off from Dartmouth, but had travelled less than
three miles along the old Exeter Road when Nurse Everdeen had
cause to wave the flag to stop the carriage.

The driver pulled up the horse and, holding tightly to his hat,
bent down to speak to the nurse, who was leaning out of the
window.

'What's the matter, Nurse Everdeen?'

'The patient's stopped breathing, Mr Brixham. I need you to take the child while I attend to her.'

The driver jumped down, came to the back of the ambulance and opened the door. The wind was howling; sturdy sheep braced against it at the side of the track. As a draught gusted inside, the child backed herself further into the corner, holding the skirt of her dress to her face. The driver glanced at the patient, shook his head.

'She looks a goner to me.'

'There is a chance she might be revived. I must try.'

The driver looked doubtful, but still he swept the sleepy little girl into his arms and tucked her into his cloak. She gave a small whine of objection, but did not fight, being too drugged or too afraid.

'Come and say hello to William,' said the driver. 'William's my horse. Do you like horses?'

He disappeared with the little one and, in the carriage, Nurse Everdeen rolled up her sleeves and leaned over the motionless woman, whose lips and skin were already taking on a blueish tinge. She unfastened the belt that restrained the woman's body, pulled open the top of her shift so that her pale skin was exposed, put the flat of her hands onto the woman's chest, and massaged her heart. It was hard work and it took all the nurse's strength, making the whole carriage rock, but she knew what she was doing and after a moment or two the nurse felt beneath her fingers that the woman's heart had begun to beat a tentative rhythm. Her breathing resumed; she was alive once more.

Nurse Everdeen continued working until she was certain the woman's heart was pumping as it should, then she sat back on her seat, held the back of her wrist to her hot forehead and looked up to the top of the carriage that was padded and the nearest she could see to Heaven.

'Thank you!' she whispered.

A few minutes after this, the child was put back in the carriage. The driver looked at Mrs March, a better colour now, took off his hat and scratched his head and then put the hat back on.

'I've never seen any doctor bring someone back from the dead like you just did,' he told the nurse.

'It's my work,' she said. 'I've done it many times.'

'Nonetheless, Nurse, you deserve a great deal more credit for your skills than that what you get.'

The nurse, unused to compliments of any kind, swept this one aside without acknowledgement. She said: 'Mr Brixham, it is imperative that we bring Mrs March to All Hallows as quickly as possible.'

'Aye aye,' said the driver and he resumed his position at the front of the carriage, flicked his whip and growled: 'G'wan, William!' and the horse picked up his big feet and heaved at the harness until the carriage wheels began to roll and they continued on their journey. The woman lay unconscious in her nest of bedding, pale lips parted, her head rocking from side to side in time with the motion of the carriage. The nurse checked her pulse intermittently and between times watched anxiously from beneath her bonnet. The child knelt on the empty stretcher rest, looking out of the window, her breath condensing on the glass, the tips of her fingers holding onto the beading. Every so often her eyes slid shut and she slept where she was, her forehead resting on the window, as far away from the nurse as she could be in that small space.

It was an old vehicle, heavy for the horse to pull, its base and wheels designed to travel the flatter, well-kept roads of London. The interior tipped and jumped and jolted as the wheels bumped over the ruts and stones in the narrow road that led across Dartmoor. The weather was dreadful: wind buffeting the carriage, rain battering its windows and roof. The horse's hooves clattered over the rough surface of the road. Eventually, the child sat on the floor between the stretcher rests, her back against the door with her arms around her knees and her face pressed into them. She stayed there, bumping about as evening fell and the interior of the carriage grew darker, until they arrived at All Hallows.

6

I was driven to my new boarding school on Dartmoor, in the county of Devon, by Tracy Connelly, my stepmother's cleaner. Tracy was a cheerful woman with a south-coast accent, three daughters called April, May and June, and six grandchildren whom she adored. We rattled down the M27 in her tinny Renault, glimpses of the sea appearing every now and then to the left. I was slumped in the passenger seat, staring out of the window. I was wearing Polly's collar and Mum's horse pendant, and my entire Goth get-up. It was one final act of rebellion against my stepmother who had, the week before, taken every single item of black clothing I possessed to the tip. She said she was too embarrassed to donate them to the church thrift sale.

My father had gone to work as normal that morning. Even though I was going away and we weren't due to see one another again until the half-term holiday, he hadn't come into my room to wish me luck or give me any fatherly words of advice, he didn't even call 'goodbye' up the stairs. As I watched his car reversing off the drive from my bedroom window, I heard Mum's voice close beside me whispering: *You know what he's like, Lewis. Just because he doesn't show any emotion, it doesn't mean he doesn't feel it.*

I stayed in my room until Tracy arrived to collect me. I heard my stepmother answer the door to let her in, and there was some to-ing and fro-ing as my suitcase and other stuff was loaded into the car. I didn't go downstairs until after the third time my stepmother called for me. She and Tracy were waiting in the hallway. My stepmother, dressed in a skirt, cardigan and matching blouse, gasped when she saw what I was wearing which was not the 'smart' clothes she'd put out for me, but a pair of faded black jeans and a black hoodie over a Green Day T-shirt, all courtesy of the Help the Aged shop on Tarring Road. I had bleached the tips of my hair the previous evening and I was wearing foundation, eyeliner, lipstick and mascara. A dangly earring brushed my right shoulder and there was a stud in my scabby eyebrow: I'd made the piercing on my own, in the bathroom.

I looked like myself. Or *not* like myself, which was how I wanted to look.

The colour drained from my stepmother's face as I clumped downstairs in my boots, making a full entrance.

'Lewis, for goodness' sake! You can't...' she began.

Tracy put her hand on her arm. 'He'll be fine,' she said.

'But what will they think?'

'It's OK, Mrs Tyler. I'll take care of it.'

Tracy made a flicking movement at me with her eyes. I ducked out of the door and went to sit in the car. A few minutes later Tracy came and sat beside me. 'You little ratbag,' she said and she shook her head, glanced back towards the house to make sure my stepmother wasn't watching, and then she laughed. She was shaking with laughter as she fastened her seat belt and started the engine. She laughed all the way to the A27.

* * *

During the journey to All Hallows, Tracy did her best to put me at
my ease, and it wasn't her fault that the closer we came to Dartmoor, the more anxious I felt. When we stopped at the services at
the edge of the New Forest, and she left me alone in the car, I
considered running away. It was only the fear of getting Tracy
into serious trouble that stopped me.

When Tracy returned, she passed me a can of Tango and a
packet of egg sandwiches. I peeled back the Cellophane. The puff
of air that was released smelled like farts.

'Ew,' said Tracy. 'Have some crisps instead.'

'It's OK,' I said. 'I'm not hungry.'

'I bet you really are.'

'I'm really not.'

Tracy sighed. She put the flats of her hands against the
steering wheel and stretched her arms.

'Listen, Lewis,' she said, 'it might not be as bad as you think at
this school. It might even be fun. And if you work hard you might
get into university and then...'

She petered off. I knew what she was going to say was: *Then
you wouldn't have to go back home at all.*

The wind was whipping across from the forestry land,
buffeting the car. I didn't know what to say to Tracy. I watched a
plastic bag being tossed about the car park. I watched a man lift a
little boy out of a car and sit him on a potty on the verge.

'You've got some eyeliner on your cheek, Lewis,' said Tracy.

She licked a corner of the paper napkin that had come with
the sandwiches and reached across to wipe the smudge away, and
the action reminded me so strongly of Mum that tears came
rushing into my eyes. I turned away so Tracy wouldn't see. The

tears ran down my cheeks and chin. I tried to wipe them away with my sleeve but they kept coming.

'Lewis...'

I opened the car door, got out and slammed it shut and went to stand at the edge of the car park with the wind making my hoodie flap.

'Don't stare, Harry,' the dad said to the little kid on the potty. The plastic bag blew up high, inflated like a balloon, and the wind sucked it away across to the motorway. Tracy came and stood next to me. Lorries and cars were whizzing past. I didn't know if they could see me or if I was just a blur. I didn't care.

'Sorry,' I muttered to Tracy.

'You don't need to say that.'

'I just...'

'I know,' said Tracy.

She didn't try to touch me. She stayed beside me and for a long time neither of us said anything at all.

* * *

By the time we arrived at All Hallows, the day was beginning to fade. The gates swung open on our approach, and as we drove through I had my first sight of the school, the huge façade with the Gothic clock tower in the centre silhouetted against a blazing sky.

'Wow,' Tracy murmured, leaning forward to peer up at it. 'It's like something out of a film!'

She parked the car behind two vans advertising flooding recovery services and another that said: 'Drainage Experts'.

The inside of the car was warm, and I didn't like the look of All Hallows one bit. I wanted to stay where I was.

'Come on,' said Tracy. 'Let's get this over with.'

We climbed out of the car. The air was cold and smelled of rain. A fierce wind gusted through the courtyard, whipping up the surface of the puddles, flattening my hair. We stared at the main building with its pointed stone arches, its mullioned windows, its gargoyles and its buttresses. Bright lights were illuminated along the first-floor corridor, and beyond the windows I could see workmen moving around inside. A stone set into the wall above the huge wooden door at the entrance said: 'All Hallows Asylum, founded 1802'.

'It's an asylum,' I said.

'It's not an asylum,' said Tracy.

'It says: "Asylum" right there!'

'OK, so it used to be an asylum, but now it's a school. I'm sure it's not at all like an asylum inside.'

'What if it's haunted?'

Tracy made claws of her hands and held them up at the side of her face. She made herself go cross-eyed and gurned. 'Like this?'

I laughed and she gave me a friendly push.

I followed her between two stone columns on either side of some steps. Each column had a pedestal on top, with a lion on each pedestal. The steps led up to an enormous wooden door. Tracy pressed the bell at the side marked: 'Pupils and Parents'. A few moments later the door was opened by a youngish, plumpish man in a suit. His clothes were a little too tight for him, his hair rather untidy.

Behind him, boys in uniform carrying musical instruments were crossing from one side of a grand, panelled hallway to the other, clearly on their way to band practice. As they passed, they stared at Tracy and me with blatant curiosity. One or two of them pulled faces, and nudged one another with their elbows, grinning.

Tracy told the man who we were and he introduced himself as Mr Crouch, my new form master. He seemed tetchy. He said he'd been expecting us an hour ago.

'Yeah, I'm sorry we're late,' Tracy said. 'We took a few wrong turns.' She smiled and Mr Crouch smiled back but his smile was insincere and this wrong-footed her. 'Lewis,' she said, 'go and get your case from the back of the car.'

'He won't need it.'

'But his things...'

'Everything Mr Tyler needs will be provided by the school.'

Tracy said: 'Oh. But what about—'

'Everything,' said Mr Crouch. 'It was all explained.' He stepped to one side and indicated that I should come past him into the hall. As I did this, a boy carrying a tuba stopped and the boy behind him, holding a violin, bumped into his back, causing a brief scuffle before Mr Crouch said: 'Excuse me, gentlemen,' and they moved on.

Tracy tried to follow me into the hall but Mr Crouch stepped forward again, subtly blocking her way.

'We don't hold with long goodbyes at All Hallows,' he said.

Tracy held my eye. 'Will you be OK, Lewis?'

I nodded.

'Well,' said Tracy. 'I feel like I ought to—'

'Goodbye,' Mr Crouch said, and he closed the door.

7

EMMA – 1903

The room in which the child and the nurse eventually found themselves after their arrival at All Hallows was one of half a dozen rooms leading off an attic corridor on the third floor, in the eaves of the asylum. Originally a staff bedroom, it had more recently been used, like those beside it, as a storeroom and had been full of old and broken pieces of furniture, and suitcases containing clothes of the insane and deceased deemed unfit for sale. The room was an ideal place to look after the child as it had access to a bathroom, and being a long way up, was safely separated from the rest of the asylum and its inmates.

Before she left for Dartmouth, Nurse Everdeen had had two of the maids empty the room, clean it and bring in and make up a bed with a clean mattress and candlewick coverlet, a table and two wooden chairs, the nurse's own rocking chair, in which she planned to sleep, and a wash-stand equipped with bowls, a large jug, towels, soap and water, so the nurse would not have to take the child to the bathroom each time she needed to wash her hands. There was a small window with heavy curtains, and a functioning fireplace. A lamp hung from a hook attached to the ceiling. The nurse had brought up from her own quarters her treasured nursing manual, some children's books and a knitted toy in the shape of a rabbit in anticipation of the child's arrival and had spread a rag-rug over the floorboards. The fire in the grate had been lit and one of the domestics had kindly placed a vase of late greenhouse roses in the centre of the table. It was not exactly homely, but the flickering of the flames gave the small room a kind of cosiness, providing one did not think too much about the dark rooms on either side of it and what they contained.

The orderly who had carried the child through all those corridors and up all those flights of stairs, had deposited her on the floorboards and immediately started complaining about the ache in his back. Down below, in the asylum, an alarm whistle sounded.

'You'd better go,' Nurse Everdeen said to the orderly. With much fussing, he went.

The child had crawled into a corner, a blanket held around her as if it might make her invisible, her eyes still heavy from whatever opioid the doctor had fed her earlier, her pupils dark and dilated. Her hair was dark, fringed, cut straight at jaw length around her elfin face. The nurse, whose eyesight was not as good as it once had been, could barely see the child in the pool of darkness. Only the darkness of her eyes against the pallor of her skin gave her away. The nurse poked the fire, shook a little more coal from the scuttle, replaced the guard and sat at the table, exhausted.

It was many years since she had had any dealings with children. The only infants ever seen at the asylum were those born to inmates, and as a rule these were removed and given back to their grandmothers or taken by adoptive families straight away. The nurse's irritation at being lumbered with the care of this child was tempered by the conviction that the situation would be short-lived. It was expected that Mrs March would either regain consciousness or die within a few hours.

Nurse Everdeen also understood that she must present a frightening figure to the child, being, as she was, an aging woman with hands so arthritic that the fingers contracted like claws. She knew some of the younger staff called her 'witch' and 'hag' and worse. But she could do nothing about her age or her appearance.

Having once been a mother herself, Nurse Everdeen had been certain that she would remember how to speak to the child. Surely, she thought, as she twisted the chain of the locket that contained the image of Herbert, her son, it would come naturally. Now the occasion had arrived, she could not think of anything she might say to make the little girl less afraid or more compliant. Because she herself was weary and anxious, a bad-tempered humour had settled upon her. She had to contain a strong urge to scold the child, to insist she show some manners. She had been shown the fine day dress her mother had been wearing when she was lifted from the boat. The doctor's housekeeper had been tasked with cleaning and mending it, but even in its wet and torn condition, its quality and style had been evident. The daughter of such a lady must surely have been brought up to be polite to her elders.

'Would you like to come to sit beside me?' she asked, patting the seat of the chair at the table beside hers. The child's frown became deeper. She backed herself more tightly into the corner. Nurse Everdeen had to bite her tongue to prevent herself from saying something unkind. 'You don't wish to come? No? Very well. You may come when you are ready.'

The nurse picked up the knitted rabbit. She had made it for Herbert and she did not particularly want this difficult little girl to have the toy that her darling had so loved, but there was nothing else to give her. The nurse held the rabbit on her lap, straightening his ears and his waistcoat; pretending to smooth his fur. She could feel the girl's eyes upon her.

With a sigh, she put the rabbit on the floor and pushed it with the toe of her boot towards the child. After a while, the child reached out and grabbed the toy, clutching it to her chin and staring at the nurse as fiercely as she could in her woozy state from beneath furiously beetled brows.

'You are to treat that toy gently,' Nurse Everdeen said. 'It does not belong to you. It was made for a very special little boy and is only on loan to you. You must take good care of it. No throwing it in anger, or making it dirty, or pulling at its ears, do you understand?'

The child gave the smallest nod.

8

I followed Mr Crouch across the main hallway. Beyond, the building became more institutional. We walked through endless corridors with pipes at waist level feeding huge radiators, past classrooms and storerooms and doors that led to staircases and study areas and toilets. Every now and then we met a pupil coming the other way. They all said: 'Good evening' to Mr Crouch and then gave me an unfriendly stare. Mr Crouch didn't have particularly long legs but he had the stride of a man who wanted to get a chore over and done with, and it was an effort to keep up. Plus, I was worried I might faint, which used to happen so often when I was stressed that, in the old days, Mum called it my 'party piece'. I doubted my father or stepmother had thought to warn the school about this. I hadn't fainted since Mum's funeral, which had been some time ago now so it wouldn't have been uppermost in their minds.

I held Mum's horse pendant between my fingers and looked about me as we walked. The corridors were either narrow and dark, or wide and dark; in both cases they had stone arches holding up the roof. It was easy to imagine hollow-eyed mental patients traipsing along these same flagstones, scuffing their feet, back in Victorian times. Me, I kept my head held low, a scowl on my face, feeling rather vampirish in these corridors in my Goth clothes. I thought that if someone was to turn up and take a picture of me now, like this, it would make a good album cover; maybe with a bit of smoke from a smoke machine winding around my ankles. And obviously some dramatic lighting. This sounds as if I wasn't feeling at all scared, but actually I was. It was just that when I was nervous and in a situation where I could talk, I always talked too much and when I was nervous and in a situation where I couldn't talk, like this one, I thought too much instead. I had so many thoughts they were literally tripping over one another in my brain.

Mum said places had personalities. Strong emotions soaked into the fabric of buildings, and if you concentrated you could feel the same feelings as the people who had been there before. Animals were better at this than people. If Polly wouldn't go into somewhere or other, then Mum said we shouldn't go in either because Polly 'knew'. Dad didn't approve of what he called 'this kind of nonsense', and although Isobel went along with it I don't think she actually believed in it, but it was true. I had a shelf full of books about unsolved mysteries of the universe such as the Bermuda Triangle, UFOs and poltergeists. Even the US army had done experiments on psychic animals. Mum encouraged my interest in mysteries. She liked puzzles as much as I did. We were addicted to detective stories in books and films and TV series.

I was absolutely one hundred per cent certain that Polly wouldn't have come into All Hallows. The great building echoed with despair. It was if it had witnessed so much suffering it had begun to suffer itself.

While I was thinking all this, Mr Crouch turned another corner and stopped beside a pair of double doors with glass windows in the top. Hundreds of teenage boys, all dressed identically, were sitting at long bench tables. The noise, even with the doors closed, was deafening.

'This is the refectory,' said Mr Crouch. 'Minced beef pie tonight. There might be some left if you're hungry.'

My belly was empty but I couldn't bear the thought of walking into that room and having all those boys turn to stare at me.

'I'm not hungry,' I muttered.

'Suit yourself. We'll go directly to Matron's office.'

We set off again, Mr Crouch striding ahead, me trotting to keep up. We went through a dark corridor with a flagstoned floor. It was partitioned along its length and a channel along the floor led to a drain. There were only a few, small windows high up on the opposite wall. The shadows cast were severe and ominous and there was a knife-sharp draught. I had thought the corridor empty, but between the last pair of partitions a boy of about my age was hunched over a desk. As we approached, he looked up.

'This is the detention corridor,' said Mr Crouch, 'known as Ward B, which was its original name. Now, it's where disgraced pupils, such as Mr Salèn here, are sent to work alone. Mr Salèn is regularly on report. He likes to wind me up. You'd think he'd know better by now.'

The boy narrowed his eyes a fraction.

As Mr Crouch passed the desk, the boy raised two fingers at his back and mouthed an obscenity, a word that Mum told me I must never use because it was disrespectful to women. In this context, she might not have minded but I couldn't be sure. Whatever. I was impressed.

* * *

Matron's office was in the east wing of All Hallows, next to the sanatorium. When we got there, Mr Crouch introduced me and Matron to one another. Then he said: 'Right, I'll leave you to it,' and he disappeared.

Apart from the grandiose architecture, Matron's looked the same as any other school office: heavy-duty beige carpet, an enormous 365-day-view calendar on the wall, filing cabinets. Matron snapped on a pair of latex gloves and looked in my mouth and ears, asked personal questions and told me to speak up when I stuttered over my answers. She passed me a flannel dampened with some astringent liquid and told me to wipe my face and remove my piercings. I stared into a small mirror screwed into the wall above the hand basin. My make-up was blurred from where I'd been crying earlier. No wonder everyone had stared at me. As I wiped it away, I glimpsed Mum reflected behind me, her eyes full of pity. I knew if I turned round she wouldn't be there, so I took my time at the mirror, watching her, wishing with every atom of my being that she was with me, that she had never left me.

Matron told me to take off my jewellery: my watch and the earring; the eyebrow stud; the tangle of bracelets; Polly's collar – she pulled a face at that – and the cord with Mum's galloping horse pendant. She put these together in a plastic tray. Then she told me to remove my boots and my clothes. I looked for a screen to go behind but there wasn't one.

'Where do I undress?' I asked.

'Here.'

'But...'

'There's nothing about your body that I haven't seen a thousand times before, Tyler. Get on with it, please.'

I turned so that I was not facing her and I took off my hoodie, and folded it; then my T-shirt, then I untied my bootlaces and took off my boots, then my jeans. I stood on one leg, then the other, to take off my socks. I could smell my body. I was conscious of every spot on my shoulders, every wisp of body hair, every bony joint; every pale inch of goose-pimpled flesh.

When I was completely naked, with my hands clasped over my privates, Matron had me stand on a weighing scale and she peered at my weight over the top of her spectacles before writing it down. Then she measured my height and lifted a laundered All Hallows uniform in my size from a shelf in the cupboard.

'Put this on,' she said. I was so relieved to be able to cover myself that I tripped over my feet getting dressed. The clothes were plain and ugly; the same green-brown colour as manure. I struggled with the tie, but I got there in the end.

'There,' said Matron, looking me up and down. 'That's better.'

She gave me another bundle, this one comprising a towel, pyjamas, a toothbrush, flannel and comb together with some basic toiletries and a change of socks and underwear.

'Take care of these,' she told me, 'because they are all you have now. If you need a replacement for anything, come and ask me. Is that clear?'

'Yes.'

'Yes, *Matron*.'

'Yes, Matron.'

She moved to pick up a file and while her back was turned, I dipped my hand into the tray and scooped up the horse pendant. I held it tightly, my heart pounding. I hated to leave Polly's collar, but Matron would be sure to notice if that went too.

Matron said: 'Follow me,' and there was another trek along corridors and up staircases. We passed a corridor that was taped off, an A-board propped up that said: 'No Entry to Pupils'. A plastic sheet hung like a curtain, blocking our view of what was beyond.

'We had a flood,' said Matron. 'A pipe burst during the cold spell. Two of the dormitories are unusable so we've had to spread pupils out amongst whatever rooms we could find whilst they're being dried out and repaired.' She shook her head. 'The building is a nightmare. Things are always going wrong. It's as if it doesn't want to be inhabited. This way.'

We climbed to the second floor and ended up on a small landing. I followed Matron into a square room. Despite the two metal-framed beds with their heads against the corridor wall, it neither looked nor felt like a bedroom.

Matron said: 'This is your room for the time being. There are only two of you here. You're lucky.' She looked at me as if I should be grateful, as if this were some kind of luxury accommodation and not a dingy room with vertical blinds at the window and the walls painted a dull, off-white.

'This is your bed,' said Matron, indicating the one closest to the door. 'Put your things in the cabinet. The bathroom is up the stairs at the end of the landing. Your roommate will explain everything you need to know.'

She held onto the edge of the door.

'Stay here, Lewis. If you leave the landing you'll get lost, which will be inconvenient and annoying for the staff who will have to track you down.'

'Yes, Matron.'

'Any questions?'

'No... but I can smell smoke.'

'It's the radiators. They always smell like that. It's nothing to worry about.'

She left and I wandered to the window and looked out. Beyond the grounds of All Hallows I could make out some features of the bleak Dartmoor landscape, drained of colour, by the drifting light of the moon. Clouds were blowing across its face, but when they cleared, a little chapel came into focus inside the boundary wall. Ivy was growing up its walls and the trees around its perimeter were straggly, their branches thrashing in the wind.

I thought of Mum, lying all alone in her coffin, and I missed her so much that the grief was like a kick to the stomach.

There was a great gust outside, which rattled the glass in the window and a groaning as the wind ran along the edge of the roof.

Then I heard a different noise.

This noise was rhythmic, careful; considered: like the sound of somebody sawing.

It was coming from above.

Nurse Everdeen folded her hands in her lap. Now she had the child's attention, she said: 'We are at All Hallows Hospital. Do you know what a hospital is?'

The child did not move.

'It is a place where poorly people, like your mother, are made better,' said the nurse. 'Although this is not a hospital for children, you may stay with me here in this room and I will look after you. You may ask me any questions that come into your mind, and I promise I will answer honestly.'

The child muttered something. The only word Nurse Everdeen could identify was: 'When?'

'When will your mother be better? We must pray that day will come soon.'

The child pulled the ends of the blanket closer to her face. She was almost hidden behind it; only the rabbit peeped over, its ears crooked.

Yes, thought the nurse, let's pray that Mrs March is soon recovered and on her way with you.

The fire crackled and spat in the grate. The flames flickered.

'It would be helpful,' said the nurse, 'if I knew your name. What is your name, child?'

There was no response.

'It's quite all right if you don't want to tell me,' said Nurse Everdeen. 'I only entrust people I know well to call me by my Christian name. So, why don't you call me "Nurse" and I will call you… what shall I call you? I know, I'll call you "Rabbit", until you are ready to tell me your real name. Rabbit. Yes. It suits you.'

'My name is not Rabbit,' the child murmured.

'I beg your pardon?'

'My name is not Rabbit!'

'Very well then, I'll call you "Not-Rabbit".'

The child gave a small laugh, which she immediately suppressed.

'Whatever is the matter, Not-Rabbit?' Nurse Everdeen asked in mock concern.

'I'm Harriet!' the child said. 'My name is not Not-Rabbit! It is Harriet!'

'Harriet?'

'Yes.'

'Well, there's a thing!'

'Harriet' had been the Christian name of the nurse, Nurse Sawmills, who had taken Emma Everdeen under her wing after Herbert's death; the nurse who had looked after her, who had taught her how to be a professional nurse; who had saved her life.

'Harriet is a very good name indeed,' Nurse Everdeen said. 'Do you know your family name?'

The child looked blank.

'Your second name?'

There was no response.

'When people speak to your mother, how is she addressed? What do they call her? Mrs what?'

She looked at the child, and the child gazed back, and Nurse Everdeen saw that she did not understand. She was, after all, very young.

The nurse's heart thawed a little. She tried to remember what the care of a child entailed. The most pressing action was evident. Harriet was grubby. Children ought to be clean.

Nurse Everdeen stood up slowly. She crossed to the wash-stand, tested the temperature of the water in the jug, and filled the bowl. She washed her own hands and forearms. Then she wet a flannel and squeezed it, and took it to the child in the corner.

'Harriet, I am going to wipe your face and hands,' she said, in a tone that was neither harsh, nor scolding, but which brooked no argument. 'Then I'm going to change you into a clean night-gown. That's all we will do for tonight. I will do my very best not to hurt you or pull your hair, but I'm not used to dealing with small girls and it would help if you wouldn't fight me.'

The child glared from beneath her fringe but she did not struggle as Nurse Everdeen gently cleaned the grime from her tear-stained cheeks, her forehead and chin. She rinsed the cloth and wiped the little girl's hands, observing the bruises on her arms and wrists, as if she'd been roughly grabbed, or held down. The delicate nails at the end of her fingers were torn and she had a mark on her cheek. She might have been slapped or perhaps her face had been bumped as she was lifted from the boat.

The nurse did one final, gentle wipe.

Then she said: 'Hold up your arms, I'm going to take off your dress.' Harriet did as she'd been told and the nurse pulled the dress over her head – it was an ugly woollen thing the Dartmouth doctor had given her to wear – took off her stays and stockings, and replaced these items with a nightgown. It was the smallest nightgown available from the hospital laundry, but it was still far too big for the little girl; she looked like a doll in a wedding dress.

Nonetheless, the gown was cotton that had been washed so many times it was soft, and it was clean. Little Harriet would be comfortable tonight.

'There we are,' said the nurse. 'That wasn't so bad now, was it?'

She lifted up the bowl of dirty water and the soiled, ill-fitting clothes and withdrew.

* * *

A little later, one of the maids, a pleasant young woman called Maria Smith, of whom Nurse Everdeen was most fond, brought up the supper tray. She was red in the face from climbing all the stairs with such a burden in her arms and muttered that she was not looking forward to having to repeat this task thrice daily for the foreseeable.

'Here we are,' she said, plonking the tray unceremoniously on the table and slopping milk out of the jug. 'You're well, I trust, Nurse Everdeen?'

'Very well.'

'I'm glad to hear it. And,' she mouthed elaborately, '*how's the little one?*'

'Her name is Harriet and she's doing her best to be good.'

Maria turned to look at Harriet. 'I'm glad to hear that too. Are you hungry, pet? Bless her heart! I hear her mother would have died if it wasn't for you, Nurse Everdeen. She's a dear little thing, the child, isn't she, and by all accounts the mother's an absolute beauty too. It's such a pity what's happened to them both. Shameful of whoever it was has hurt them and sad to think there is such wickedness in the world. Anyway, just so as you know, Nurse, Mr Uxbridge said I was to lock the door at the top of the stairs on my way out just to be on the safe side. There was an awful to-do this afternoon with one of the men and we don't want him coming up here in the middle of the night and...' She caught a glimpse of Harriet's face, and said: 'Anyway, it's best we shut you in. So, if you need any more coal or anything, ask me now.'

'We have sufficient, thank you.'

'Good. Well, I'll be off then. I'll bring you a breakfast tray up in the morning and collect this one. I wish you both a good night!'

She waved her fingers at Harriet and then she left and they heard her footsteps on the corridor and then the sound of the door at the top of the stairs closing and the lock being turned. Night had fallen completely and the nurse felt a prickle of unease at being imprisoned here in the attic. Then she considered the busyness of the wards below: the onerous and often unpleasant tasks that had to be undertaken at this time of an evening, the complaints and tears of those who had been locked up all day, and she looked at her situation in a different way. They could hear, distantly, the sounds of patients being moved about the hospital: the clanging of doors; the occasional, awful wail. The asylum wards seemed a very long way from where they were now.

She and the child were shut inside, yes, but everyone else was shut out. And it was a pleasant enough space for the two of them. It was cosy.

The child was too exhausted to eat, or to kneel to say her prayers. Nurse Everdeen lifted her into bed and tucked her in with the knitted rabbit beside her and she whispered the child's prayer:

> Now I lay me down to sleep
> I pray the Lord my soul to keep.
> If I should die before I wake
> I pray the Lord my soul to take.

She dimmed the lamp, picked up one of the children's books, a book that she hadn't opened since Herbert's death, and moved over to the rocking chair. She put the spectacles that hung on a chain around her neck onto the bridge of her nose and began to read aloud and at the same time she tipped the chair backwards with her feet and rocked it. The words of the story fell into a rhythm with the movement of the wooden runners. The child lay, curled like a bean. The nurse, holding the locket in her hand, continued to read. The child pulled the blanket over her head and closed her eyes, clutching the rabbit to her chest.

After a few more pages, she was asleep.

The noise was persistent. It sounded as if someone was in the room above.

I left the bedroom and went out onto the landing. It was a gloomy corridor, the floorboards covered in a threadbare old carpet. There was a door at one end and a steep staircase at the other. I went to the foot of the stairs, looked up, and began to climb, keeping one hand on the wobbly handrail fastened to the wall. The frame and hinges of a door that was no longer there remained at the top. Now I was in the attic space.

The landing below was claustrophobic, but this was truly oppressive. A narrow corridor in the eaves of the building, windowless and with a steeply sloping ceiling so low that I could stand straight only if I kept to the left – and I wasn't even tall. There were five closed doors on the left-hand side and an open door at the far end that I could see was the bathroom.

The sawing noise that I'd heard downstairs was louder here. Actually, it wasn't a sawing, more of a creaking. The hairs on my arms stood on end and I felt a shiver of fear. The darkness didn't help.

I patted my hand along the wall until I found a light switch and pressed it down.

Old-fashioned strip lights flickered along the landing, their shades speckled with the bodies of dead insects. The light was muddy yellow and menacing, as if I had disturbed the darkness; woken something that should have been left to sleep.

I tried the handle of the door closest to me. That was locked, and the next door, and the one after that. But the fourth door groaned and swung open when I turned the handle and I walked into a small room. Despite the gloom, I could see it was empty save for an old metal bed frame and a wooden rocking chair that was tilting backwards and forwards on its runners. That was the origin of the noise: the chair, creaking as it tipped forward and back. The runners had rocked so many times they had worn grooves into the floorboards. I stepped into the room and put my hand on the back of the chair to still it. The plaster on the walls was old and crumbling in places, stained black with mould, and a draught sneaked from the fireplace, cold fingers creeping around my ankles. It must have been the draught that was making the chair move. The smell of smoke was stronger in this room although there was no radiator; perhaps it was soot clagged to the chimney walls.

Far away, I heard the clock on the tower chiming the hour.

* * *

I was sitting at the head end of my bed when the door swung open and my roommate strode in – the same boy who'd been in the detention corridor earlier. Close up, he was taller, broader-shouldered and more developed than I was. He had a wary expression that reminded me of the cat that used to live on the allotments. I wished I still had my Goth clothes and my make-up.

Without them, I was just a shy teenager, small for my age, without a mother.

'Hi,' I said.

The boy walked past me without a word, opened the door to his bedside cabinet, took out a packet of cigarettes and a lighter, went to the window and opened it. The wind snatched the window from his hand and banged it back hard. He put his hands on the sill and hoisted himself onto the frame, and then he disappeared out through the window, leaving it open so the cold air tumbled into the room. He had not acknowledged me at all.

I went to the window and peered out. The boy was sitting a few feet to the left on the ornamental ledge that ran around the entire building at this level, his feet dangling over the edge between the shallow ramparts. The wind was blowing so hard that his shirt and jumper appeared glued to one side of him, his hair pulled back. He was smoking the cigarette on the leeward side, the wind snatching the smoke and whipping it away. He was an awfully long way above the ground and it was a sheer drop.

I went back to my bed and waited for him to return, praying that he *would* return and wondering how long I should leave it before I disobeyed Matron and went down into the school in search of help if he did not. After what felt like about three hours had passed, he jumped back into the room, wind-battered and bringing a new rush of cold with him. I was so relieved I started talking at once.

'Hi. I'm your new roommate, pleased to meet you, it's going to be great sharing with you, I hope it's OK with you that I'm here.'

He ignored me. He crouched in front of his bedside cabinet and poked around inside it.

'I saw you in the detention corridor,' I said, 'I liked the way you did the Vs up at Mr Crouch's back. He's my form master. Is he yours too? Are we going to be in the same class? Is Mr Crouch all right? I thought he was a bit of a dick, actually.'

I pushed my hair out of my eyes and waited but still the boy did not speak.

I imagined Mum saying: *Give him time. You know he's had a rotten day.* So, I was quiet for as long as I could bear the silence and just when I couldn't bear it any longer he asked: 'What's wrong with your hair?'

'What d'you mean? There's nothing wrong, it's like this because I'm a Goth.'

'Real Goths are from Sweden,' said the boy, 'from the island of Götaland. They do not have hair like that.'

'How do you know?'

'I'm Swedish.'

He lay down on the bed with his back to me and curled one arm above his head. It was a gesture so obviously intended to make me stop talking to him, that I stopped talking to him.

I sat cross-legged on the end of my bed, twisting the cord of my mum's pendant around my fingers, one way and then the other, thinking that this was worse than I'd imagined, being stuck with a sullen roommate who didn't want me to be there. I thought of Polly's collar on Matron's desk and prayed she wouldn't throw it away. I thought of my father and stepmother eating dinner at the table in the dining room of the Worthing house. I wondered if they had dressed up for their first dinner without me; if my stepmother had made an effort to cook something nice; if they were playing music, feeling more at ease because I was not there.

'What's that?' the boy asked.

'This? Oh, it was my mum's.'

I tossed the pendant across the space between our two beds and the boy caught it. He looked at it, turned it over, made the little horse stand up as if it was galloping over the palm of his hand.

'Does your mum like horses?'

'Yeah. Well, she used to.' I swallowed and scratched an insect bite on my arm. 'She's dead,' I said. The two words came out awkwardly, as they always did. I'd tried lots of different ways to say them and realised there was no good way. You either sounded like you didn't care or you sounded like you felt sorry for yourself.

'How did she die?'

'It was a riding accident.'

The boy frowned. He laid the little metal horse down on his palm.

I looked down at my fingers. There were still faint traces of the varnish my stepmother had insisted I remove in the corners of my nails.

'An accident?'

'Yeah,' I said. 'She was riding up on the Bristol Downs and there was a Fried Chicken bag caught in the hedge and the horse, Zephyr, he's nervy and when he saw the bag he panicked and his hooves slipped on the road. It had been raining and she...'

The boy was hunched over now, his head low between his shoulders.

I cleared my throat.

'She fell off and her neck was broken. Some people saw it happen and they tried to help. Mum was lying on the road and Zephyr was standing beside her, pushing her with his nose. He didn't want to let anyone else get too close, like he was protecting her. The people felt sorry for him. They came to the funeral. They wanted me and my sister to know that it wasn't... that she didn't...' I tailed off.

'Didn't feel any pain?'

'Yeah. I mean no. It was very quick.'

'People shouldn't throw litter out of car windows,' the boy said quietly.

'No,' I said.

I rubbed the bottom of my nose with the back of my hand.

The boy reached across the divide to return the pendant to me.

'My name's Isak,' he said.

'Hi, Isak. I'm Lewis. Lewis Tyler.'

11

Dr Milton Milligan arrived at All Hallows Hospital the afternoon after Harriet and Mrs March. The fly was sent to collect him from the station at Exeter – he having travelled by railway from his mother's cottage outside Birmingham where he had repaired for a few weeks' rest after his tenure in Vienna. He had not been due to take up his position at the hospital until the following week, but cut short his break in order to be able to attend to Mrs March from the offset. Maria Smith made sure that Nurse Everdeen was aware of the situation. They were at the table in the attic room, drinking tea. Little Harriet was on the other side of the bed, whispering to the knitted rabbit.

'And how does Superintendent Pincher think he's going to pay the wages of some fancy new doctor?' Nurse Everdeen asked grumpily, none of the staff having had a pay rise for several years, and those same staff having to work inordinately long hours to make up for there being not enough of them.

'He's not any fancy new doctor, but one with unrivalled experience in dealing with injuries of the head and brain,' said Maria.

'An *expensive* fancy new doctor, then,' said Nurse Everdeen.

'Mr Pincher thinks Dr Milligan will attract the attention of a wealthier class of clientele. He's written to the newspapers to inform them of the appointment.'

Nurse Everdeen sighed.

The new doctor, Maria told her, had alighted from the fly beside the steps that led to the main entrance, where he was greeted by Mr Francis Pincher, his very self. Mr Pincher was a portly man, with sandy hair on either side of a bald pate, watery blue eyes and a small moustache. Maria Smith acted out his bluster for Nurse Everdeen's pleasure. She had him down to a T, his pomposity and the self-regard of a man who had spent all his life at boardroom tables, managing business.

Mr Pincher had asked one of the orderlies to take charge of Dr Milligan's luggage and then he invited the doctor into the asylum. They had climbed the steps, crossed the grand hallway and gone into the superintendent's office. Dr Milligan had apparently sniffed and pulled a face at the odour inside the asylum, it, presumably, being baser than the more refined air of the hospitals in Austria, which was hardly surprising seeing as most of the All Hallows patients didn't get any fresh air from one day to the next and rarely encountered a bath. Mr Pincher asked Maria to open the window a fraction and to put some more coal on the fire. The doctor sat on one of the shabby Queen Anne-style Chesterfields while Mr Pincher briefed him on the history and ethos of All Hallows. It was a speech he had given many times before, and he sounded as if he was reciting from a guidebook as he stood with his back to the fire, rocking on his heels.

'Just like this,' Maria said, standing in front of Nurse Everdeen's fire with her hands clasped behind her back and her chin raised importantly. The nurse, who could picture the scene exactly, smiled.

'So, he did his usual talk about All Hallows being a place of refuge from the rigours of daily life, et cetera, et cetera, but he rushed through it because he was so keen to tell the doctor about Mrs March and the child.'

'And what did he have to say about them?'

'He said that Mrs March is not the woman's real name. The fishermen who found her named her after their boat. That nobody knows who she is, nor where she came from, nor how she was injured, nor at whose hand, nor how she came to be in the boat. That her heart stopped in the ambulance but she was revived. That she is still unconscious and is being treated in one of All Hallows' finest private rooms. A nurse sits with her at all times in case of any change.'

'Did he mention the child?'

'Only to say that she is being cared for by All Hallows' most experienced nurse. That would be you, Nurse Everdeen!'

'Hmm.'

'The doctor asked to see Mrs March and the little one, and Mr Pincher said he would show them to him in due course. In the meantime, he had had a small apartment prepared for the doctor, which he hoped would be to the doctor's satisfaction and the doctor said he was certain it would be. Although when I took him up there, Nurse Everdeen, he seemed a little disappointed. He said it rather lacked the finesse of the apartment he'd had in Vienna. Now that *was* an apartment! All polished wood and sash windows with a view out across the Platz to the theatre and a café downstairs that served the most exquisite pastries. He even had his own dedicated maid.'

'Exquisite pastries *and* a dedicated maid! Well, I never.'

'And he did rather a lot of sniffing and holding his handkerchief to his nose. Still, once he'd got over his disappointment, he told me the rooms had their own charm and he was sure he would be able to make himself comfortable because he is not, he assured me, a natural pessimist. If he had been, he would never have chosen to work in a profession that involved the exploration of the darker recesses of the human mind.'

Nurse Everdeen rolled her eyes.

Maria raised her teacup to her lips, and smiled.

On the other side of the bed, Harriet held the knitted rabbit to her ear as if she was listening to the secrets he was telling her. She was quiet as a mouse.

12

It took me ages to fall asleep that first night. Outside, the wind had grown in ferocity; it was howling, battering the building, shaking it as if it was angry.

I thought I heard something falling; imagined the whole building being brought down by the wind, all of us buried beneath rubble. When the great storm swept across the UK in 1987, people had been killed by chimneys crashing through their ceilings. Who was to say that it was not happening again?

I thought I felt the building move, and I put my hands above my head and held onto the bedstead, thinking the metal frame might protect me if All Hallows collapsed and we plummeted through the floors. And then, over the noise of the storm, I heard a different noise. It was the sound of the runners of the rocking chair in the little room on the floor above.

Backwards and forwards, creak, creak, creak, like the beat of a song; like a lullaby.

* * *

When I slept at last it was a drifting, half-sleep where I kept imagining myself in different places: one moment at home in Bristol, lying on a towel in the back garden, Mum pegging out the washing and singing; the next hanging out in the park with my old friends. Then I found myself on the outskirts of a beach, somewhere I didn't recognise. The sand was a dark grey and pebbled, a cliff rose behind me and I was crouched behind a cluster of rocks. I looked around the rocks, and saw a woman running towards me with her hand raised as if to strike me and I cowered down and covered my head with my hands.

I was woken by something hitting me on the shoulder. I opened my eyes; couldn't work out where I was, tried to scramble away and fell off the bed with a thump.

'Fuck's sake!' muttered a voice to my left.

Then I realised where I was. I climbed back up onto the bed.

'Did you throw a shoe at me, Isak?'

'Yes. To make you shut up. You were making stupid noises.'

'Sorry.'

What I needed was a kind word, some sympathy; a mug of peppermint tea with my mum in the kitchen; she wearing her raspberry-coloured dressing gown, pushing her long hair back behind her ear, the horse on the cord around her neck, asking about my nightmare then analysing it with me, telling me some funny story about her class at the primary school, fishing the teabags out of the mugs with a spoon.

What I had was a bad-tempered roommate.

'Sorry,' I whispered again.

'Just shut the fuck up and go back to sleep.'

I lay quiet and still for a few moments, then I asked: 'Isak?'

'What?'

'Can you smell smoke?'

'No.'

Silence.

Then Isak said: 'Will you stop that!'

'Stop what?'

'Fucking sniffing.'

'Sorry,' I said.

I wasn't sure if the smoke smell was worse than before. Probably it wasn't. It was probably just how All Hallows smelled, the radiators, like Matron said. But I was worried now that the storm *might* have caused an electrical wire to spark and it might be crackling away in some deep corner of the building and there might be a teeny little flame that would creep along the edge of the wallpaper and then the curtains might catch fire and then the fire would sweep through the lower rooms and we'd be here, trapped on the second floor with no obvious means of escape. If there *was* a fire, someone needed to be vigilant.

Isak grumbled for a while, but soon enough his breathing became regular and slow and I knew he was sleeping. I lay awake, huddled beneath my thin duvet, trying to get warm and not to think about flames sneaking around our beds.

The night seemed to last forever, but eventually dawn broke: a watery grey light, like smoke, hanging in the room. The wind was still gusting, but less violently and the coo of wood pigeons announced the dawn chorus. It was short-lived but reassuring.

I rolled onto my side, feeling the loneliness of the beginning of a new day in a place where I was a stranger. The future stretched ahead for ever, all of it bleak.

I slipped out of bed and padded across the worn old carpet to the window, pushed back the greasy blinds and looked out. The countryside colours were dulled by the grey sky and the great, wet, looming clouds hanging heavy over Dartmoor. High up, a flock of white birds drifted on the wind. I watched, envying them their freedom, and then I noticed that a tree had fallen behind the little chapel. It lay at a jagged angle, like a broken bone, its crown resting on the far side of the chapel roof.

13

EMMA – 1903

Maria made an extra journey up through All Hallows to the room in the attic to bring some clothes for Harriet; items donated by Mrs Collins, mother of Sam, the All Hallows' groom and Maria's sweetheart. Mrs Collins had six children, all but Sam were girls, and the youngest was now ten so the clothes had been outgrown.

The clothes had been passed down between the Collins's daughters, but Mrs Collins was a good seamstress and the dresses, pinafores, a jacket and undergarments were all in a good state of repair. Maria presented the pile of folded items with pride, rather shyly. Nurse Everdeen was touched by Mrs Collins' kindness but also surprised at the speed at which the news of Harriet's being at the asylum had reached the woman's ears.

'Sam Collins is a most thoughtful young man,' Nurse Everdeen said, taking the clothes.

'Indeed,' said Maria, blushing a little. 'He is.'

14

A prefect came to our room. He told Isak to go to the refectory for breakfast as usual and said I was to follow him to Matron's office.

'Why?' Isak asked the prefect.

'How should I know?'

'I don't see why he should go with you if you don't even know why he's supposed to be going.'

'Shut up, Salèn.'

'Shut up yourself.'

'Jesus, you're an irritating little prick.'

'Don't call me a prick, you dickhead!'

Isak ran at the prefect but the prefect was bigger and stronger. He pushed Isak, hard enough for him to stumble backwards and bang into the wall. It wasn't much violence, but it was more than I was used to. I felt panicky. Isak's expression was bitter and hard.

On the way to Matron's office the prefect grumbled about Isak.

'He's such an arrogant little bastard. I feel sorry for you having to share with him.'

'He's not that bad.'

'You don't know him yet. Give it time and you'll hate him as much as the rest of us do.'

* * *

Sheets of newspaper were spread over the carpet in Matron's office, and a chair placed in the middle. A broad woman with a ruddy complexion and sleeves rolled up to the elbows was standing behind the chair.

'Lewis Tyler?'

'Yes.'

'I'm here to give you a haircut.'

'Are you a hairdresser?' I asked.

'Oh, Good Lord, no! I'm a domestic. But I've got two lads of my own and I know my way around a pair of clippers. Now sit down and I'll have you sorted in no time.'

She seemed a reasonable woman.

'Thank you for explaining,' I said, 'but I don't want my hair cut.'

The prefect, who was leaning against the door, snorted.

'You don't want your hair cut?'

'No,' I said. 'Thank you anyway.'

The woman leaned down so her lips were close to my ear. 'I'm afraid it's not up for discussion,' she said.

My mother had drummed into Isobel and me that we were in charge of our bodies and nobody else was allowed to do anything to them unless we wanted them to.

'Actually, it's my hair and I'm in charge of it,' I said.

The woman chuckled. 'Did you hear that?' she asked the prefect.

'He's sharing a room with Isak Salèn,' said the prefect. 'That's where the attitude's coming from.'

'Actually, it's nothing to do with Isak,' I said.

The woman squeezed my shoulder. '*Actually*, Lewis, you are going to have your hair cut no matter what you think about it. You can either make it easy for yourself, or difficult. I would strongly recommend the first option.'

I fidgeted throughout but did not stop the woman giving me a grade one buzz cut around the back and sides. I was horrified by the length of the hanks of cut hair that lay on the newspaper, dreading to think how badly my ears must be sticking out. I put my hand on the back of my head and felt the prickly fuzz. I imagined what my mum would have to say if she knew what had been done to me.

The woman came to stand in front of me.

'Right, Lewis Tyler,' she said. 'I didn't appreciate the behaviour back there. Matron told me that if you misbehaved I was to put you on report for two days. So that's what I'm going to do. That means no games, no free time, no privileges. Understand?'

This seemed very unfair to me. I hadn't really done anything wrong.

'What about breakfast?' I asked hopefully.

'It's too late now. Jacob here will take you directly to your classroom. You'll get a bun to eat at break.'

She leaned down so that her eyes were on the same level as mine.

'A word of advice, young man. Don't try to fight the system, because the system has had plenty of experience with boys a lot tougher than you and none of them wins. Ever. Not one.'

15

EMMA – 1903

The first few days spent in the attic room were long and tedious. Nurse Everdeen was obliged to keep reminding herself that she was better off being upstairs with the recalcitrant child than she would have been downstairs in the asylum carrying out her usual duties. Although she was glad, in many ways, to be away from the sounds and smells and drama of the wards, they were what she was used to. The quietness, the absence of the ever-present threat of some kind of violence, were unfamiliar and therefore disconcerting.

In the old days, Nurse Everdeen's skills and experience had ensured she was tasked with the more complicated nursing jobs: caring for patients who had suffered so much in their lives that they had become emotionally crushed; helping those poor souls afflicted by tumours of the brain and other diseases that affected their mental capabilities. But in the old days, the asylum had a more progressive superintendent, one committed to a 'no restraint' policy, a superintendent who endeavoured to stimulate the minds of the patients. In its heyday, the asylum had resembled less a hospital than a grand country estate, with the patients taking on different roles in the house and gardens; and being rewarded for their efforts with dances and entertainments. Only the genuinely, medically sick were kept bedridden in the wards. But the asylum's charitable status, its benefactors, its kindly old superintendent and the former board of governors were gone, replaced by a company set up to run it as a business. Corners were cut, savings made wherever possible. Now, it seemed to Nurse Everdeen, the asylum and its inmates and depleted staff were constantly on the brink of disaster. Only opiate drugs and the threat of violent punishment kept a lid on the simmering tensions within the wards. It was only a matter of time, surely, before some tragedy occurred.

Lately, because she now struggled with heavy tasks, Nurse Everdeen spent most of her time working in the women's dementia ward. It was more homely than the other wards, with Prince Valliant, the parrot, dividing his time between this ward and the men's equivalent. The patients, desperate for any object on which they could ply their affection, adored the parrot, who was all that remained of a number of 'therapeutic' animals kept at All Hallows in the good old days. He did not look as well as he used to. Once he had been encouraged to fly free in the Great Hall for exercise, the brilliant colours of his plumage flashing against the dark panels that covered the walls and ceiling. Now he was permanently caged he was losing his feathers and had become ill-tempered, nipping at the fingers of anyone who attempted to feed him titbits.

Nurse Everdeen, like the Macaw, was grumpy and well past her best. Nonetheless, she could still manage the requirements of the majority of the dementia patients. Most did not know what they had forgotten, could not miss what they no longer remembered. Most were kindly souls.

Now, stuck in the little attic room, she missed her ladies. She had not expected the time here to pass so slowly. Harriet still refused to engage with her. She ate a little food at mealtimes, was quiet when Nurse Everdeen washed her, and did as she was told, yet she did it in a way that was so resentful it made the nurse feel helpless.

In the end, Nurse Everdeen spent most of those early days sitting in her rocking chair, peering through her spectacles at her sewing, or reading one of the books that she used to read to Herbert; thinking about Herbert and his short, wonderful life; resting, certainly, but without feeling any benefit from it; observing the child, but not interacting with her.

When the child fell asleep, Nurse Everdeen took a nip of gin, and then a small dose of the special narcotic liquor that was given to the patients downstairs at night, and settled in her chair, and slept.

I followed the prefect back through the school. On the way we passed hundreds of boys, some bigger than me, some smaller, all of them seeming to take up a lot of space in the corridors. Now I looked the same as them, they didn't take any notice of me, except for the few who stopped to point at my ears. Most were in pairs or groups, laughing and jostling and messing around, but some were on their own with their eyes downcast, looking as if they wished they were somewhere else.

At my old school in Bristol, some of the older pupils volunteered to act as lookouts for anyone who was lost or unhappy or who might be being bullied. They were called Friendship Monitors. Mum thought it was brilliant. Dad said children needed to learn to stand on their own two feet; that if they couldn't cope in the school environment how would they ever manage in the real world?

I remembered Mum saying: 'They're children, Geoffrey, why should they be miserable if they don't need to be?'

* * *

My first day at All Hallows taught me the shape of the days to come. It also taught me that rewards came to those who conformed. Anyone who bucked the system or who tried to steer his own path was punished.

I was in form 3B, one of twenty-five boys aged thirteen to fourteen. Our classroom was in the main part of the building. The windows overlooked the terrace and then the front gardens but we had to sit with our backs to them, at old-fashioned wooden desks with lids covered in scratches and graffiti; desks that had a hollow for pencils carved into the flat part above the hinge, and a hole where, in the olden days, pupils used to put their inkwells.

Mine was the only empty desk in the classroom. It was towards the back, which was a relief because it meant most of the other boys wouldn't be spending their lessons staring at my ears. Isak was already slouching at his desk. I noticed how the other boys moved around him, giving him space. I kept trying to catch his eye but he ignored me.

A baby-faced boy with inky-black hair, who said his name was James but everyone called him Mophead, looked after me. He explained that we had registration first. Mr Crouch came rather dramatically into the room, pink in the face and straining the fancy tortoiseshell buttons of his waistcoat. He stood at the front and called out everyone's surname and we had to say: 'Present.' I was pleased that 'Tyler' came immediately after 'Salèn'. I know it didn't *mean* anything, but at least I was next to Isak in the register. After that, Mr Crouch introduced me to the class and asked everyone to treat me courteously and 'show me the ropes'. Everyone except Isak turned to look at me. One boy crossed his eyes and made a hanging man face at me that Mr Crouch couldn't see.

After that, we filed into the Great Hall for assembly. Mophead walked next to me amongst the river of boys in brown uniforms and gave me some background information about our classmates; who was 'sound' and who was best avoided. When he nudged me and pointed to Isak he said: 'Be careful of him, he's a psycho. Beat up some boy last term. Put him in the san. He would've been expelled but his dad coughed up a load of cash to help with the flood repairs.'

'Why did he beat up the other boy?'

'No reason. It was random.'

'Isak's my roommate,' I said.

Mophead whistled.

'You'd better watch your back then. Make sure he's asleep before you are.'

I watched Isak's gingery head rising above the heads of the other boys in our age group as we moved down the corridor. He was walking by himself, looking as if he didn't care that he was alone.

There was something a bit odd about him. But also heroic.

As I watched, a group of older boys caught up with Isak and formed a semi-circle around him, jostling and pushing him.

'Uh-oh,' said Mophead. 'That's Alex Simmonds and his mates. Isak and Alex hate one another.'

The older boys were nudging Isak with their elbows, pecking at him like crows. It was obvious they were trying to rile him to get him to lash out. I imagined how I would feel if they were doing that to me.

I had to push past them to reach Isak.

'Leave him alone,' I said, pushing them back.

'What's this?' one of them asked.

'Will you look at its ears! It's Mickey Mouse!'

'Who stuck those handles on the side of your head?'

Isak glanced at me and then carried on walking, just the same as before. The only difference now was that I was walking beside him.

17

EMMA – SUNDAY, 4 OCTOBER 1903

In the room above the attic, nothing of note happened until the fourth night after the arrival at All Hallows of Mrs March and the child. On the fourth night, Nurse Everdeen, asleep in the rocking chair, was awoken suddenly. She was disorientated and it took her a few seconds to work out what was happening.

Then she realised the cries of a terrified child were emanating from the bed beside her.

Still woozy from the sleeping potion, the nurse leaned over the bed.

'Harriet! *Harriet!* Wake up!'

Harriet did not wake.

Over the years, Nurse Everdeen had witnessed all manner of odd behaviour from the asylum patients. She was familiar with night terrors and the ways in which they manifested. Yet what was unsettling in adults was unbearable to witness in a child. She crouched down, and lifted Harriet into her arms. The little girl was twitching and trembling, her eyes wide open but rolled back, her mouth fixed in a rictus grimace. It appeared that she was trying to scream but her brain had paralysed her and the nurse was afraid she might be trapped in her terrors and swallow her tongue, or forget to breathe.

'Harriet! Wake up, *wake up!*' the old woman cried. She sat on the bed, cradling the child, shaking her gently and when that didn't work, cried: '*Harriet!*' into her face and pinched her. The child's eyes snapped shut and then opened again. She was trembling. She looked about her and the nurse watched recognition dawn as she realised where she was. Then she threw her arms around the nurse and buried her face into her body.

'Mama!' she cried. 'I want my *mama!*'

Nurse Everdeen patted the child's back awkwardly. 'There, there; it's not Mama, it's Nurse Everdeen. It was only a silly dream that frightened you. We're quite safe here in this room. You may go back into bed and go to sleep again now and—'

'I want my mama! Where is Mama? *Where is she?*'

'She's here, in the hospital. You came together. Perhaps you don't remember. You were very sleepy.'

The child sniffed. She took a large gulp and a swallow. She lifted up the hem of her nightdress to wipe her eyes.

'The lady said Mama was dead,' she said miserably.

'That's nonsense. Of course, she's not dead.'

'*But she said!*'

'Which lady, Harriet? Was it a lady in your nightmare?'

'I fink so.'

'Well, that lady is not real and she doesn't know anything. It's true that your mama is poorly but the doctors will make her better.' The nurse hesitated, reluctant to make a promise that she might not be able to keep. 'I'm sure they will make her better,' she qualified. 'We'll keep praying to our dear Lord to help her too.'

Harriet brightened slightly.

'God looks after good people, doesn't He?'

'Yes,' said Emma Everdeen. 'He does.'

He hadn't looked after Herbert, though, had He, she thought with a pang of resentment, and then she was ashamed of herself for this terrible, unchristian thought.

'Come, Harriet,' she said. 'It's cold. Get back underneath the covers and I shall tuck you in, safe and sound.'

Harriet obligingly wriggled off the nurse's lap and put herself back into the bed. Nurse Everdeen wrapped the blankets around her. 'There,' she said, 'isn't that better?'

'Where's my rabbit?'

'He's not your rabbit, Harriet, he's Herbert's rabbit and you are borrowing him. Here he is.'

Harriet tucked the rabbit under her chin and put her thumb into her mouth. Nurse Everdeen thought that really she was too old for thumb-sucking, but not having any experience of children beyond Herbert, who had not sucked his, she was unsure. She decided not to scold Harriet for now.

'Nurse?'

'What is it?'

'What if that lady *is* real?'

'She's not real.'

'I fink that she might be.'

'No. She's a nightmare lady and I promise she will never hurt you. I will not let her.'

18

The cloakroom was a vast, low-ceilinged space at the back of the main building, lower than the front façade because of the way the land sloped downhill. There was no natural light, only dim orange strip-lighting, like the lighting in the attic. This was where our overcoats were hung, hundreds of them on pegs in lines, with outdoor shoes in racks underneath. The pegs were arranged by year groups and alphabetically; mine was almost at the end of the line on my year, next to Isak's. At the far end of the cloakroom were a line of toilet cubicles and next to them, a communal shower.

Most of the other pupils had been out for their lunch break already; clods of dirt and streaks of mud littered the flagstones that covered the cloakroom floor. It smelled of disinfectant, socks and lavatories. It was vast and echoey and creepy. One of the boys in our class had told me that an asylum patient had hanged himself from the beam in the ceiling of one of the cubicles. I couldn't stop thinking about the hanging man; imagining that I heard the rope creaking. Lots of people must have died in All

Hallows when it was an asylum. It must have been a place full of sorrow. It wasn't all that much better now.

I wasn't the only pupil on report, but I was the last in the cloakroom, because I'd got lost on the way. I'd hoped Isak might have waited for me, but he hadn't. I assumed he and the others were already outside exercising. I wondered if anyone would notice if I stayed inside, in the cloakroom. Then I thought of the hanging man and I pulled my coat around me and hurried to the door. It opened onto a courtyard area, enclosed on three sides by the back of the main All Hallows building, and the two wings that stretched on either side behind it. I looked up at the west wing, grim from this perspective, like a prison. Up there, somewhere, was the corridor above the bedroom that Isak and I shared.

The duty teacher beckoned me forward. I pulled up the hood of my coat so it covered my ears and looked around for Isak. I couldn't see him. I walked up to the teacher who checked my name off a list.

'Right,' he said, 'you can go where you like as long as you don't go out of the courtyard, OK? You stay in this area here, within the paths.'

'OK,' I said.

'OK, *sir*.'

'OK, sir.'

I snapped my back straight and saluted. The teacher shook his head and turned back to his cigarette. I expect he'd seen it before.

The courtyard had been landscaped into a formal garden area that must have been the same in the days of the asylum. In the centre was a great stone bowl, which formed the base of what once was a fountain but now was merely a grim statue of a great, muscular, bearded man breaking free of his shackles and rising up out of the water like a rocket being launched. Pathways radiated from the fountain with lawned sections in between. There were no flowerbeds or trees; it was all lines and angles.

I walked around the stone man. Two boys squatted on their haunches on the other side, hidden from the view of the supervising teacher. Others were walking around the edges of the courtyard. I looked for Isak but he was nowhere to be seen.

I wished Jesse was here. Or Isobel. Or someone I'd known a long time, one of the kids I'd played with on the street, a friend since I was Wingnut at primary school. Someone who knew that sometimes I laughed at the wrong things and in the wrong places; or that I could be too keen, too needy, too talkative, too quiet. Someone who didn't mind about me blushing and fainting.

I'd never been good at making new friends.

Thinking of Isobel made me sad again. As soon as Dad told me about boarding school, I'd told her over the phone during her weekly call. I'd hoped she might be able to think of a way to rescue me, but she'd put another 10p in the slot and said: 'Lewey, I'm in Durham in women's halls. I love you but I can't do anything to help you this time.'

She said she'd speak to our father, and she'd been good to her word. I'd crouched at the top of the stairs behind the banisters, eavesdropping. I heard Dad say: 'Boarding school is the best thing for him, Issy. We didn't make this decision lightly.'

At the other end of the line my sister said something and Dad had replied: 'It's nothing to do with his nonconformity. It's to do with his living a decent, respectable life.'

'Respectable' and 'decent' were not words my mum used often. She preferred 'creative' and 'fulfilling'. As I walked along the gravelled path towards the far end of the All Hallows courtyard, I realised how different my parents had been from one another: she a free spirit, he so committed to doing things properly.

Dad and Mum used to argue all the time. Well, not *argue* exactly. Mum would sometimes shout at Dad but he would just walk away. He said it was impossible to have a proper conversation with Mum when she was being 'like that'.

I hated it when they got angry with one another. Isobel said not to worry. She said opposites attract and that was what had happened with Mum and Dad. She said they'd 'had to get married', which proved how much in love they were – although it sounded like the opposite to me.

And now it was clear that Isobel had been wrong.

Dad didn't love Mum. He didn't love any of us.

I didn't realise how much he didn't love us until after Mum had died and he was free to be the unloving person he'd always been all along.

* * *

I'd reached the far end of the courtyard and now the wind was no longer blocked by the west wing, it blasted me, making my trouser legs flap around my ankles. The chill was biting, sweeping off the moor. I held the hood tight around my face. It was a good, heavy coat, the kind a spy might wear. I liked the feeling of being a spy, in enemy territory.

I was technically still inside the boundaries of the courtyard. I took another few steps out into the longer grass beyond, and then looked behind me. The supervising teacher's head was tucked inside his coat, trying to light a cigarette. With my head low, I crept across the grass to a clump of hydrangea bushes in exactly the same way as a prisoner of war might slip out of the sight of his captors, and crouched behind it.

To the right of me now was a lake with an island in the middle. Some kind of building, like a shelter, stood in the centre of the island with an angel on either side holding up a plaque; it was too overgrown to work out the details.

Still crouching, I peered around the dying leaves. The teacher still had his back to me. I headed in the opposite direction, towards the chapel. I wanted to get a closer look at the fallen tree and see how much damage it had done.

In full POW mode, I loped across the unmown grass, flattened in patches by the weather, the water caught in the seed-heads soaking the legs of my trousers. Above the beech copse behind the chapel, the rooks were cawing, flapping their untidy wings as the wind tossed them about. As I drew close, I saw how big the fallen tree was; its great canopy, branches still half-full of turning leaves, enclosed the roof of the chapel. Some of the branches had made holes in the roof, breaking and displacing tiles, and smaller branches and twigs were scattered everywhere.

'Wow!' I breathed.

Wow! Mum echoed.

I followed the small wall that encircled the chapel round behind the building and soon the tree was in front of me: the great, grey-green column of its trunk resting at a shallow angle.

The beeches had clearly been planted to shelter the chapel. They had lasted this long, had even survived the great storm, so it must have been a massive gust of wind that brought the tree down. As well as toppling itself, the giant beech had brought down a smaller tree, one that had been planted closer to the chapel wall. This was a thorn of some kind, and its roots still contained the cake of soil and stone to which they had been clinging before it fell.

I crouched down to creep beneath the trunk of the beech, behind the thorn. This would be the perfect place to dig an escape tunnel; out of sight of the windows of All Hallows; sheltered by the graveyard wall.

I put my hand against the bark of the beech, keeping my head low. I was out of the wind now, and the organic, peaty smell of earth and leaf and rain was familiar to me. This was a secret hiding place all of my own. Right now, nobody in the whole world knew exactly where I was – except me. I slipped without thinking into a game that Jesse and I used to play in Bristol, commentating on my imaginary situation.

This is where the prisoner has to make a decision. Should he hide here until nightfall and then make a dash for the wall; knowing the dogs will be out searching for him, knowing there will be searchlights and guards with guns? Or should he start to dig now?

Jesse would be all for making a den. He would love this!

I crouched on my heels, conscious of the weight of the great tree above me, knowing that if the chapel were to collapse, the tree would fall with it and I would be crushed. There was something exciting about being in danger. Not real danger – I didn't *really* believe I was going to be flattened – but it definitely might happen. Here I was, a hero in the making, wrapped in my greatcoat, my future depending on chance. Would anyone notice if I didn't go back to All Hallows, but stayed here? I could catch rabbits, steal food from the kitchens, grow feathers, fly away…

I was so lost in these thoughts that I didn't notice at first, not for several minutes in fact, that something was tangled amongst the roots of the thorn right in front of me; it was brown-grey and smooth, streaked with dirt; not a stone but circular in shape, as if man-made, the size of a melon.

What's that? Mum asked.

I don't know.

I held on to a thick tuber for balance, reached forward and

prodded the thing with my finger and it swayed a little on its root-hook. I pushed it again, harder and it swivelled towards me and I saw what it was. It was not a ball. It was the top half of a human skull, the smaller rootlets fingering their way through the dark sockets where the eyes once used to be.

19

EMMA – 1903

After Nurse Everdeen and Harriet had breakfasted the next morning, two visitors came to the little room in the attic: Superintendent Francis Pincher and the new doctor, a slight young man with thinning, fair hair, a smooth complexion, a soft moustache and an eager smile.

'This is Dr Milligan,' said the superintendent. 'He is an expert in the treatment of head injuries and he's going to be taking charge of the care of Mrs March.'

'We're honoured to have you here, Doctor, I'm sure,' said the nurse.

'Mr Pincher has sung your praises to me, Nurse Everdeen,' said the young doctor. 'He says you are one of the most reliable members of the female staff.'

Nurse Everdeen tried not to feel patronised.

'And this must be the little one,' said the doctor, taking a step towards Harriet.

'Don't go too close,' said Nurse Everdeen. 'She's frightened and in my experience—'

'Your *limited* medical experience,' said Mr Pincher.

'In my limited experience, it's best not to make frightened patients feel threatened.'

The young doctor didn't comment but did not go any closer to Harriet. He tilted his head this way and that to have the best look at her as if she was an exhibit in a museum. She watched him, steely-eyed, over the head of the knitted rabbit, which she was clutching to her chest.

Mr Pincher, having decided to make absolutely clear his lack of regard for the opinions of his subordinate, came forward past the doctor. His hair was slicked back with Macassar oil. As he approached, the child pressed herself back into the wall and although he was not a large man, he was so much larger than the child that Nurse Everdeen had an urge to rush at him and shoo him away with a tea-towel, as if he was a hungry crow and Harriet a defenceless kit. The strength of her desire to protect the child took her by surprise.

'She's very young,' he said, peering at Harriet over his spectacles.

'About five years, I'd say,' Nurse Everdeen said tersely. It was the same age as Herbert had been when he died, that was how she knew.

'Has she spoken at all?'

'A little. She's had some bad dreams.'

'That's only to be expected,' said the young doctor. 'Dreams are a window into the subconscious mind. It might be helpful, Nurse, if you would be kind enough to write down anything the child tells you about her dreams. They might help us piece together some of the puzzle about what happened to her and her mother.' He hesitated. 'You do know how to write?'

'I do.'

Superintendent Pincher spoke again. 'Have you found anything about the child's person that might help us identify her?'

'She has a birth mark.'

'May we see it?'

The nurse stepped forward. 'I need to show the two gentlemen your wrist, Harriet.'

She leaned down and gently she lifted Harriet's left hand, pushed back the sleeve of her dress and turned the arm so that the wrist was uppermost. There was a brown stain in the shape of a birch leaf just beneath the base of her thumb, close to veins that were slender as threads.

'Her mother has one almost exactly the same,' said the doctor.

'Someone who knows them well would recognise the two of them by these marks,' said the superintendent.

'Will you put an appeal in the newspapers?' asked Nurse Everdeen.

Mr Pincher sucked in the corners of his lips.

'Not yet. Not until we know what happened to them, and why. If they are in some kind of trouble, we feel it would be unwise to advertise it while they are so vulnerable. We don't want some scoundrel turning up and laying claim to Mrs March's jewellery. We'd like you stay up here with the child, Nurse, if you are willing to bear the inconvenience, until Mrs March has regained consciousness.'

'It's no inconvenience, sir. Is there still no improvement in Mrs March's condition?'

'I'm afraid not, Nurse Everdeen.' The doctor glanced towards the child, and next time he spoke, his voice was low. 'One would have expected Mrs March to have shown some signs of sensibility after this length of time if all she had suffered was a blow to the head. Her continued lack of responsiveness is of grave concern.'

'I will keep her in my prayers, Doctor. And so will Harriet.'

'We are still hopeful for a positive outcome, but you may be confined to this attic corridor for some length of time.'

'We shall manage. This corridor suits the two of us very well.'

'You're a credit to your profession, Nurse Everdeen,' said the doctor.

Mr Pincher rocked on his heels, praise for the nurse reflecting on him.

'We'll have Maria continue to bring up your meals and anything else you request, Nurse Everdeen. Besides yourself, only she and Dr Milligan will have access to the child.'

'Very good, sir,' said Nurse Everdeen. Then she added: 'May I ask, will Harriet and I be permitted to attend chapel on Sunday?'

'Not for the present. But you can pray as well here in the attic, Nurse Everdeen, as in the pew.'

It wasn't the praying, it was the visiting of Herbert's grave that Emma would miss. Since her son's death more than half a century earlier, she had visited at least once a week. She'd felt Herbert's presence there each time, and although she knew a pure soul such as his must surely be safe in the arms of God, she imagined He allowed Herbert a few moments' grace each week to give comfort to his mother.

Still, she could see the chapel and the wall that surrounded the graveyard through the glass in the small window. She could look over to where Herbert lay and she was confident he would know that she was thinking of him, even if she was not there in person. If it was God's will that she stay here in the attic to care for the child, then so be it.

Life was a series of checks and balances. Emma Everdeen knew this. So far, her scales had weighed more heavily on the side of pain and misfortune. God willing, caring for little Harriet March would help to even things out. And then, when eventually she was called, she would be laid to rest in the same grave as Herbert, and they would be reunited for ever, and grass would grow above them, and the birds would sing, and the seasons would change, and she would be eternally at peace.

Should I go back into the courtyard and tell the teacher about the human skull caught up in the roots of the thorn tree and be punished for breaking the rules, or not say anything and leave it for someone else to find?

You have to tell someone, Mum whispered. *What if an animal comes and takes it away?*

I could always write an anonymous note, slip it under the head-master's door...

You could do that, yes, but you couldn't be sure he'd see it.

I inched forward and looked down into the hole left by the roots of the thorn. A number of other bones lay in the wet soil, some fine and curved as if they'd been carved from wood, others thick and brown and knobbled. As the argument about whether I should do something about them or not went backwards and forwards in my mind, I heard voices approaching.

Keeping my head low, I crept forward and peeped over the wall. A man, who had to be the chaplain because he was wearing a dog collar, was talking with another man, who looked like he might be the caretaker, about the damage caused by the fallen beech. I couldn't hear the details of what they were saying but it was obvious that they were about to come round to where I was hiding and that I was certain to be discovered.

What would Steve McQueen do if this was *The Great Escape*?

He would give himself up before he was found. That way it would be like he was the one in control.

My heart was pounding. Even so, I bravely crept out of my hiding place, stood beside the wall, raised a hand and, hardly showing any fear, called: 'Excuse me!' Neither of the men heard me so I said it again, only louder this time and the caretaker man turned.

'Hey!' he said. 'What are you doing here? You're not supposed to be here!'

The chaplain held up a hand to shush him.

'Don't,' he said, 'he's very pale.' Then to me he called, 'I say, are you all right, young man?' and that was when I felt the ground beneath my feet tilt alarmingly as it came rushing up to meet my face.

It wasn't really that surprising that I'd fainted given that, a) I'd just found my first ever shallow grave, b) I knew I would be in trouble about it, and c) I had eaten hardly anything since my arrival at All Hallows. Luckily for me, the faint, for once, got me out of a sticky situation. The chaplain clambered over the wall to come to my rescue and it was while I was slumped on the grass with his arms around me that I opened my eyes and blearily came to. I told him about the bones and he checked to see that I was telling the truth and when he found that I was, he squeezed my shoulder and said: 'Not to worry, old chap,' exactly as if we really were in some old black-and-white war film.

He and the caretaker took me to see Matron, who gave me a jam doughnut (delicious) and a cup of sweet tea to boost my sugar levels. She treated me like an invalid until after she'd spoken to my father, who told her the fainting was nothing to worry about. 'He does it deliberately to get attention,' he said, which wasn't true, I couldn't control it. It was another unfairness on top of everything else made me feel even more sad and helpless.

A little while after that, I was packed off to the headmaster's office. I sat on one of the straight-backed wooden chairs that stood against the wall outside, waiting for my fate. The corridor smelled of wax polish and of the dust scorching behind the huge old radiators, which wasn't at all like the burning smell upstairs. I wound a length of cotton that I'd pulled from my shirt cuff around my finger, one way and then the other, carving red welts into the skin, wondering exactly how much trouble I was in.

The chaplain was in the office with Dr Crozier, the headmaster, the headmaster's secretary and two police officers. I wasn't sure if they were there because of the bones, or whether I had committed an actual crime. Perhaps I had and I was about to be arrested and sent to borstal. That would be the end of my dreams of becoming a detective. I was pretty certain you weren't allowed to join the police if you had a criminal record.

I wound the thread round my finger. The clock on the wall ticked and tocked and each time the second hand reached the vertical, the minute hand clicked as it moved forward. Time moved very slowly at All Hallows, I'd noticed. The hour turned but the clock tower bell didn't ring. Actually, I hadn't heard it all day.

When the door to the office finally opened, I sat up straight. The police came out and stood directly in front of me so my eyes were at the exact levels of their stomachs; one man and one woman, both bulky in their uniform, and behind them was the headmaster's secretary. The policeman smiled at me, and winked.

'Looks like we've got a right troublemaker here,' he said to his colleague. 'Criminal mastermind in the making, I'd say.'

I knew he was teasing but still I felt myself flush from the bottom of my neck to the top of my exposed, sticking-out ears.

'Dr Crozier is waiting for you, Tyler,' said the headmaster's secretary.

I stood up and walked miserably into the office. The headmaster was standing behind an enormous desk, a tall, thin man with a gaunt face; the folds of his black gown and his beaky nose giving him the appearance of a crow. The chaplain sat on a chair beside the desk, an egg-shaped face rising above a podgy body, his legs crossed at the knee with the trouser of the upper leg ridden up so that I could see a stretch of hairy pink ankle above the elasticated top of his sock. The office was cavernous: a huge stone fireplace; a grand Gothic window, fancily framed portraits and acres of ornate, dark panelling.

I thought of all the hundreds of boys who had been caned in this office and my stomach turned to liquid. I wondered if they had to bend over the desk or how exactly the punishment was administered. Did they have to pull down their trousers? Did they put exercise books in their pants to protect themselves? Nobody was ever hit at my old school – they wouldn't have dreamed of it. I'd been smacked across the legs once at primary school. Mum had gone ballistic when I told her and complained to the governors; it didn't happen again. Other than that, my only experience of corporal punishment at school came from books and films. I couldn't quite believe it might be about to happen to me. I tried to be Steve McQueen again. I tried to stand brave and tall but also insolent in the enemy's spotlight. I tried not to care.

'Sit down, Tyler,' said Dr Crozier, looking at me over the tops of his spectacles. 'The chaplain has something to say to you.'

'Thank you, Headmaster.' The chaplain cleared his throat and leaned forward. 'Now, Lewis, I know what happened this morning was a shock for you. It would have been a shock for anyone. You're probably wondering why the unfortunate person to whom those bones belonged had been buried on the wrong side of the graveyard wall. I want to reassure you that there was nothing irregular about the burial. We've spoken with the police and showed them our records. They concur that the remains exposed had been buried legally in that spot ninety years ago.'

'Why weren't they in the graveyard?'

'I'm coming to that. In the old days, Lewis, there were rather a lot of regulations about who could and could not be laid to rest in the chapel graveyard, the land being consecrated. Those who weren't eligible for burial inside the graveyard, but who died at the asylum, or in this case, *belonged* to the asylum, were buried on the other side of the wall, as close as they could be to God, without breaking any of the aforementioned rules. It happened surprisingly frequently; not just here, but in other graveyards, in other places.'

He glanced to the headmaster, who gave a small nod to signify that he should continue.

'Most of the souls buried on the wrong side of the wall were unbaptised infants. Obviously, the bones uncovered beneath the blackthorn tree were adult bones. I've checked the chapel records and only seven adults were ever laid to rest beyond the graveyard wall. Six were male convicts transferred from Dartmoor Prison during the nineteenth century, and the third was a female nurse who died at the beginning of this century.' He paused and then continued: 'It looks as if the bones in question belonged to the nurse. They will be removed and laid to rest in a more suitable location.'

'Why was she—' I began, but Dr Crozier interrupted.

'There's no need to dwell on this, Tyler. Once you leave this office, you are to put it from your mind. I forbid you to discuss it with the other pupils. Is that absolutely clear?'

'Yes, sir.'

Dr Crozier turned to the chaplain. 'Thank you, Chaplain, that will be all.'

The chaplain stood and dusted the thighs of his trousers. I stood too. That hadn't been anywhere near as bad as I'd expected.

'Not you, Tyler,' said Dr Crozier.

Uh-oh.

I sat down again.

The chaplain left, closing the door behind him. Dr Crozier returned to the desk, resting his knuckles on the surface. He stared at me. It made me uncomfortable but he kept staring. I looked away, skewered by his gaze.

At the exact moment when I thought I could not bear it for a single second longer, he asked: 'What am I to do with you, Tyler?'

Don't answer, whispered my mother. *It's a trick question.*

'You've been here no time at all, you seem an insignificant, rather pathetic little chap and yet you've shown a complete disregard for instructions, you've broken rules and disobeyed orders. Do you think they don't apply to you? Do you think you're better than everyone else here? Different? Special?'

'No, sir.'

'You're on report already, yet you went to the chapel this morning, having clearly been told that you must stay in the courtyard, knowing the chapel was out of bounds, without any care that you were transgressing.'

'I'm sorry, sir.'

'Do you have any excuse for your behaviour?'

'I wanted to see the fallen tree, sir.'

'Have you never seen a fallen tree before?'

'Yes, but this was a big one and...' I tailed off. 'Sorry, sir,' I said. I really was.

'I can't put you on report when you're already on report,' said Dr Crozier. His voice was low and calm, so quiet that I had to strain to hear it. 'You leave me no alternative but to use a different form of punishment.'

Oh Jesus! said my mother.

I prayed for my mother. I prayed for her to materialise and barge into this huge, dark office and push Dr Crozier aside and take me by the hand and say: 'Come on, Lewis, we're getting the hell out of this godforsaken shithole.' No, better, she could come riding in like the Lone Ranger and scoop me up onto Zephyr's back and then turn the horse and we'd gallop through the corridors of All Hallows, only stopping to rescue Isak on the way out. And maybe Mophead too, if there was room.

If I concentrated hard enough I might be able to summon her by force of will alone; hers and mine. I did my best but she didn't come. Obviously.

Dr Crozier adjusted the shoulders of his gown and stood up straight.

'Stand up, Tyler,' he said.

I stood. My knees felt very wobbly but I didn't wobble. I was Steve McQueen and Crozier was the camp commandant and I would never let him see that I was afraid.

He picked up the cane that had been lying on his desk. He weighed it in his palm.

'Hold out your hand,' he said.

Steve McQueen kept his head high as he held out his hand. His hand might have trembled but other than that he showed not a single sign of weakness.

21

'Miss Harriet March! Look what I have for you!' Maria Smith came around the door into the attic room, waving something in her hand.

Harriet looked up from the table, where she was drawing on a tablet with a piece of chalk.

'What is it?' Nurse Everdeen asked.

'It's a catalogue from a toy shop in Exeter!' said Maria, dancing the few steps to the table and laying it down in front of Harriet. 'Mrs Collins thought Harriet might like to look at it.'

'Well!' said Nurse Everdeen. 'A toy catalogue! I never knew such a thing existed!'

Harriet did not move from her drawing but her hand had stilled.

'I understand there's all kinds of dollies in there,' said Maria. 'And tea sets and clockwork toys and puzzles and games.'

'My goodness!'

'Indeed!'

Maria took the chair beside Harriet's and began to turn the pages of the catalogue, humming and making appreciative noises as she did so. Nurse Everdeen continued to sit in her rocking chair and knit but she smiled as she noticed Harriet lay down her chalk and lean closer to Maria.

Soon enough, the child was engrossed in the catalogue and Maria moved closer to Nurse Everdeen to tell her the latest news from the asylum. A visitor had come to see Mr Pincher and Mr Uxbridge that morning, a 'very fine gentleman' – a *lord* no less! – who had come to discuss possible treatment for his debauched daughter. His lordship and his lordship's wife were visiting several asylums to find the one that would best meet their requirements. As the lord had a great deal of money, Mr Pincher was most eager that All Hallows be the one he picked.

'Debauched?' Nurse Everdeen had repeated. 'I've never heard such a word.'

'It means that the daughter is disobedient and vulgar,' Maria replied in a low voice. 'I asked Dr Milligan.'

Nurse Everdeen had heard of similar complaints by fathers, and indeed mothers, about their headstrong daughters before. No doubt some unfortunate young woman would soon be arriving at All Hallows to be taught a lesson at great expense to her parents.

'Mr Uxbridge told the lord that he'd take the girl in hand and break her in, like you'd break a horse,' said Maria darkly.

Nurse Everdeen shuddered. 'Mr Uxbridge is a vile man.'

'He certainly is. Did I tell you about Dorothy?'

Dorothy was Mr Uxbridge's niece and had been hired as a nurse at All Hallows despite rumours that she'd been dismissed from her previous position as companion to a crippled woman after accusations of neglect. There was no evidence – at least none that Nurse Everdeen could see – of the girl having any innate desire to care for others, nor did she demonstrate any tenderness. She certainly had no patience with the slower and sadder patients, yet she was not above poking fun at them, even teasing them. Nurse Everdeen had complained about her behaviour to Mr Pincher who told her it was a matter for Mr Uxbridge's attention. Mr Uxbridge had laughed when Nurse Everdeen told him what Dorothy had done. 'Oh, she's a livewire!' he had said and that had been the end of the matter. All Nurse Everdeen could do was endeavour to protect the patients from Dorothy's cruelty. Unfortunately, Dorothy was not the only member of staff who seemed to derive pleasure from tormenting the most vulnerable and the most afflicted.

'What about Dorothy?' Nurse Everdeen asked Maria cautiously. 'What's she done now?'

'Mr Uxbridge has only gone and appointed her personal nurse to Mrs March. In the Royal Suite!'

'The Royal Suite?'

'Indeed.'

The Royal Suite was what All Hallows' staff called the grandest, most luxurious and costliest of the private rooms on the ground floor of the asylum. A personal nurse attending to a patient there would have the benefit of all its comforts.

Nurse Everdeen was about to exclaim her anger at this state of affairs, but on reflection, she thought perhaps it was for the best. While it was wholly unfair that Dorothy Uxbridge should enjoy Royal Suite privileges when she had done nothing at all to deserve them, it did at least mean that she would be away from the other patients, and not making their lives more miserable than they already were.

'I hope she will be kind to Mrs March,' Nurse Everdeen said quietly.

'Dr Milligan is there almost constantly,' said Maria. 'Dorothy will have to mind herself; he watches Mrs March like a hawk.'

* * *

That evening, after supper, Harriet took off and folded her own stockings and held up her arms for Nurse Everdeen to take off her dress, her fine hair catching on the wool. She knelt down beside the bed to say her prayers, with the knitted rabbit tucked under her arm, and then settled down beneath the blankets without any fuss. Nurse Everdeen poked the coals to warm up the little room, then read a story by the light of the lamp, and Harriet soon fell asleep. The nurse spent a quiet ten minutes at the window, waiting for moonlight to illuminate the chapel and its graveyard.

'Sleep tight,' she whispered as the clean, white light fell at last over the place where Herbert lay and then she went back to her rocking chair. She put a pillow behind her and settled with a blanket over her knees.

Her mind drifted back to Herbert's last days. His troubles had begun with a cold on his chest. He was prone to them and this one seemed no worse than usual; nothing to worry about. Emma had kept him warm in her room and Nurse Harriet Sawmills had come to see him and reassured Emma that this was normal for a child. When the gurgling in his lungs had become worse, they had applied a mustard plaster to his back and given him honey and vinegar to sip from a teaspoon. Emma – she was not a nurse then – had not left her son's side. She had sung to him, played counting games with him; anything to persuade a smile to his lips.

Herbert's forehead grew hotter and hotter. Soon, it was so hot that Emma could hardly bear to hold her wrist against it.

She took off his clothes, his covers and then he cried and said he was cold, even though bubbles of sweat were seeping through his pores.

He began to hallucinate, telling Emma that spiders the size of cats were in the room, climbing the curtains. She had shooed them away. When Herbert at last slept, Emma lay beside him and closed her eyes. She woke to find her son fitting.

'What can we do?' Emma had asked Nurse Sawmills, and Nurse Sawmills no longer told her not to worry, no longer said that Herbert would soon be back on his feet, running around, back to his cheeky, naughty, happy little self. Instead, she said that they should pray.

Herbert grew weaker.

Two days later, he stopped breathing.

Simply stopped.

In the attic room, Nurse Everdeen rocked her chair slowly and wiped the tears from her tired eyes.

'I'm sorry, my angel,' she whispered. 'I'm so sorry I couldn't save you.'

22

When I came into the bedroom, Isak was changing for bed. He paused, the pyjama top halfway over his chest. His stomach and chest were milky pale.

He let the pyjama top fall and turned to me.

'Where have you been?' he asked. 'I haven't seen you all day.'

'Where have *you* been? I looked for you at lunch and you weren't there!'

He shrugged. 'Crouch called me in to do some cramming.'

'Oh.'

I clenched my sore hand tightly as I sat on the bed. Humiliation was like a sour taste in my mouth. That and anger. I did not know who I hated more: Dr Crozier for caning my hand six times, or my father and stepmother for sending me here in the first place.

'What's happened?' Isak asked.

'I had the cane from Dr Crozier.'

'Shit. Why?'

In one breath, I remembered that Dr Crozier had forbidden

me to talk of the bones. In the next, I recalled Mum saying: *Anyone who asks you to tell a lie does not have your best interests at heart.*

'I found some bones. Human bones.'

'*What?*'

'Under a tree, on the far side of the graveyard wall.'

'A skeleton?'

'Yeah, basically.'

Isak whistled.

'And he beat you for that?'

'For going out of bounds...' I tailed off, my bravado gone. 'I was already on report; he said he had no option.'

'He had an option to *not* fucking hit you, didn't he?'

I hunched over my knees. Isak moved over from his bed and sat beside me. I could feel the warmth of him, smell the carbolic soap on his skin. His fringe fell forward over his eyes. He put his arm around my shoulders like a brother would. His palm patted the prickly, tufty stubs of my hair.

'He's a bastard,' he said quietly. 'He's as bad as my father.'

Before I could ask about his father, he took hold of my hand and uncurled the fingers; looked at the red welts on my palm.

'Hurts, huh?'

'Yeah,' I said.

He closed the fingers, gently, over the welts and let my hand fall back onto my thigh.

'Come up to the bathroom,' he said. 'We'll run it under the cold tap.'

* * *

That evening, all I wanted was to wash away the day, to get rid of the pain in my hand, the memory of the self-satisfied expression on Dr Crozier's face – I was certain I'd detected a hint of pleasure as he hit me. It had been a horrible day and I wanted to wash it all down the plughole.

We stood together at the basin in the bathroom, Isak supporting my hand in his and cold water splashing onto my sore palm. It was so nice to have someone looking after me. It brought to mind Isobel and I thought that I must write to her and tell her everything that had been going on. She'd want to know.

When my hand had almost stopped hurting, Isak went downstairs and I had a shower, standing in the bath. After that, because it was cold in the bathroom, I went back into the rocking chair room with my towel wrapped around my waist to dry off. I sat on the chair, feeling the give of the old seat beneath me, the press of the tenon in the small of my back and the crest rail at the back of my head. I pressed my toes into the floorboards and tipped the chair backwards.

My hands rested on the towel on my lap. The light coming through the window strengthened in colour as the sun sank to meet the horizon. Backwards went the chair and forwards. The runners creaked. I closed my eyes and I sat there until the light faded and without its golden glow the room became shadowed and chilly and I thought I saw a shadow dart across the room, from one side to another, and I heard the clock tower bell chime the half-hour.

And then all at once the atmosphere changed. Suddenly, I felt a chill far colder than anything I'd felt in the bathroom and I had the sensation of something huge coming into the room and dread ran through my blood. It was a kind of dread I'd only experienced once before, at the Bristol Royal Infirmary when Dad and Isobel and I were in the family room and the doctor came to talk to us, and I could see from his face that there was no saving Mum. It was like that.

I couldn't get out of the room quickly enough. I stumbled to the door, ran through it back along the corridor and down the stairs, taking them two at a time: I dashed into our room, pulling the door shut behind me. Isak was lying on his back on his bed, reading. I was grateful not to be alone. I changed into my pyjamas and rubbed my head with the towel.

'Better?' Isak asked.

'Yeah,' I said. I didn't know how to start to tell him about the experience I'd had upstairs so instead I raised something else that had been bothering me. 'Isn't it creepy how you can hear the big clock chiming in the room above, but nowhere else in the school.'

'What do you mean?'

'The clock in the tower. I heard it just now chiming the half-hour.'

'No, you didn't. The clock doesn't work. It hasn't worked since I've been at All Hallows.'

'Must've been some other clock then.'

'There is no other clock.'

'Maybe your ears just aren't very good.'

The moment I said that I realised I'd set myself up for him to say something about my ears being the size of radio telescope dishes, but he didn't say anything.

I put the towel down, got under the covers, and picked up my notebook to write to Isobel. I was engrossed in the letter when Isak asked: 'Lewis, do you feel angry?'

'About what?'

'Everything.'

'I don't know,' I said. 'Sometimes. A bit.'

Isak pushed himself up and stood between the foot of his bed and the window. 'I get so angry that sometimes I feel I'm going to erupt, like a volcano. *Boom!*' He described a mushroom cloud of exploding anger above his head with his arms.

I remembered what Mophead had said about Isak being a psycho and pulled the bedspread up to my chin.

'Sometimes I go down into the cloakroom and punch the coats hanging on the pegs: I pretend they're teachers.' He mimed the act for my benefit, fists raised close to his chest, skipping about with his eyes narrowed, punching imaginary coats, jabbing them violently. 'Sometimes I grab one by the neck and throw it on the floor and kick it. Usually it's Crouch, but next time, for you, I'll make it Crozier.'

'Thanks,' I said.

Isak mimed the murder of a coat. His skin was flushed, sweat beading on his forehead. The muscles on his arms and back and shoulders were defined. He was strong.

'Why are you so angry?' I asked.

Isak froze mid-punch. Then he started again, more furiously than before.

'Is it your family?' I persisted.

'What do you mean?'

'Is it your dad? Your mum?'

He doesn't want to talk about them, Mum whispered urgently.

'Has someone said something to you?' Isak asked.

'No,' I said.

He leaped across so that his face was close to mine, his green eyes staring into mine, his breath on my face. 'What have they said?'

'Nobody's said anything!' I cried, and then as he continued to glare at me, I repeated it more loudly. '*Nothing! I don't know anything about your family, OK?*'

I went back to my letter. I had already written about the bones and the caning. I'd asked Isobel if she could find out anything about the nurse who'd been buried on the wrong side of the graveyard wall and why she'd been buried there. I started a new paragraph.

By the way, I wrote, *my roommate is Swedish, he's called Isak Salèn and everyone says he's mental. I think they're probably right.*

Anyone who was at All Hallows could not fail to notice the constant thrumming of the dehumidifiers that had been set up in the parts of the building affected by the flooding. Because the noise was there all the time, sometimes it faded into the background, but at other times it became really annoying and you just wanted to yell at it to shut up. Mophead, whose father worked in construction, told us that water could do terrible damage to old buildings. It made the wood that held up structures like All Hallows go soft and rotten. It wet the old concrete, causing mould to grow and the mould had spores that weakened the concrete. It rusted metal. And water was sneaky. It could find its way into the tiniest cracks and gaps and lie there, waiting for a frost, and then when the frost came the water would turn into ice and expand and crack the bricks and stones in which it was hiding.

I kind of wished Mophead wouldn't tell me all this stuff. It made me feel even less easy about the place. And with that constant vibrating noise going on all the time, it was difficult to forget about it.

During lessons, we heard the workmen moving around and above us; the clomp of work boots, furniture being dragged across floors. A pile of damaged chairs, cupboards and beds was forming on the front courtyard outside the converted stable block like a stack for a giant bonfire. Ruined bedding, blackened by mould blooms, was draped over and across it.

A family lived in the converted stable block. I saw the woman who lived there come out and talk to the contractors about the pile of old furniture. It was almost as high as her home. I bet she was asking them when they were going to take it away.

23

EMMA – 1903

Emma put her wrist against Harriet's forehead to make sure that she was not too hot. She listened to her breathing; could hear no obstruction in the child's lungs. Reassured, Emma then put the pillow behind her own head, and pulled the blanket around her in the chair, and she settled down to sleep. Her rest did not last for long. She was woken by a cry and found that Harriet was out of bed.

The child was standing in the middle of the room, in her nightdress with her toes peeping out from the hem. Her arms were outstretched and her fingers too and she was pleading: 'Stop it! Stop it! Oh, please, please don't hurt her! *Don't hurt her!*'

Nurse Everdeen went to her at once, but the child's appearance was disconcerting, her face oddly shadowed by the glow from the fire. The nurse was, for a moment, afraid to touch her, and then she reminded herself that this was only a little girl who had witnessed unimaginable horrors; only a terrified child.

The nurse guided the child back into bed and tucked her in for a second time, hummed hymns to her until she fell back into a deep sleep without ever really waking. Then Emma prayed that the horrors that plagued Harriet would leave her alone for the rest of the night.

It was one thing for the child, but after the fright she'd had, Nurse Everdeen couldn't fall asleep for a second time, no matter how many sheep she counted nor how many sweet memories of Herbert playing in the grounds of All Hallows she summoned to mind. She worried that Harriet might sleepwalk again, and go too close to the hearth so the hem of her nightdress caught fire, or fall and bang her head or otherwise hurt herself. The nurse was immensely relieved that the door at the top of the stairs was locked, and that there was no way for Harriet to wander from this part of the landing. She could not bear the prospect of the child injuring herself while in her care.

By the time dawn broke, the nurse was exhausted. She made up the fire that had died almost to nothing and put some water in a bowl beside it to warm, and then she sat back on the rocking chair and pushed it backwards, and despite everything she must have dozed as the room grew warm because she didn't hear the key turning in the lock of the landing door, nor the footsteps approaching. What woke her was a muted cough on the other side of the door. The polite nature of the cough was enough for her to recognise that it was made by Dr Milligan and the fact that the door was ajar made her suspect that he had come into the room, seen her sleeping and withdrawn again to preserve her dignity. She pushed herself to her feet and fought away the feeling of disorientation that came with being woken from a deep slumber, the guilt of being caught shirking in her duty. She stretched out the ache in her knees, smoothed her skirts and went to the door.

'Good morning, Dr Milligan,' she said, attempting to make her face bright and alert. 'Do please come in.'

The doctor entered and Maria was behind him, carrying the

breakfast tray, which she placed on the table. 'Good morning!' Maria cried cheerfully.

The sound of this disturbed Harriet, who woke and yawned, stretching in the bed like a little cat. She pushed herself up and looked around, observed that the doctor was present and asked: 'Is my mama well again now?'

'She's still sleeping,' said the doctor, 'but her bumps and bruises are healing very nicely.' He smiled at the child. 'I have told her that you are being a good, patient girl. I'm certain that she hears me and that it pleases her to hear your news.'

The child nodded, and her hair swung about her chin, but the disappointment was written clearly on her little face.

The doctor continued: 'I've been reading all the articles I can find about how best to care for someone like your mother to bring about the best possible conclusion for her. I've even written to my colleagues in Austria asking their opinions.'

'Do you hear that, Harriet?' asked Maria. 'Doctors all over the world are trying to help your mama!'

'But also, they want to know about you, child,' the doctor said. 'So, I'd like to make a photograph to accompany the article I intend to publish. I have already made a picture of your mother.'

Maria and the nurse glanced at one another. Nurse Everdeen had little experience of photography and was not certain of the etiquette. The picture of Herbert that she wore in her locket had been cut from a much larger image of All Hallows staff and their families taken many years earlier. It had taken an age for the photograph to be made and nobody was supposed to move in that time. Herbert hadn't been able to keep still. That was why his face, in the picture, was blurred.

'Will it take a long time to make the photograph?' she asked.

'No time at all.'

'Even so, I think maybe another day might be better.'

Dr Milligan rubbed his hands together.

'There's no time like the present, Nurse Everdeen. Mr Pincher, who is this child's legal guardian, *in loco parentis*, is in agreement that we should proceed.'

Nurse Everdeen's lips made a line. Maria observed her expression and interjected: 'Harriet is not yet dressed.'

'It will take a while to set up the apparatus. I shall take the photograph in the corridor outside. You prepare the child and I shall be ready when she is.'

Maria helped Nurse Everdeen wash and dress Harriet. They put her in the fanciest of the available dresses: a balloon-sleeved cotton dress with buttons at the back, a satin belt and a lace trim. She pulled up her stockings herself and the nurse laced her original boots, which she had cleaned and polished to a shine. Maria tied a bow in the child's hair. Nurse Everdeen disapproved of the bow – it seemed an affectation, and not an honest one – but Maria insisted that Harriet look 'as dear as she can for posterity'.

When she was ready, Maria took Harriet's hand and led her out into the corridor for the photograph.

Nurse Everdeen sat on the edge of the bed and waited, and after some minutes the little one came back into the bedroom.

'Is the photograph taken already?' Nurse Everdeen asked.

Harriet nodded. She came to Nurse Everdeen, climbed onto her lap and put her thumb into her mouth. The nurse pulled one end of the ribbon and the bow slithered apart. She placed the ribbon on the bed, and smoothed the child's silky hair with her hoary palm. She felt the buttons of Harriet's spine and the little ridges of her ribs beneath the dress. The child smelled sweetly of sleep and soap. It was a perfume that reminded Emma Everdeen so strongly of her beloved Herbert that time kaleidoscoped and she became dizzy, losing track of which child was hers, love for the one mingling with concern and affection for the other, like ink poured into water.

Maria came back into the room.

'Dr Milligan has packed up and gone downstairs,' she said. 'He promised to make a copy of the photograph for you to keep, Nurse Everdeen.'

She busied herself, removing plates and other items from the tray and setting them on the table. 'I brought you a breakfast fit for a princess, Harriet March,' she said cheerfully. 'You get better service up here than the fee-paying patients downstairs.'

She took a beaded cover from a cup and brought it around to the side of the bed.

'Milk and honey,' she said. 'Specially for you!'

'Fank you,' Harriet whispered.

She took the cup between the palms of her hands, held it to her lips, tipped back her head and drank. When she'd had all she wanted, she passed the cup to the nurse, who wiped the white moustache from the child's upper lip with her handkerchief.

'Good girl,' she murmured.

Harriet smiled shyly.

Something stirred inside Emma, something tiny but strong, like the casing of a seed opening so the first tiny shoot could begin to finger its way out of its shell. It was not a comfortable feeling exactly and so much time had elapsed since she last felt it that she had completely forgotten how powerful, how intoxicating, how gently consuming that feeling could be.

She had forgotten how to name it.

She had forgotten how to love.

24

After school, I reported to Ward B with Isak and the other pupils on report and we were allocated desks in the partitioned booths. Isak was several booths removed from me and I couldn't see him. The supervising teacher told us to sit down and get on with our allocated work.

My task was to read a section of *Hamlet* and then answer questions about the text. I hadn't understood any of it when we were reading it in class and didn't hold out much hope for now.

I opened the textbook and turned to the page where I was supposed to start. I stared at the words but couldn't make head or tail of them. The more I looked, the less sense they made and after a while they began to dance around the page like tiny black devils. My eyes hurt. We had studied *Macbeth* at school in Bristol, but the teacher there had explained the whole story before we started and I was sure it was a better story than this. I wished I was back in Bristol. I wished I could go back in time to the day when Mum had her accident and tell her not to go riding.

Sorry, Mum whispered.

It wasn't really your fault. It was whoever chucked that bag.

I looked back at the page. The words were dashing all over the place, pulling faces at me. I jabbed my finger at the page, trying to squash them to death.

This whole punishment was a waste of time; a waste of an hour of my life. I couldn't answer questions about something I did not understand. I thought of all the other kids around the world wasting their lives carrying out pointless detentions; it was so stupid.

Ward B was a gloomy place. I imagined what it would be like to be a patient in this ward when All Hallows was an asylum. That little window behind me would have been the inmates' only connection with the outside world and yet from where I was sitting I could see hardly anything, only a tiny patch of dull sky. Imagine being trapped here for days and weeks and months and years, and only a few inches of sky to let you know what life was like beyond.

There was something of the crypt about this ward. It was deep within All Hallows and the windows couldn't be opened so the air was old air. Probably I was breathing the same air as the patients in the asylum; the same air as the nurse whose remains I'd found.

That was an odd feeling.

'Stop fidgeting and get on with your work, Tyler,' said the supervising teacher.

'Yes, sir. Sorry, sir.'

I looked back at my book.

The copy of *Hamlet* I'd been given was an old one, its spine broken and every page was heavily annotated. I entertained myself for a short while searching for the teeny tiny cocks-and-balls meticulously drawn and cunningly hidden amongst the text by some former pupil. Then I made myself concentrate and read a page and had a brief attempt at deciphering Shakespeare's blank verse.

My mind, once again, wandered.

It went first to what there might be to eat for supper. The food at All Hallows was basic but there was plenty of it, so as long as you weren't a fussy eater you would be OK. I was not fussy. Mum used to say I had hollow legs. Mum and I shared a taste for chip-shop chips and curry sauce. That was our favourite. Even the thought of those slack brown chips, the tang of vinegar, the glossy sauce, steaming and speckled with raisins, nestling next to the chips in a polystyrene container was enough to make my stomach rumble. I doubled over to try to shut it up before anyone heard and told myself to think of something else.

I recited the lyrics of a Kirsty MacColl song that my mother liked to sing: 'Don't Come the Cowboy with Me Sunny Jim'. She used to call me 'Sunny Jim'. Or maybe it was 'Sonny Jim'. I wasn't sure. That song took me back to the North Somerset countryside, to her favourite pub garden in summer, us children playing on the swings and Mum drinking cider, and the musicians sitting hunched over their guitars and banjos and flutes, making music; butterflies, smoke, the scent of the sweet peas growing up the trellis attached to the brick wall; a large white goat in the paddock on the other side of the wall eating brambles.

Where was my father in these memories? Did he ever come to the pub with us? I couldn't remember him being there. He wasn't really a pub type of person. I remembered Mum calling to him that we were going out and him coming out of his study, formal even at home, still wearing his tie, his shirtsleeves buttoned to the cuff, the hem of his shirt tucked into his trousers.

'Won't you come with us, Geoff?' she'd ask. 'You might enjoy it,' but he always said he was too busy.

Isobel and I had been so close to Mum that we hadn't paid a

great deal of attention to our father. Perhaps if we had, things would have been different now.

This thought made me feel sad. And it made me miss Mum so much that tears filled my eyes and I had to press the heels of my hands into my eye sockets until they hurt to stop myself from crying.

I wiped my nose on the inside of the sleeve of my jumper and looked over my shoulder at the clock on the wall. There were still ages to go. I turned back to my desk. *Hamlet*. 'When he himself might his quietus make with a bare bodkin? Who would these fardels bear...' I literally did not understand a word of it. I felt like throwing the book at something. At the wall.

The wall in front of me was plastered; a lumpy, old-fashioned plaster that seemed to have been used a lot at All Hallows. Probably it was cheap; made out of horse manure or something. There was a metal bracket fixed to the plaster with two large bolts at about waist level. The supervising teacher was marking exercise books and paying me no attention so I leaned over the desk and touched the bracket, trying to work out what it was for. At some time, something must have been attached to it. The first time I saw these partitions they'd reminded me of stables and I wondered if horses had been kept here, but of course, they hadn't. We were on the ground floor of the building, but deep inside it. And it was a *ward*! The clue was in the name! Duh!

What if the brackets had been for chains? What if this had always been a punishment ward? What if Ward B was where people came to be tortured?

As soon as the thought occurred to me, prickles ran down my back: I had a strong feeling that I was right. This was a bad place. It was the dark heart of All Hallows. It was the place where people came to suffer.

Is there any evidence to support your theory? Mum whispered.

I could not leave my booth because the teacher would see me, but I could slip from the chair and creep to the wall in front of me, hidden from the teacher's view by the partition. I crouched down and ran my hands over the plaster. It must have been replaced and painted since All Hallows was an asylum, but the wooden floorboards would always have been there. I examined their black-and-gold patina, searching for some disruption to the grain of the wood that wasn't natural; a message from the past.

And there it was.

The marks were tiny, two letters, each less than one centimetre long, not deeply grooved, but enough for me to be certain they had been made deliberately by a human hand, a thumbnail probably, working into the wood. Two strokes making a 'T' and three to form an 'N'. TN. Somebody's initials.

I tried to dig my nail into the wood but it was hard, and my nail was badly bitten so I couldn't make any impression. I glanced behind me to check the teacher wasn't looking, then I put my hand into the collar of my shirt and I pulled the cord of my mother's pendant over my head. I used the hoof of the little metal horse's extended front leg to scratch my own initials, LT, beside TN's. The old marks were blackened with age and dirt and the new ones pale and clean. It was a most satisfying piece of work.

Feeling a little more cheerful after this small act of solidarity, as if I'd somehow got one over on the staff of All Hallows, I returned to my chair and sat at the desk with my chin in my hands staring at the *Hamlet* text but not reading it. Who was TN? Why was he or she here? When had he or she made their small marks on the floorboards? Did they have any inkling when they made them that they'd be found decades later by a thirteen-year-old Goth boy?

I doubted it!

Inspector Paul of the borough police rode up to All Hallows on his piebald mare. His arrival was announced by the clatter of hooves in the courtyard, a livelier and more skittish clanging of metal on cobblestone than was made by the feet of the sensible black cob, William, according to Maria Smith.

She was describing the inspector's visit to Nurse Everdeen over a pot of tea in the attic bedroom. Maria had made an extra visit, ostensibly to bring Harriet a gift of some doll's house dolls that she had ordered from the toy catalogue but really to share her news with her friend.

At present, the little girl was making a home for the dolls under the bed, and was engrossed in her play, making the dolls speak to one another in a charming manner. Neither Emma nor Maria had had toys anywhere near as delightful as these in the course of their own childhoods, which made their delight in Harriet's delight all the more enchanting.

'What is he like?' Emma asked.

'The inspector? Hmm… well, he's shorter, but of a more robust build than Dr Milligan; in his forties. He said he had come...' Maria glanced at Harriet to check that she wasn't listening, then continued in a lower voice, 'to discuss Mrs March's condition with Dr Milligan!'

'Oh!'

'I showed him into Dr Milligan's office. Dr Milligan is using the small office at the far end of Ward Four – do you know the one I mean? Really, Nurse, you wouldn't believe how he has filled up that office with books and medical equipment and papers and goodness knows what.'

'I would believe it,' said Emma.

'Anyway, the doctor asked for refreshments – I was ahead of him there, they were already on the way – and he invited the inspector to sit.'

'And you were party to their conversation?'

'Better than that, the doctor asked me to stay and make notes! As you know, he is preparing an article about Mrs March's case, she being the first comatose female patient he's ever treated, and he wanted me to write down what was said so there would be a permanent record to which he could refer when he comes to publishing his research!' Maria's eyes were glowing with pride.

'I'll tell you what, Nurse Everdeen,' she continued, 'it's my good fortune that you taught me to read and write because otherwise I'd have been out of there and Mr Pincher's secretary brought in, and then I wouldn't have heard the half of it.'

The nurse checked that the child was still concentrating on her dolls then said: 'Go on then, what did the inspector say?'

Maria took a deep breath and puffed out her chest in a parody of the man.

'He said: "We are not making much progress with this case, I'm afraid, Doctor!"'

'No?' asked Emma.

'No,' said Maria. 'He said: "Even my good lady wife, Elizabeth, who is generally rather expeditious at hypothesising when it comes to unusual cases, is failing with this one."'

"'Expeditious at hypothesising"?'

'That's what he said. "Anyway", he continued, "Elizabeth and I were discussing the 'lady in the boat' only last night and she said: "James, why don't you ride to All Hallows and have a word with the doctor treating Mrs March, find out more about her injuries and how she came by them and then you'll have more to go on." And, of course, she's right. So, Doctor, I'm rather hoping you'll be able to help us shed some light on the inquiry."' Maria paused for breath. 'That was the inspector saying that to the doctor,' she explained.

'Yes,' said the nurse, 'I'm with you.'

'And Dr Milligan was leaning forward in his chair, all keen and eager. He said: "Certainly, Inspector, I'm willing to help in any way that I can. What is it that you'd like to know?" and the inspector said: "Would you be willing to share with me, Doctor, your observations of Mrs March? Anything, even the smallest detail, might be important."' She paused to catch her breath. 'Would you care for a little more tea, Nurse Everdeen?'

'Perhaps just some more hot water in the cup to refresh it. Thank you, dear.' She waited while her drink was attended to and then said: 'Go on.'

'Dr Milligan said he would share the facts he believed to be relevant. The gist of it was that Mrs March's injuries are extensive and indicative of a violent struggle.'

'I'd gathered as much myself.'

'Beside the stab wound in her arm, she has a large bruise on her temple that's caused severe swelling. He said this injury concerned him more than the knife wound. He'd had the nurse apply a tincture of arnica thrice daily and in between place a cold compress on the affected area. He said that, superficially, Mrs

March's body appears to be mending but she remains unconscious, which indicates the original trauma caused by the blow that caused the bruise was extreme.' Another glance at the child and then, speaking so softly that her voice was barely more than a whisper, Maria said: 'He fears some injury might have been done to Mrs March's brain, internal bleeding or perhaps a fracture to the skull.'

'Oh dear.'

Maria shook her head. 'It's dreadful. A dreadful situation. The inspector asked him how he thought Mrs March came by this injury and he said she must have been struck by some heavy object.'

Emma thought that any fool could have worked that out, but did not say as much because she did not want to offend Maria, who was doing such an excellent job of remembering the discussion.

'After that,' said Maria, 'the inspector asked the doctor if he could tell how long Mrs March and her daughter had been in the boat and the doctor said no more than two or three hours or they would certainly have died of cold. The inspector said he was trying to establish whether they got into the boat themselves to escape their attacker, or if they were put into it and sent out to sea against their will. The assailant might have wagered that the currents would take the craft away from land where it would take on water, capsize and the bodies be lost. The tide was on its way out, the currents strong and those waters are unpredictable. The inspector surmised it would be a simpler, quicker and less dangerous way of disposing of two bodies than, for example, trying to hide them on land or bury them, and even if the tide brought them back to shore it would seem to everyone as if they'd drowned by accident.'

Emma glanced at little Harriet, playing so nicely with her

dolls, and a cold chill ran down her spine. It was horrific to think that anyone would have a heart wicked enough to wish harm on an innocent child.

Maria continued: 'Dr Milligan said he couldn't say whether or not Mrs March and Harriet got into the boat themselves. So, then the inspector asked if she,' a nod to Harriet, 'had said anything that might help the police narrow their search and the doctor said she hadn't. He said it is a common coping strategy for young children to block the memory of an event as distressing as this must have been.'

'She recalls it in her dreams,' said Emma. 'I've been making notes in the back of my nursing manual. I could have shown the notes to the inspector if Dr Milligan had thought to come and ask me.'

'I think Dr Milligan rather enjoys being the sole authority when it comes to his two special patients, Nurse Everdeen.'

'Hmm.'

The nurse stood up and wandered over to the small window. Outside, distantly, the male patients were exercising, a line of men in coats and hats walking the length of the inside of the asylum's perimeter wall, crossing between it and the beech copse behind the chapel. The men's heads were bowed against the wind. Fallen leaves blew about their ankles. They appeared forlorn; without hope.

She felt a small pressure at her side and looked down. Harriet had left her position by the bed and had come to stand beside the nurse, looking up.

'What can you see?' she asked.

'I'll show you.'

The nurse reached down and picked up the child and held her on her hip. 'See the men walking?'

'Yes.'

'See the trees and the chapel?'

Harriet nodded.

'See the rooks? Those black birds dancing amongst the tree tops. If you look closely, you can see their nests, dozens of them. Can you see?'

'Yes.'

'Perhaps we will go out there, one day, you and I. Would you like that?'

Harriet nodded and tucked her head into the crook of Nurse Everdeen's neck.

Maria came over to stand with them. She stood just behind the nurse, her hand on her shoulder.

'Have you noticed how the child speaks?' she asked. 'Her accent is not local.'

'What *is* her accent? Do you recognise it?'

'We have a patient who hails from Pickering, in Yorkshire,' said Maria Smith. 'How that child speaks sounds pretty much the same as him, to me.'

Emma looked at the child in her arms.

'Do you come from Yorkshire, Harriet? Is that where you and your mama live?'

The child put her thumb into her mouth. She turned her face and pressed it into Emma's shoulder. She could not, or would not, answer. Or perhaps she didn't know.

26

From the window of the room that Isak and I shared, I could see the chapel, and what remained of the fallen beech tree. Its trunk had been sawn into logs, the roots and branches piled in a heap and a temporary fence erected around the hole. Every piece of the thorn tree was gone. Behind the fence, the remaining bones had, I supposed, been uncovered and taken away. The question of why the nurse had been buried on the wrong side of the wall bothered me, buzzing round my brain like a trapped fly.

What had the nurse done to deserve being buried outside the churchyard with a bunch of convicted criminals? It must have been something really bad. Perhaps she'd treated the asylum patients cruelly. Maybe she'd befriended them and then secretly stolen from them. Or perhaps she'd poisoned them. The Victorians and Edwardians were always poisoning one another; Mum had had a book about it. It was much easier to kill people with poison back then – at least much easier to get away with it – because forensic science hadn't been invented.

I hoped Isobel would hurry up and get back to me. I sent her a second letter to remind her and went all out for the sympathy vote, telling her how I was struggling with *Hamlet*. I imagined her sitting on her bed at university reading the letter and feeling guilty because she hadn't replied to me sooner. I could picture the stripy legwarmers she wore, the oversized shirt; her dark hair, hanging in pigtails, on either side of her head, her fingernails each painted a different colour.

While I waited for Isobel's reply I settled into life at the school. I began to find my way around. I learned what lay behind some of the doors: a stationery cupboard, a tiny passageway leading to a kind of cell like a priest's hole; some grand offices that now were used for storage. Because I'd come to All Hallows after term started, I'd missed out on joining the clubs, so while the other boys were doing band practice or chess club or whatever, I wandered around the great building by myself, trying to keep out of the way of both the staff and Alex Simmonds and his gang.

On one of these excursions, I pushed past the plastic sheeting that covered the entrance to one of the water-damaged parts of the building and found myself in a corridor whose boards had been lifted, a corridor full of scaffolding and tools and bright lights plugged into temporary sockets. I thought the contractors had all finished for the night, but a short, stocky man dressed in orange hi-vis came round the corner and said: 'Oi! You! You're not supposed to be here.'

It turned out he was Polish, his name was Pavel. The contractors were staying in a Travelodge on the edge of the moor and all there was to do at night was watch TV so Pavel preferred to stay on at All Hallows and work. Pavel was a film buff. He shared a can of Fanta and a KitKat with me and we talked about Edward Scissorhands.

After that, I used to hang around that part of the school often and whenever he saw me, Pavel beckoned me over and gave me a piece of chewing gum or an apple or whatever else he had in the pocket of his overalls.

At mealtimes, I learned the importance of being towards the front of the queue in the refectory, because that way the food you were served was still hot and the dinner ladies weren't yet tired and bad-tempered and were more inclined to give bigger portions. Isak said the ladies felt sorry for me because of my ears. I didn't know if that was true.

I also learned that I hated the sports teacher, Three Rolls, but liked the art master who was the only teacher to call us by our first names. I learned that the best way to get through lessons was to be as quiet and un-obvious as possible. I never put my hand up. If I was picked on by a teacher to come up to the front and write something on the blackboard, I avoided eye contact. If I didn't know the right answer I either wrote something deliberately funny or I didn't write anything, because it was better to be punished for insolence than it was to be mocked in front of the whole class for being stupid. Regularly, I was hit with the ruler or cane during consecutive lessons and the palm of my left hand was burned and bruised.

It made no sense. Hitting me would not make me cleverer.

I was coping with school life, but inside my head I felt as if I was becoming smaller every day. It was partly because, no matter what I wrote to Isobel, I had not really made any friends. Mophead was friendly towards me but he already had his other friends, and although Isak and I were roommates, we didn't do anything together outside the room. Also, I had never realised how thick I was. I'd never felt stupid at my old school, but at All Hallows it was pointed out to me all the time that I was a slow learner. I was useless at everything except art.

My nickname was Dumbo and it wasn't only because of my ears.

Still, no matter how bad it was for me, I did not have it as bad as Isak.

Nobody liked Isak. Not the teachers, not the pupils. It was partly his own fault because he was so unfriendly and also he genuinely did not seem to care that he was in trouble all the time.

Mr Crouch was the worst with him. He went on and on at Isak; always making him stay behind after class or giving him detention or telling him to go to his office.

I tried to stay close to Isak to show him solidarity, and sometimes he tolerated me but other times he'd tell me to go away and leave him alone. More and more he reminded me of that allotment cat, which would scratch you if you tried to help it.

* * *

At last, I heard from Isobel, not just a letter, but a package! I took it up to the room to open, picking at the sticky tape and then tearing the brown paper. In the package were several Curly Wurly chocolate bars, a copy of *Melody Maker* magazine with the band Nirvana on the front, and a book, *Hamlet for Beginners*. It wasn't the best present I'd ever had but it would be useful.

With it was a letter that ran to several pages.

Everything you need to know about Hamlet is in the book.

She'd written.

And if you get stuck again, ask the school librarian. They're bound to have books to help you in the library.

She had underlined the word 'library' three times.
I should have thought of that myself.

Isobel then went on to talk about the bones I'd found. She had looked up the rules about being buried in church graveyards.

It was important for people to be buried in consecrated land in the old days, because if they weren't, they thought their souls wouldn't go to Heaven.

Also… I asked around and it turns out that your bones, the ones you found, have been taken to Exeter University. They belonged to a nurse called Emma Everdeen who was buried there on Boxing Day 1903. She must have done something really bad to have been buried outside the graveyard wall.

At the bottom of the package was a piece of paper. A cutting from a newspaper.

The headline was:

Hopes run high for Salèn US visit.

Isobel had drawn an arrow pointing to the face of a fleshy, fair-haired man in the photograph below. In the picture he had a flag in each hand and was waving them above his head.

Above the arrow were the words:

Is this your roommate's dad?

I read the article.

The controversial Swedish politician Elias Salèn arrives in America today to launch a charm offensive on the White House in advance of the latest round of trade talks between the two nations.

Salèn, who is renowned for his flamboyant lifestyle, is

hoping to strengthen links already forged with Mr Clinton during a previous visit...

I looked to the end of the article, which was where, Mum used to say, all the juicy details were hidden. And there it was.

Elias Salèn is gaining back some of the political ground he lost following revelations about his affair with the young American actress Phoebe Dexter who, at twenty-three years old is a quarter of a century younger than he is. After details of their relationship were exposed, Mr Salèn left his wife, Anna, for Ms Dexter. Anna Salèn, who gave up her own career as an actress in order to support her husband's political ambitions, was subsequently found dead in woodland close to the family home in the north of Sweden. She is believed to have committed suicide.

The couple had one son, Isak, now 14.

'Do you know, I haven't seen Dr Milligan since he came up here to take the photograph,' said Emma.

'He doesn't care about the child like he cares about the mother,' said Maria. Her tone, when she spoke of Dr Milligan, had become disparaging of late. 'His mind is wholly taken up with the progress of Mrs March.'

'Or lack of it.'

'I think he is infatuated,' Maria said darkly. 'He barely leaves her side. Some nights, Dorothy says, he even sleeps in Mrs March's room. In a chair, of course. But still.'

'Do you believe Dorothy?'

'On this occasion, yes.'

Emma didn't mind about Dr Milligan's lack of interest in Harriet's progress. She was thankful that she and Maria were left to care for Harriet as they thought best. She was taking pleasure from the present and she was looking forward again, for the first time in decades, to the future. She was imagining, for example, there being snow in the hospital grounds during the winter and if Mrs March remained unconscious and Harriet was still in her charge, she thought she might wrap her up warmly and, all being well, take her outside to play. It would be quite safe; the other patients would not be allowed out when the weather was icy. Harriet could have the whole of All Hallows' vast gardens as her own personal playground.

In the last days, Emma Everdeen and Harriet had begun to explore the other attic rooms. They were full of old clothes and objects, including, beneath a tumble of broken furniture, a wooden sledge. It was the same sledge that Harriet Sawmills had given to Herbert when he was three years old. It hadn't been used in fifty years, but if Maria would bring some wax to Emma, she would polish its blades and make sure it was sound, and then she would be able to take Harriet sledging as she used to take her son. Emma's heart quickened at the thought of herself, striding through the snow, pulling the sledge behind her and Harriet sitting upon it, holding onto the sides, squealing with delight.

She imagined the child's bright eyes and rosy cheeks, and Herbert's face transposed itself on Harriet's.

Of course, Mrs March might regain consciousness at any time and when she did, Dr Milligan had told Maria, her prognosis would be clearer. If there were no obvious impairments, there would be no reason to retain either the woman or the child in All Hallows. However, in the head injury cases that Dr Milligan had treated previously, many of the patients were not the same when they awoke. Their personalities had changed, or they struggled to speak, or they had physical difficulties.

There was a good chance that Harriet would still be here for Christmas.

And if she was, Emma would buy a book for her; a gift by which she could remember Emma, just as Emma remembered Nurse Harriet Sawmills by the nursing manual that had been given to her. The manual had pride of place on the shelf in the room in the attic, beside Emma's nursing chatelaine to which were still attached her mercury thermometer, her scissors, spatula, a set of tiny measuring spoons and the tool she used to administer medicine. Emma no longer used the manual as a reference; much of the medical information it contained was outdated. But the blank pages at the back were useful for recording Harriet's progress, and even if the words had faded from every page, Emma would still treasure that manual as she hoped Harriet would value the book that she would, one day, give to her.

Harriet enjoyed being read to. She reported that her mama used to read to her every night and she was truly delighted when Maria brought up a bundle of children's books that were amongst several boxes of adult novels donated to the hospital. Amongst the books was a well-worn copy of *The Bad Child's Book of Beasts.* 'We have this one at home!' Harriet cried, holding up the book as if it were the greatest prize ever. 'This is Mama's favourite book! Please may we read this book, Nurse! This one!'

They settled down in the rocking chair to read, the child on the nurse's lap, her head resting in the space between Emma's chin and her shoulder.

'Where is "home"?' Nurse Everdeen asked Harriet, when they had reached the end of the book amongst much deliberating on Harriet's part about which of the poems she and her mama preferred.

Harriet turned to look up at the old woman, her eyes bright beneath the straight, dark fringe, but also suspicious. 'By the sea,' she said carefully.

'That's nice,' said Emma. 'I have always thought I should like to live by the sea.'

'Mama and I go paddling in the summer,' Harriet confided.

'You do?'

'Yes.' The child nodded. 'And we fish for crabs. Sometimes we have a picnic on the rocks.'

'How lovely.'

'Yes,' said Harriet. She busied herself tracing the outline of a dodo with her finger, following the illustration.

'What can you see when you sit on the rocks?' Nurse Everdeen asked.

'The sea.'

'What else?'

'Fishing boats.'

'Is that all?'

'On the other side of the bay, we can see the ruins.'

'Which ruins, Harriet?'

'The ruins of the abbey.'

* * *

'They live by the sea,' Emma told Maria later. 'At night time they can see the lamps of the fishing boats out on the water. And on the other side of the bay there is a ruined abbey.'

'It must be somewhere along the East Coast,' said Maria. 'I shall ask the patient from Yorkshire if he knows where it is.'

* * *

'Whitby,' Maria told Emma the next day. 'I asked my patient and he said the only place he could think of that fitted the description was Whitby on the coast of the North Riding of Yorkshire. It's not a million miles from where he hails from and the ruins are famous. I understand they feature prominently in Mr Bram Stoker's vampire novel. Do you know it, Nurse Everdeen?'

'The vampire novel? I do not.'

'From what I've heard of it, I don't think it would be your cup of tea.'

'The North Riding of Yorkshire is a good distance from Dartmouth,' said Emma.

'At least a day's travelling. And not an easy journey, whichever way you look at it.'

'It's not surprising nobody is searching for Mrs March and Harriet in Devon.' Emma tapped her fingers on the arm of her rocking chair.

'What do we do now?' asked Maria.

'You must tell Dr Milligan what we have discovered and he can pass the information on to Inspector Paul. If the inspector gets in touch with his colleagues in the north, perhaps the true identities of Mrs March and Harriet will soon be known.'

I felt guilty every time I thought about Isak's parents. He'd had plenty of opportunities to tell me about his father's infidelity and his mother's suicide and he never had which could only mean that he didn't want me to know.

I hadn't asked Isobel to send the cutting but still I felt as if I'd betrayed Isak by uncovering the secrets he'd done his best to keep hidden.

To stop myself obsessing about this, I obsessed about Emma Everdeen instead. Who had she harmed, and why? Had she been motivated by greed or jealousy or something else?

I stole an exercise book from the stationery cupboard and I wrote 'Emma Everdeen' on the front, and made different chapter headings inside. I wrote down what little I knew and made sketches of All Hallows building, inside and out. My friend, Pavel the builder, helped me. During and between lessons, I explored the different floors, mapping the rooms and corridors; working out which parts had changed and how. It was exciting, ducking out of sight of the teachers and the other boys to walk along some panelled corridor that I'd discovered was a short cut to another part of the building. I found remnants from All Hallows' asylum days; a door marked 'Pharmacy', for example, which was locked; another, grander door on the floor above that said 'Boardroom'. I tried the handle to this door, not expecting it to open, but it did. Inside was a fully panelled room with a huge great stone fireplace. A massive table, big enough for about thirty people to sit round, ran the length of the room. Paintings of whiskery men hung on the walls. I made a mental note to go back and copy down the names of the men because it would be easier to find information about them than it would about a nurse who was buried without a headstone. I figured that Emma Everdeen's path must have crossed with at least some of them.

My exploring was not without its dangers. Sooner or later, I was bound to be spotted sneaking out of the bounds of the established school. Worse, if Alex Simmonds or any of his friends saw me snooping about in the unused rooms and corridors, they might ambush me. But it hadn't happened yet.

This new obsession occupied my sleeping hours as well as those when I was awake. More and more I dreamed about the asylum. In the dreams I was usually an observer, drifting through the same places that I'd been exploring. I moved amongst the inmates; hid in the corners of wards.

Still, the dream that came most often was that of being on the beach. The dream of being afraid. The dream of the woman running towards me.

* * *

It was a Wednesday, hours after lights out. All Hallows was settling beneath the moonlight, the old wood of its great beams creaking and stretching, the pipes sighing and gurgling, the dehumidifiers thrumming and the hundreds of boys and teachers inside the buildings settling to sleep. As everything else quietened, the rocking chair runners began their rhythmic creaking on the floorboards in the room above ours.

Isak had fallen silent a while back and I thought he must be asleep.

I rolled over and pulled the pillow over my head, but I could still hear the runners moving on the floorboards: creak, creak, to and fro. I swung my legs out of bed, picked up my school jumper, pulled it over my head and went out onto the landing. I walked barefoot along the threadbare old carpet, to the narrow staircase. The glow of the nightlight plugged into the wall showed me the way, a dim orange passage through the gloom. I hesitated at the foot of the stairs, but then I heard something else beside the rocking. It sounded like laughter.

Someone was up there.

I put my hand on the wooden banister and I climbed those steep stairs up onto the attic floor, my curiosity stronger than my fear.

At the top of the stairs, I hesitated. The bathroom door was open at the end of the corridor. The other doors were closed, but a thin line of light was shining beneath the bottom of the fourth door.

It wasn't a constant light but one that flickered as if people were moving about. I crept closer.

Someone *was* inside the room. I could hear movement on the other side, a rustle of fabric, the scrape of a chair being moved. The voice, or voices – I wasn't sure – were distorted, like the voices on a record being played at the wrong speed. I leaned my ear as close to the door as I could and strained to hear but then I felt a hand on my shoulder and almost jumped out of my skin.

'It's me.'

'Isak! You idiot, I could have had a heart attack. There's someone in the room.'

'I know. I heard them downstairs.'

'What should we do? What if it's Alex Simmonds?'

'If it was him, he'd have come straight into the bedroom to beat us up.'

We listened again, but no sound at all was coming from inside the room now, only the light shone beneath the door. It was as if whoever was inside had heard us and was listening on the other side.

'Someone's definitely there,' I whispered.

'Sod it,' said Isak. He reached past me and knocked on the door. 'Who's there?' he called. 'What are you doing?'

Silence.

I grabbed the sleeve of his pyjama jacket. 'Come on, leave them alone...'

'I want to see.'

'Isak!'

He took hold of the knob and turned it. The door swung open and the ice-cold air trapped behind it spilled out.

Isak gasped. I blinked; looked again.

Inside the room was nothing but darkness; not even a silvering of moonlight.

And it was empty.

No light was glowing, no flame flickered, nobody was there.

Only the rocking chair moved, rocking forwards and backwards as if whoever had been sitting in it had, a moment earlier, got up and left the room.

The next night, Emma was woken by the sounding of All Hallows' emergency siren. It was used to warn the inhabitants of farmsteads and shepherds' cottages that inmates had escaped from the asylum and were loose on the moor.

Emma held Harriet on her hip at the window, looking out, the two of them spotting the beams of torches flashing in the night, and the swinging of hand-held lamps. They heard the baying of the dogs although they could not see them, it being a dark night.

'What are they doing?' Harriet asked.

'Looking for people who have run away.

'Why have they runned away?'

'Because they didn't like being here, I suppose.'

'What will happen to them when they are caught?' Harriet asked.

'They will be brought back to the asylum and...' Nurse Everdeen tailed off, 'After that I don't know.'

The last escapee had been a young man – a boy, really – the son of a wealthy trader who had become addicted to drink and probably other substances besides, for he had suffered dreadfully while he was at All Hallows, kept in a padded cell, always crying for thirst, yet vomiting everything he swallowed while he sweated and gasped through the tremors. After two weeks he'd been deemed well enough to move onto one of the less secure men's wards. He had run away that same night and been lost on the moor for several days. Superintendent Pincher had been desperate to keep the news of his absconding a secret because he feared his father would transfer him to a different establishment if he found out.

The young man had eventually been found half-dead in a hollow. Mr Collins had brought him back slumped over his horse's shoulders like a hunted deer.

The young man had been punished, of course. He was returned to the cell and his family told they could not visit until they were summoned. When they eventually came and the young man told his father of his escape onto the moor, Mr Uxbridge had denied this version of events.

'He was hallucinating,' he told the father. 'Being lost in the wilderness is an internal metaphor for his external struggle.'

The father had believed Mr Uxbridge. It was possible the son believed him too.

Emma and Harriet eventually returned to bed and in the morning Maria filled in the details of what had taken place the previous night. It was three women, this time, who had escaped. They were caught quickly and brought back to the asylum. There was not room in Ward B for them all, because one of the stalls was being kept vacant ready for the arrival of the lord's debauched daughter, so they were put in individual cells. They would not be returned to the wards until they demonstrated suffi-cient remorse for their actions. That should be enough to deter them from trying such a trick again.

Maria knew the name of the lord's daughter now. It was Thalia Nunes, and she had failed to take heed of any of her parents' warnings to moderate her behaviour. Downstairs in the asylum they were expecting a call from her father summoning them to go and fetch her any day.

Back in our beds, in our room, I told Isak everything I knew about Nurse Emma Everdeen.

Isak listened, sitting cross-legged on the end of my bed with the duvet wrapped around his shoulders like a cloak. We had unplugged the nightlight from the landing socket and brought it into our room. Whispering to Isak like that, in the almost-dark, in the room surrounded by empty rooms in that great building, felt significant, as if we were on the cusp of something, although I could not have said what.

I told Isak about my experiences in the room in the attic. He did not laugh or mock or tell me I was stupid.

'The first time I heard the chair rocking was the night of the storm,' I told him, 'the same night the trees came down and the bones were uncovered. It can't be coincidence, can it?'

'So, you're thinking that the tree falling and the grave being exposed released the nurse's spirit somehow and that maybe her ghost is up there, in the room above?'

'Yes. And that she came into All Hallows to haunt us. Or me, actually, because I was the one who found her.'

'But it didn't start then,' said Isak. 'It started before you even came.'

He dropped his head forward so his fringe fell over his eyes. 'After the flood, when they moved me into this room, I heard noises from the room above. I thought it must be rats and I told Mr Crouch. The caretaker came and said there was nothing there.'

'Why didn't you tell me?'

'You might have thought I was stupid.'

'No, I wouldn't.'

'You might have. And also if I told you and *then* you heard rocking, it might have been because I put the thought into your head.'

'You think too much, Isak.'

'What do you think it is, up there? Do you really believe it's the nurse's ghost?'

'Perhaps, someone died in that room or was murdered or something.'

'Murdered?'

'I don't know. But I know that sometimes when things die, they don't go away.'

He didn't say anything, but he was listening.

'When our dog, Polly, died, Mum told me that if you love someone, they never really leave you.'

Isak remained silent.

'When Mum died,' I murmured, 'I thought she couldn't be *gone;* nothing that existed could ever be gone. She must be somewhere and I thought that if I looked hard enough, I would find her...'

Isak pulled the duvet more tightly about himself and he shrank down a little.

I wanted *him* to talk to me. I wanted to ask him if he felt the same as I did, if he missed his mother every day, if ever she came to talk to him, but I couldn't say anything because he didn't know that I knew his mother was dead. I waited, making a big space, hoping he would fill it, but he didn't say anything.

'What if I'm right and Emma Everdeen's spirit is in the room above?' I asked when the silence became uncomfortable. 'If it is her, we might be in danger.'

'How do we find out?'

'If we could get into the chapel and look at the burial records, we might be able to find out *why* she was buried outside the graveyard.'

There was a noise from above.

The rocking chair had started to move again.

'Jesus!' whispered Isak. He crawled up the bed until he was sitting beside me. We didn't actually hold onto one another, but the sides of us were touching all the way down.

'How can we get into the chapel?' he whispered.

I'd already spent a lot of time thinking about this.

'We sneak in during cross-country,' I said. 'It's the only way.'

31

EMMA – 1903

Emma pulled a clean nightdress over Harriet's head and helped feed her arms into the sleeves. Harriet was struggling to stay awake. Still, she knelt at the side of the bed, put her hands together, squeezed her eyes tightly shut and said the child's prayer. The words gave the nurse a chill.

If I should die before I wake.

But you won't, my lamb, Emma thought. You won't die because I won't let death take you. I will keep you safe until the day when I must give you back to your mother.

Harriet moved on to her 'God blesses'.

'God bless Mama and make her better soon. God bless Harriet, God bless all the little children in the world and all the animals and birds and fishies too. God bless Nurse Everdeen.'

She had never added this last phrase before.

'There's a good girl,' said Emma, speaking over the lump in her throat. 'You say your prayers so nicely.'

She pulled back the covers on the bed and the child climbed

up and in with the rabbit and snuggled down. She put her thumb into her mouth and rubbed the bridge of her nose with her fore-finger. The nurse covered her over and tucked her in.

'There,' she said, 'snug as a bug.' She smoothed the top cover with the palm of her hand. 'Night night, sleep tight.'

'Hope the bed bugs don't bite.'

All Hallows staff were very keen on making us pupils go outdoors to exercise, no matter how bad the weather. Three Rolls was fond of telling us that regular, rigorous exercise was essential to the formation of strong moral fibre. Isak said they wanted to make us too exhausted to think about sex. Whatever, every morning, regardless of whether or not it was blowing a gale, we boys were obliged to change into our sports kit and go for a 'cross-country' run around the grounds, mottled legs, runny noses and all. Isak and I usually ran together, trying to get ahead of Alex Simmonds and his mates so we couldn't be ambushed by them later.

That morning was miserable, with a bitter wind blowing across the grounds and rain in the air, the sun hidden behind heavy, low cloud. The lawns were puddled, the ground slippery. As Isak and I emerged from the cloakrooms out into the cold, we shivered and hunched our shoulders, kept close together amongst the pushing, stamping, jostle of older boys, holding on to the residual warmth.

Three Rolls clapped his hands. 'Right, boys, you know the score,' he called. Even he was hunched in his tracksuit against the wind. 'Start on my first whistle. Three laps, stick to the track; anyone caught cheating will be in deep doo-doo.'

He raised his whistle to his lips and blew, a piercing sound. And we were off: the athletes powering away at the front of the pack, the rest of us starting more slowly, breath puffing around us before the wind snatched it away; the asthmatics, already fumbling for their inhalers, bringing up the rear. Alex Simmonds was calling insults to a boy who'd won a prize for maths and paying no attention to Isak and me. We ran together, going over the plan one last time.

The cross-country route was one with which I was utterly familiar by this point. Starting from the courtyard, we headed in a straight line for the beech copse, then veered towards the boundary wall and ran all the way round it until we found ourselves parallel with the far end of the west wing, from where we were to return to the courtyard. The whole distance of one lap was approximately a mile.

Within minutes, my fingers were purple with cold. Isak's nose was red, his cheeks pale, and his ankles and lower legs as mud-spattered as mine, but he was more agile, taller and a better runner. As the group began to string out, he looked over his shoulder and gave me the thumbs-up.

I raised my thumb in return and he quickened his pace and loped off ahead. As soon as we had cleared the courtyard, he tripped dramatically and fell to the ground, rolling over twice before ending up on his side, clutching his knee and groaning. It was a spectacular fall, which brought down a couple of the lads behind him. The whole group stopped to help and Three Rolls headed over too. I veered sharply to the left and ran as fast as I could towards the hydrangea clump. The plants were dead now, but their old brown heads still offered cover. I crouched there until the group had moved on, including Isak who was limping for full effect. I ran low towards the chapel and jumped over the wall, feeling like James Bond except I tripped and almost went head first onto the nearest grave. Nobody was around to see so I dusted myself down, trotted to the chapel door and turned the great black metal handle.

It wouldn't open.

I put all my weight behind it and tried again. No luck.

'No!' I cried. I couldn't have come this far to be frustrated now! I heaved on the handle, tried to turn it, but it still would not budge. I kicked the door and bruised my toes through the thin rubber of my trainers. I hopped about for a minute, holding my painful foot and muttering swear words. It made no difference. The chapel was still locked.

Almost crying with frustration, I went to the side, ducked under the tape put around the area damaged by the tree and tried to find another way in. If I'd climbed up the scaffolding that had been put up ready for the roof to be mended, I might have been able to crawl through the hole, but even if I managed to lower myself down to the floor, how would I get out again?

I circled the chapel like a cat. There was a small arched door, no more than three feet high, at the very back, but that had been secured with a heavy bolt. The windows were high up and sealed. There was no other way in.

Desperately disappointed, I turned back into the graveyard. I had a few minutes until the running group began their second circuit and came this way again, when I'd have to somehow join them without being spotted by Three Rolls.

The closest gravestone was grand, the perimeter of the grave marked by a small stone wall and its surface covered in green chippings. 'Here lies Mr Francis Pincher, Superintendent at All Hallows 1895–1924, his faithful wife, Constance, and their son, Algernon.' Next to Mr Pincher was 'esteemed cook', Dulcie Steward, and next to her, orderly Edward Simpson, and his daughter, Susan. So this must be the part of the graveyard reserved for asylum staff and their families. Behind Edward and Susan's grave was a small headstone on its own at the head of a small grave, unremarkable and overgrown. The weeds that covered it were dying now, but a few weeks earlier it would have been completely hidden. It was very old and the stone had eroded. I knelt on the wet grass and traced the outlines of the letters with my fingers, working out each word, one at a time.

Herbert Everdeen, aged five years and two months, taken to live amongst God's angels on 7 November 1857.

Always beloved by his devoted mother, Nurse Emma Everdeen.

Emma heard the key turn in the lock of the door at the end of the corridor, and a few moments later Maria flounced into the room with a bottle of gin tucked under her arm. She banged the bottle onto the table.

'Shh!' Emma slapped her gently on the arm. 'Harriet's sleeping. Whatever is the matter?'

Maria took two small glasses from the shelf, turned them over and placed them on top of the table.

'You will not believe what's happened, Nurse.'

'Oh, I'm sure I will.'

'This afternoon, being Dorothy's afternoon off and the first time I was alone with Dr Milligan, I took the opportunity to tell him that Mrs March and the child are from Whitby, in the North Yorkshire Riding. I was expecting him to be pleased at this news. Grateful, even, that we had gone to the trouble of establishing this fact when he and his policeman friend, as far as I can tell, have established exactly nothing! Not one thing!'

'And was he not grateful?'

'He barely listened to me. I would go so far as to say he was dismissive.'

'Ah,' said Emma.

'I explained how we had come to this realisation, you and I, with the help of little Harriet and the patient from Yorkshire, and asked if he would convey the information to Inspector Paul at the police station, and he said he did not think the inspector would welcome being distracted from his work by the whims of a serving maid and an old nurse.'

'Oh.'

'"Women's tittle-tattle" was the phrase he used.'

Maria took the stopper from the bottle and filled both glasses.

'I asked him if he did not wish Mrs March to be identified and he said it wasn't his main priority at the moment. His priority was helping her back to full health.'

She pushed one of the glasses towards Emma who took it and chinked it against the side of Maria's glass.

'In his heart, I don't believe he wants the poor woman to be reclaimed by her family. He wants her to stay here so he can continue to have her companionship all to himself.'

'And is Mrs March still comatose?'

'She is, but that doesn't stop the doctor admiring her! Dorothy says when Dr Milligan goes into her room, he sighs over her.'

Emma raised an eyebrow. '*Sighs*?'

'As God is my witness. And here's another fact for you. Now, as well as turning Mrs March over in her bed to prevent the formation of sores, Dr Milligan exercises her limbs, one at a time, *twice a day*! He takes her right arm, for example, like this, and flexes it at the shoulder, wrist and elbow, rotating the joints and stretching the muscles. He says it's to prevent atrophy and to improve the blood flow. He moves every single joint on each finger separately, and rotates her hand. He says it's the modern treatment, pioneered in the European hospitals. Dorothy says it's positively immodest.'

'Dorothy is in the room when the doctor is repeating these exercises?' Emma asked anxiously. 'Mrs March is chaperoned?'

'Yes, yes. And, indeed, she is also chaperoned when he, Dr Milligan, lifts her half out of the bed in order to move her hips, and torso, letting her fall forward like a doll and then lifting her up so that the spine and its associated muscles will retain their flexibility, her hair falling over her face so that he has to tidy it when she is upright again. Dorothy says it's as if he's dancing with her; his hands all over her body and she still fast asleep. What do you think of all that, Nurse Everdeen?'

The nurse considered her response. She did not like the sound of it one bit, but she did not think Dr Milligan was a lascivious man. She was as sure as she could be that his actions were well-intentioned. She tried to dampen the flames of Maria's ire.

'It makes sense, Maria,' she said levelly, 'to keep the blood flowing through a comatose body and to stretch the muscles. Perhaps in Europe such exercises are routine.'

'You think it's appropriate for him to handle Mrs March in that way?'

'Are you suggesting some impropriety?'

'Not impropriety. No. And yet...'

'What, Maria?'

Maria drank her gin and put the empty glass back on the table.

'It doesn't feel right, Nurse Everdeen. If you were Mrs March, and some man you'd never met was doing all that to you, how would you feel about it when you woke up and found out?'

Emma said, 'I don't think I'd be best pleased.'

Maria took the stopper out of the bottle. 'Neither would I, Nurse. Neither would I.'

She filled her own glass and went to refill Emma's, but Emma put her hand over the top. She didn't want to drink herself into a stupor. She needed to be sure that she would wake at once if Harriet needed her in the night.

It had all been a great big disaster.

Not only had I *not* managed to get into the chapel to read the notes on Nurse Everdeen's burial records, but I had managed to get myself spotted sneaking back into the running group when it came back round for the second circuit. I'd been back behind the dead hydrangeas, crouched, tense, alert like a big cat, a lion – or perhaps a panther, anyway – waiting my moment to zip out and back into the group when someone grabbed me by the collar. I thought it was Alex Simmonds but it was Three Rolls, who'd come over to relieve himself behind the bush.

Fortunately for me, Three Rolls had rugby coaching straight after cross-country and he didn't want to risk being late, so rather than taking me to see Dr Crozier, he told me to report to my form tutor's office. I trailed through the corridors to the door to Mr Crouch's office and knocked.

'Come!' said Mr Crouch.

I went inside and found him sitting behind his desk, with newspapers strewn across it. He pushed them to one side as I stepped forward, but I caught a glimpse of a headline and caught two words, 'Sex Scandal', above a photograph that I'd seen before: the one on the cutting about Isak's father that Isobel had sent me. I crooked my head to try to read but he put his arm over it.

'What can I do for you, Tyler?' he asked.

I told him I'd been sent by Three Rolls because I'd skipped a circuit of cross-country. I said it was because I was tired.

'Couldn't be bothered, more like,' said Mr Crouch. 'Lazy little tyke. Back on report, Tyler.'

'For how long, sir?'

'Two days.'

Shouldn't have asked, my mother's voice whispered in my ear. *Should have just taken a day.*

I made my way back to the cloakrooms. By the time I got there, the showers were full of boys and the cloakrooms were full of steam, the floor was covered in chunks of mud and it smelled of sweat and wet socks. I sat down on the bench beneath my peg and took off my trainers.

Isak, damp-haired and rosy-cheeked, frowned at me over the shoulders of two dozen other boys, making a question mark with his eyebrows. I tried to push my way closer to him but it was impossible with everyone rushing to get changed; I couldn't get through the sea of elbows and hips and towels.

We couldn't catch up at lunch, either, because of me being on report and later that same afternoon, I found myself back in Ward B. I managed to sit in the same booth as before, which was about the first thing that had gone right that whole day. 'Right' wasn't the correct term, but at least it was a positive. I felt almost as if this was 'my' booth now. As if I belonged there, me and TN, whoever they used to be.

Hamlet was finished, thank goodness. We'd moved on to *Jude the Obscure* in English, which was not, in my opinion, much of an improvement.

I would go to the school library as Isobel had suggested and ask if they had a book that would explain *Jude the Obscure* so I didn't have to read it all. But for now, I had some history home-work. History should have been a good subject for me because I was really interested in the past and how people used to live and so on, but what I didn't like was stuff about war and religion, which were the two main subjects covered at All Hallows. Plus Mr Crouch was not what you'd call an inspirational teacher.

I opened the sheet of paper with the homework questions; three of them.

1. Write an account of the martyrdom of Ridley.

Who was Ridley? Well, I knew he was something to do with the Reformation. And the fact that he met a sticky end was obvious from the question. I did vaguely remember Mr Crouch talking about Ridley – was he a bishop? – but I'd been thinking about Nurse Everdeen at the time so hadn't paid an awful lot of attention. It was sad that the nurse already had a beloved son buried in the chapel graveyard ages before she died. Perhaps it was grief that turned her into a criminal.

I now knew that Emma had planned to be buried in the same grave as Herbert. There was an empty space beneath the inscrip-tion on Herbert's headstone; space for someone else's name. There was no mention of Herbert's father on the gravestone, so the space must have been reserved for Emma. The fact that she'd been buried outside the graveyard's boundary despite her plans now seemed even more sinister.

I tapped the lid of my pen against my teeth and looked at the next question.

2. Why was the vestments controversy important?

I was in big trouble with this homework. Again, I'd heard Mr
Crouch talking about this but the subject had been boring in the
extreme and I'd made a decision about thirty seconds in not to
waste another second of my life on something which I was
ninety-nine point nine per cent certain would never be relevant to
my future self. But I had to write something because I had to
hand the work in at the end of detention, and if nothing was
written down I'd end up on another report or even worse.

Please, I prayed, let question three be an easy one.

3. Explain the three main arguments used by Hooper and
Ridley in their debate.

I dropped my pen. It rolled under the desk. The supervising
teacher heard the clatter and looked up.

'Dropped my pen, sir,' I said.

He looked back at whatever it was he was reading. I pushed
back my chair and knelt down on the boards. I could see the pen,
but something else caught my eye first.

There were the two old marks, TN. There were the fresh
marks that I had made, LT. But next to those were four new
marks, new in the sense that I hadn't noticed them last time I was
here.

I touched them with my fingertips. They were cruder than the
first marks, less deeply scratched, but the word they formed was
clear: 'HELP' only the P was more of a |> made of three straight
lines.

I crawled forward to look round the partition. The teacher
was not paying any attention to me. As I watched he yawned, and
then picked up his coffee mug and peered into it.

I reached up to the top of my desk and took down a piece of paper and a pencil and copied the marks onto the paper as accurately as I could. Then I scratched a really basic question mark in response, before I sat back up at the desk and stared at the letters. The HEL|> *must* have been there before because those four letters, like the T and the N were old, black, worn.

They must have been there when I carved out my initials.

But I was a hundred per cent certain that they hadn't been.

35

Emma sat at the chair by the table and she put the lamp above her and dipped her pen into her bottle of ink, and she wrote a letter to the police station in Whitby.

Dear Sirs,

it began,

You will not know me and I doubt you will have heard of All Hallows Hospital in Devon but we have two Patients here who there is strong reason to believe come from the Town of Whitby and I wonder if anyone is missing Them. They are a Woman and a Female Child. I do not Believe there is a Husband for the Child does not ask God to Bless Papa when she Says her Nightly Prayers.

She wrote the letter carefully and when she was satisfied that she had communicated all the relevant information, she folded it and placed it in an envelope. Maria would put it with the mail to be taken to the post office in Dartmouth in the morning. The address she wrote on the envelope was simply:

Police Station, Whitby, North Riding of Yorkshire.

She could not see how that could possibly go amiss.

After that, Emma sat in her rocking chair with a pillow behind her back and she permitted herself one more small glass of gin while she thought about all that Maria had told her. She did not doubt Maria's version of events downstairs. Mrs March was a beautiful woman, and Dr Milligan a sensitive young man in a position of almost God-like authority over his unconscious patient. Emma had seen similar relationships forged before. A vulnerable patient, one who could neither tell her own story nor express her personality, was effectively a blank canvas on which a doctor could paint any picture he so desired. This case was so unusual, Mrs March's background so beguiling and her appearance so appealing that it was no wonder she was an irresistible prospect to a naïve and inexperienced man such as Milton Milligan.

Still, it did not make the situation *right*.

Somewhere, someone would be looking for Mrs March, whatever her real name might be, and her little daughter. Even if there was no husband, there might well be parents somewhere, worried half out of their minds, or siblings; at the very least there would be friends. And much as Emma was beginning to enjoy looking after Harriet, it was only right that she and her mother went home, where they belonged. Indeed, all that the nurse wanted was for her little charge to be happy and if that meant giving her back to her family, so be it.

Emma doubted she would be thanked for taking matters into her own hands and writing directly to the police, especially if Dr

Milligan's attachment to Mrs March had become so strong that he could not bear the thought of losing her. But her priority was not Dr Milligan's happiness. It was Harriet's.

She thought of the doctor, ensconced in the fine bedroom with his patient. There were twelve good rooms at the asylum: six reserved for women on the ground floor of the west wing, with the men's equivalent in the east wing. These rooms – of which the 'Royal Suites' were the grandest – had large windows, facing out over the grounds, and there was a terraced area outside where the patients could sit, if they were well enough and the weather clement, and take the air without having to observe any of the less salubrious aspects of hospital life. The occupants of these rooms and their visitors could pretend this was a grand hotel, rather than an asylum. The rooms were expensive, yes, but the patients who resided in them were treated like royalty. There was a dedicated cook in the kitchens, who only prepared food for the patients in these rooms – and for the asylum's directors, of course, when they came for their monthly board meetings. In the old days, when All Hallows was a charitable institution run by volunteer governors, there had been no such private rooms, no such cooks. All patients had been treated as if they were equally important.

Those halcyon days seemed a lifetime ago.

A chill came over Emma. She looked to the window and saw that the curtains were not properly drawn and the window was open an inch. She stood to close it, and was stopped by a twinge in her back. In that instant between rising and moving towards the window, it seemed as if darkness poured through the gap, darkness so intense that Emma believed, for a moment, that this was death, come for her. She had a feeling as if she were being carried away and the next instant the feeling was gone and she was back in her chair, feeling horribly afraid. It was the kind of fear she'd seen in the eyes of patients who knew death was imminent, those who had not made their peace in this world, who were not ready for it.

It was probably no more than an owl that interrupted the moonlight falling through the window frame that had brought the sensation of darkness. Nonetheless, the conviction that something evil had entered the room would not leave the nurse and filled her with a visceral dread.

'You are a silly woman,' she said to herself, and she tried to shake the fear away.

She crossed to the window, pulled it shut and secured the clasp. Then she drew the curtains properly. She grunted as she hefted the scuttle to put more coal on the fire, and as the flames licked around the new lumps of fuel, she placed the guard in front of it, and dimmed the lamp. She took a small dose of the sleeping medicine, took away the taste with a mouthful of gin, washed her hands, and then plumped the pillow to settle as usual in the rocking chair. In the bed, Harriet sighed.

Emma looked down on her little charge. She looked at her chair, and she looked at the bed, and she shuddered at the memory of the fear she had felt a few minutes before. She did not want to sleep on the chair alone.

She pulled back the cover on the bed and lay herself, very gently, beside the child. Harriet murmured in her sleep and Emma put an arm around her.

She closed her eyes. She clutched the locket with Herbert's picture inside in the palm of the other hand. The fire crackled and spat in the grate but other than that, in the attic, all was quiet.

36

I couldn't wait to show Isak the paper with the marks from the floorboards copied on it but when I got to our room he wasn't there. I fidgeted about for a while; and then went off in search of Pavel, who I thought might be interested, but when I reached the plastic curtain at the entrance to the flood-damaged corridor, I could see that all the lights had been turned off. I looked out of the window into the front courtyard. The contractors' vans were all gone.

The woman from the converted stable block was out again, walking her dogs and a young girl was with her, about the same age as me. I watched them for a while, my elbows on the window ledge, my chin in my hands, then Mum said: *You'd better get back to your room now,* and I knew she was right.

I bumped into Mr Crouch on the way back and he asked what I was doing in that part of All Hallows at that time of night and I said I was looking for the library because I wanted to find out more about Bishop Ridley, and Mr Crouch said that the library closed at 5 p.m., but he was pleased I was taking such an interest. He put his warm hand with its pudgy fingers on my shoulder and guided me through the main part of the building to a pair of double doors with glass in the top half and the words 'School Library' written on the doors in gold letters.

'There,' said Mr Crouch, leaning down so his face was almost on a level with mine. 'You'll know where it is in the morning.'

'Thank you, sir,' I said.

He tweaked my ear. 'Can't quite work you out, Tyler,' he said. 'Can't work out why a boy like Salèn would be friends with a boy like you.'

'He didn't have much choice, sir,' I said.

I didn't like the feeling of Mr Crouch's skin touching my skin. On the way back up to the room, I diverted to the drinking fountain outside the refectory and I leaned my head over and washed my ear.

Isak was back in the bedroom when I arrived for the second time. The window was open and he smelled of cigarette smoke and he had a prickly attitude about him.

'I've got something to show you,' I said. I took the piece of paper out of my pocket and unfolded it and showed it to him. He gazed at the letters.

TN LT HEL|>

'The "TN" is the initials of someone who was in Ward B as an asylum inmate,' I said. 'You know those brackets on the wall down there? I think TN was chained to the wall and had to sit on the floor and the only way they could leave a mark was to scratch the floorboards. It must have taken ages but I don't suppose they had anything else to do.'

Isak grunted but I could tell he was interested.

'I wrote the "LT",' I said. 'They're my initials. Lewis Tyler.'

'No shit, Sherlock.'

'And that last word says "Help",' I said.

'Yeah, I can read.'

'It sounds like someone is in trouble. They want us to help them.'

'Lewis, those marks were made years and years ago. It's way too late to help whoever it was who made them.'

'But I didn't see the "help" message last time I looked.'

'Then it must have been made by someone at the school.'

'It wasn't. It's old. Like the first one.'

'It can't be.'

'It is.'

We were both quiet as we considered the implications of this.

'Did you make another mark?' Isak asked.

'Just a question mark. It wasn't very good as I had to do it quickly. But also, I had a good look round the floorboards in that area, a careful look to make sure I wasn't missing anything else and I wasn't. If another mark appears, we'll know it's new.'

'Good thinking, Läderlappen,' said Isak, and then he blushed furiously. 'It's Swedish for Batman,' he said. 'My mama used to...' he tailed off.

'She used to what?' I asked.

'Nothing.'

'Call you Läderlappen?'

'*Shut up!*' Isak said angrily.

I changed the subject immediately to Herbert Everdeen's grave and the space on the headstone that had been left for the inscription of his mother's name.

'Maybe,' I whispered, with a glance up to the ceiling, 'Herbert died in that room and that's why she stays there.'

'Shit,' whispered Isak, cowering beside me.

'I'm going to go to the school library tomorrow,' I said, 'to see what I can find out.'

'OK.'

'You can come too, if you want.'

Isak shrugged.

'Will you?' I asked.

'I might.'

37

EMMA – 1903

Winter came in properly and settled on the wild and rugged South-West of England. Mists crept over Dartmoor, dropped into its hollows and swathed its landmarks. The summer lambs were taken for slaughter and without the to-and-fro bleating between ewes and lambs, the moorlands around All Hallows Hospital fell quiet. The buzzards mewed overhead and leaves withered on the stunted blackthorn trees beyond the hospital walls while the berries grew round and darkened to blood red. The last of the leaves of the beech trees in the copse that stood guard over the chapel changed colour, grass stopped growing and lost its bright greenness, rain fell in curtains that blew over the moor, and the lawns were waterlogged. Fallen leaves spun on the surface of the lake. The swans dipped their long necks into the black water and the cygnets were as big as the parents and their dark juvenile fluff began to turn into brilliant white feathers.

Emma waited for a reply to her letter to Whitby police station but none came. She asked Maria if she had checked the staff pigeonhole so often that Maria became quite bad-tempered about it. In all this time there was only once a letter for Emma and that was from Joan Fairleigh, one of the girls she'd taught to nurse before she started working with Maria. Joan had written to let Emma know she was going to Africa to work in a military hospital, tending to soldiers injured in the course of quashing challenges to the Empire. She thought the nurse would be interested in her career and thanked her for giving her the requisite skills to take up this post. Emma had been fond of Joan: a serious young woman, prone to melancholy. She folded the letter and sighed and remarked to Maria that she very much hoped Joan would be able to cope with the trials she would inevitably face in Africa.

Maria was more than a little jealous of Joan and her adventures.

'Is Whitby a large place?' she asked, to bring Nurse Everdeen's mind back to the matters in hand.

'I have no idea.'

'Perhaps it is and the police are going about trying to discover if any persons are missing and it's taking them a long time, and that's why they haven't responded to your letter.'

'Perhaps.'

Maria had brought up clean bedding from the laundry. She and Emma were so used now to working together, that they did not need to communicate to know when the other was ready to begin work. Maria stepped forward and pulled back the sheets from the bed while the nurse set to removing the pillowcases from the pillows.

Maria dropped the old sheets into her basket and shook out a clean undersheet, taking hold of the corners and flapping it to unfold it. 'Are you well, Nurse?' she asked. 'You look tired.' She reached across to touch the nurse's forehead with the back of her wrist. 'You don't feel as if you have a fever.'

'I'm perfectly well,' said Emma, but there was a tremor in her voice that she could not quite hide. 'I'm just a little tired of being confined to this small area, that's all.'

It was not all. But she could not tell Maria Smith what was in her mind: that lately, since that night when she'd sensed some malevolence come into the room, she had not felt right. She couldn't tell her about the darkness she was certain was present in the room – not a normal sort of darkness – or that sometimes the rocking chair moved of its own volition; that once she'd tried to still it and she'd felt a pull, as if some opposing force was at work. She could not tell the younger woman that she'd seen shadows moving when everything solid was still, that the door opened and closed by itself, that she'd sensed the presence of another being, even though nobody was there. How could she say such things when she'd spent all her life attempting to quell the superstitious nonsense that sometimes bubbled up amongst the staff of the asylum?

How could she talk of her fears, Emma Everdeen, who for all her years at All Hallows had professed adamantly that there were no such things as ghosts, that spiritualism and seances were contrary to the natural order of the world and its life, that the only possibility of any form of existence beyond death lay in the hands of God Himself?

How could she do that?

38

'This is one of the few remaining entirely original parts of All Hallows,' the librarian, Mrs Goode, told us as we followed her through a long, dark room divided by multiple partitions.

I'd recognised Mrs Goode the moment I saw her. She was the woman from the converted stable block. The one with the dogs and the daughter.

'Yes,' she continued, answering a question neither Isak nor I had asked, 'it was built both as a facility for the medical staff and a resource for the patients – those who were capable of using it. See the sign on the panel there: "Reference", so this is where all the psychiatry, medical, legal and philosophy manuals were kept, and then over there we have "Fiction". Novels were very big in Victorian times. Not everyone approved. Indeed, I read an article that cited one of the reasons women were admitted to asylums in the nineteenth century was because they read too many books. But that's probably apocryphal. Now what exactly was it that you wanted?'

She addressed the question to Isak, which was what always

happened when he and I were together. People tended not to notice me; he simply shone more brightly.

'We're interested in the history of All Hallows,' Isak said, 'before it was a school.'

'Ooh, me too!' said Mrs Goode. 'It's so nice to meet kindred spirits. Follow me!'

Mrs Goode was the kind of person my mother would have liked. Her skirt didn't match her top. She was wearing a bright orange shirt beneath a baggy, hand-knitted cardigan that was buttoned on the wrong holes. Her fir-green satin skirt was tied with a bow at the side, and the ribbons dangled almost to her ankles, and she wore long, silver earrings beneath hair that didn't lie flat, despite the clips stuck into it. Her fingernails were painted duck-egg blue and a great big charm bracelet rattled about her wrist.

Isak and I followed Mrs Goode around the partitions until we reached a corner by a window in the furthest reaches of the library.

'Here we are. This is where everything pertaining to the history of All Hallows has been kept for more than one hundred and fifty years. Whoever designed this space wanted to make a little nook for themselves where they could escape the rigours of the asylum, don't you think?'

By this time, we had gone round so many turns that I wasn't sure if we would be able to find our way out. We were certainly in a nook. There was a mullioned window with a ledge wide enough to sit on, in a Gothic arch. The window was shielded by two shelved partitions full of books. It was a cosy place in this huge great uncosy building.

'So...' said Mrs Goode. 'The history of All Hallows is particularly interesting for me because both my great-grandmother and my great-grandfather worked here. That was how they met!'

'Wow!' I said.

'Yes! Without All Hallows I wouldn't be here and neither would my father or my children or... Anyway. She, my great-grandmother, was a local girl, uneducated. She joined as a domestic maid but one of the older nurses encouraged her to train to become a nurse. During the War years, she assisted with the care of the injured soldiers who came here after the asylum was requisitioned. Her name was Maria Smith and she married the hospital's groom, Samuel Collins. I'm very proud of my ancestors.' She beamed at Isak, who gave her a winning smile in return.

'Very few pupils have ever asked to come to this part of the library,' she continued, 'in fact I can't remember the last time anyone did, but there's a wealth of information here. Whatever it is you're looking for, I'm sure we can find it.' She waved a hand in the direction of the shelves. 'Some of these books are contemporary accounts of staff and patient life. There are others about the architecture and biographies of various dignitaries who worked here, some of which are,' she lowered her voice, 'a bit dull, if I'm honest. A better bet are the staff diaries, patient case notes, records and so on. I'll show you something!'

She stood on tiptoe and reached for a small and obviously old book, which she took down and held lovingly between the palms of her hands. 'It's a manual of nursing first published in the nineteenth century,' she said. 'It's very rare. Look!' She opened the book. The endpaper was in a fancy pattern, but when she turned the page there were several lines of handwriting. She passed the book to Isak.

'Read it!'

I leaned forward to look over Isak's shoulder. The writing was small, ornate, and spidery. Isak read:

To my pupil and friend, Emma Everdeen, with affection Nurse Harriet Sawmills, July 1858.

Beneath that was a second inscription in a different hand.

To Maria Smith, a most Capable Nurse at the Start of her Career. With Affection from Nurse Emma Everdeen, 23 December 1903.

I heard my mother's voice whisper: *Good work, Lewis! You've found her!*

It was almost too much to take in. Emma Everdeen had been given this actual book the year after the death of her son. She had held it in her hands, just like Isak was holding it now. This same, actual book! And then, decades after that, she had passed it onto Mrs Goode's great-grandmother. She must have written the second dedication shortly before her death. These were amazing facts and made me feel so victorious that I punched the air. Mrs Goode looked startled and took a step away from me.

'Sorry,' I said. 'I just...'

'He's really into history,' said Isak. 'He gets a bit carried away sometimes.'

'It's so lucky they wrote the inscriptions at the front,' I said, 'otherwise we wouldn't have known who the book belonged to.'

'Books were far more valuable and harder to come by back in those days so they tended to be passed on much more than they would be today,' said Mrs Goode. 'Even so, this one's pretty special.'

'Do you know anything else about Nurse Emma Everdeen?' Isak asked.

'Our family has a lot to thank her for,' said Mrs Goode. 'It was she who taught Maria Smith to nurse. Without her, Maria would never have made it out of the servants' quarters.'

'What happened to Nurse Everdeen in the end?' Isak asked.

'Oh, it was awful. An absolute tragedy. Maria could hardly bear to speak of it. I don't know if I should tell you boys.'

I heard my mother sigh, as if she knew what was coming. Suddenly, I wasn't sure that I did want to know after all.

Then Mrs Goode said: 'I suppose you'll find out, whether I tell you or not.' She hesitated, then said: 'Emma Everdeen was hanged on the prison gallows at Dartmoor. She'd been convicted of murder.'

'Murder?' Isak repeated.

'I'm afraid so. She was convicted of killing a little child in her care.'

'The daughter of the lord is coming tomorrow,' Maria said.

'Oh, yes?' said Emma, her brow furrowed as it always was these days.

'Her name is Thalia Nunes. She has cut her hair short like a man's and she wears trousers even when she isn't riding *and...*' Maria lowered her voice and said theatrically, 'she is involved in the movement demanding votes for women!'

Emma sniffed. 'And why shouldn't she do those things if that's what she wants to do? Because by doing so she causes embarrassment to her family? Because they're hoping to marry her off to some chinless wonder with more money than manhood, some... some milksop who would be humiliated to stand beside a woman who shone more brightly than he?'

Maria said. 'You didn't hear that, Harriet!'

'Yes, I did,' said Harriet. 'What's a manhood?'

'Take your ball and play on the landing, there's a good girl.'

'Really, it boils my blood,' said Emma, 'these men who send their wives and daughters to the asylum because it is the only means left to control and silence them.'

Maria glanced at her friend sideways. 'You have strong feelings about this, Nurse Everdeen.'

Emma tensed. She felt a rush of shame, a flashback to the shame she had felt when she was first brought to All Hallows.

'Is the father bringing her himself?'

'No. The carriage is being sent to Ivybridge. They're expecting the patient to put up a fight so they're sending a couple of orderlies and a nurse with a pocket full of morphine vials.'

Emma was silent for a moment, imagining a scene playing out in the courtyard of some stately home that she would never visit: the rebel daughter in her trousers haring towards the gates, some sour-faced old lord shaking his fist after her. Then she came back to the real world and sighed and went back to making the bed, tucking in the corners of the sheets. On the landing corridor outside, little Harriet threw the ball that Maria had brought for her against the wall and let it bounce before she caught it. The sound of the ball hitting the wall and then the floor was a rhythm like a heartbeat.

Isak was sitting on the rug beneath the table in the library nook with his back against the bench, looking through a book of photographs of Victorian asylums in Britain. I sat on the window ledge with the nursing handbook that had once belonged to Emma Everdeen. I held the book to my face, and sniffed its pages.

'Weirdo,' Isak muttered, and went back to his disturbing pictures.

I flicked through the manual. There were chapters on everything from concussions of the brain (this section was heavily underlined and annotated), to nosebleeds, sprains, fractures, burns and scalds. Notes had been written on many pages by several different hands. The typeface was small and the pages busy, but the manual was instructive and easy to read. I was pretty sure that most of its advice was wrong and some of it positively dangerous.

Strychnine for constipation? Mum said. *Good grief! Strychnine was what Victorian serial killers used to use.*

If Emma Everdeen had access to such stuff, it would mean murdering someone would be easy.

But a child!

I tried to imagine how it would feel to be Maria Smith, having someone like Emma Everdeen believe in you and teach you and bring you along. It must have been a pretty good feeling for a girl who'd expected to spend her life cleaning up after mad people. Pretty good right up until the part when Nurse Everdeen turned into a murderer.

There had been a boy at my old school; everyone called him Tyson as if he was a Rottweiler, and he was big and thickset and struggled to make a sentence. But our maths teacher, Mr Munro, noticed Tyson had a gift for numbers and he gave him extra coaching, and Tyson won a scholarship to a private school. He never went. He said he wouldn't have fitted in. But for a while he was famous in our school for all the right reasons and all because one person saw his potential. And after that everyone treated him differently. It must have been the same for Maria. And afterwards, when it turned out Nurse Everdeen was a murderer, Maria must have felt like Tyson would have felt if Mr Munro had turned out to be a paedo.

The bell rang to signify the end of the lunch break.

Isak looked up from his position on the floor. The autumn sunlight fell through the old glass, turning his hair the colour of quince, and the freckles on his face were illuminated too. Catching him like this, peaceful, took me by surprise.

'What?' he asked.

'Nothing.'

'Stop staring then.'

He pushed himself up to his feet in one hop.

* * *

Our first lesson that afternoon was history. I'd forgotten this, which was a good thing as I hadn't had time to worry about the Ridley homework. Perhaps Mr Crouch wouldn't have had a chance to look at it yet.

He came into the room, waistcoat buttons straining over his belly, with something of a spring in his step. He pushed the door shut behind him, stood on the podium, lay down the pile of papers he was holding and said: 'Good afternoon, gentlemen!'

'Good afternoon, sir.'

Mr Crouch's cheeks were flushed. This wasn't a good sign.

'I hope you're all well today and looking forward to another hour of absorbing information that will help you become more rounded and educated adults,' said Mr Crouch. 'I hope at least *some* of you will pay attention to the teaching I am about to impart. After thirteen years at school, three at university, two at teacher training college and several more spent absorbing information pertaining to the history of Great Britain and the Commonwealth, it would be disappointing if I were to stand here, holding forth about my subject of expertise, only to discover that certain pupils were not paying one iota of attention.'

Uh-oh.

He picked up the piece of paper on top of the pile.

'"Question one",' read Mr Crouch. '"Write an account of the martyrdom of Ridley..."'

My heart sank. I tucked my left hand under my right armpit to warm it in preparation for the inevitable beating. I felt the discomfort of all the boys around me, each wondering who it was who had failed so spectacularly in their homework; who the poor sod was who was about to be called to the front of the class to be punished in front of everyone with Mr Crouch's cane.

* * *

Ironically, it was an actual relief when the academic day was over and I was back in Ward B. I wanted to be by myself somewhere where nobody could see me or jostle me or slap me on the back and call me a hero. The fifty per cent of my classmates who were rebels had assumed that I'd deliberately messed up my homework to rile Mr Crouch; they thought I was emerging as a troublemaker, a desperado, someone with a complete disregard for authority. But actually, that wasn't me at all. I didn't want to be that kind of person. And especially I didn't want the teachers to think I was like that. I didn't want to keep getting beaten. It hurt, and I didn't like being hurt and I didn't like being humiliated either. I didn't like to think of how upset my mum would be if she knew what was going on here, and lastly, I didn't like imagining my father's face when he opened my academic report at the end of the year and discovered the number of my transgressions.

Fortunately, 'my' booth in Ward B was free. I scuttled to it before anyone else could claim it and took out my homework, part of which was to read the chapter in my history textbook about Bishop Ridley and learn that which I'd failed to learn before. I found the chapter and stared at the words but my eyes had started to glaze over with boredom before I'd even read one paragraph.

Was this it? I wondered. Was I to be stuck forever at page 170 of my *Reformation* book, never being able to climb the hill that was the martyrdom of Ridley, never being able to move on to other topics?

I stared at Bishop Ridley's picture. He had a black hat and a pointy beard and laughter lines at the corners of his eyes. From the little I knew of him he hadn't seemed like someone who might have a good sense of humour, but the person who painted him obviously thought he did. He was holding a book which was must have been a bible but that looked ever so similar in size and shape to Emma Everdeen's nursing manual.

Frustrated, tired, I took the lid off my pen and began to make notes, resenting every ounce of energy and concentration that the task demanded. The pen lid rolled towards the edge of the desk. I pushed it with my finger and it went all the way and fell onto the floor. I dropped down to retrieve it, my heart thudding with anticipation; but I could see at once that there were no more marks on the floorboards.

The disappointment was like a lump in my stomach. But what had I been expecting? Did I really think some person decades ago, chained to this wall, would have been somehow able to see my question mark and write back? It was stupid. I was stupid.

Still, I didn't feel ready to give up just yet. I pulled my mother's pendant from my neck and took the little horse in my hand and I began to scratch another question with its hoof.

'Tyler?'

I jumped and looked up. It was the supervising teacher.

'Tyler,' he repeated, 'what on earth are you doing?'

41

EMMA – 1903

Two days later, Maria was back in the little room in the attic with the Sherlock Holmes novels that Nurse Everdeen had asked her to bring up from the library. Maria also brought some distressing news that she conveyed at once although in a roundabout manner, to her friend.

'I knew Inspector Paul was back because I was out pushing a patient in a Bath chair when I heard a clattering of hooves,' she told Emma, 'a great to-do, nothing like the plodding of old William. I pushed the chair around the corner and I saw Samuel leading the piebald mare towards the stables. He was grumpy because she, the mare, was all of a sweat and a fluster. He said it wasn't right the inspector riding her so hard over the moors unless he was trying to stop a murder, which, of course, he wasn't. He said it was lucky the poor creature hadn't stumbled and broken a leg. Anyway, that's all by the by. I asked one of the other nurses to look after my patient and I went running inside and up the stairs to see if Dr Milligan required any notes to be taken.'

'You left an old woman in a Bath chair outside on her own?'

'It was a man and no, I told you, I asked Nurse Ashcroft to

take care of him. He wouldn't have been on his own for more than a few minutes. Don't look at me like that, Nurse. Do you want to know the news or don't you?'

'I do. So, did the doctor require you to take notes?'

'No, but he asked me to fetch Superintendent Pincher because Inspector Paul had some grievous news that he believed they should hear together. So I ran to fetch the superintendent and the three men repaired to the boardroom where I was to serve them tea and I overheard every word. Shall I tell you?'

'Yes, please.'

'See, if I hadn't left the patient, I wouldn't have been there to listen to them and you'd never know.'

Nurse Everdeen narrowed her eyes.

Maria adopted a smug expression and continued: 'The gist of it was, Nurse, that the corpse of a woman has been found washed up in a cove a little way along the coast. The body had been in the water for some time but bore wounds that almost certainly had been inflicted by the same weapon used to attack Mrs March. Don't ask me how they know, but know they do.'

Emma's eyes widened. She went to the door of the room and looked round it to check that Harriet was still playing safely in the corridor. Then she returned to her place and asked: 'What does this mean?'

'That's exactly what Mr Pincher asked. He drew on his pipe and puffed out his chest and said: "Does this mean there is a maniac on the loose in Devon, hunting down and attacking women at random?" And the inspector said: "We don't know what it means! But the woman's clothes were respectable and her purse was still about her person. Neither rape nor robbery appear to have been the motive. One thing they *do* know is that, given the state of the corpse, both this attack and the attack on Mrs March must have taken place at around about the same time."'

'Dear God! And is this second victim a local woman?'

'They haven't identified her either. The inspector went on about his dear wife, Elizabeth, again.' Maria paused to roll her eyes. 'She is mining the seams of local wisdom to discover if anyone is missing any servants. Last year a body was found in woodland and it remained unidentified for weeks, nobody having reported a person fitting its description missing. It turned out to be a young lad who had been let go by one of the big houses. They thought he'd gone home to Sussex but he never left Dartmoor.'

'His poor mother.'

'Indeed. There is so much sorrow in the world.' Maria fidgeted with a loose button at the cuff of her sleeve.

'Is there something else, Maria?'

'I'm not sure if I should tell you... but I will. Last night, one of the old women in the dementia ward, Ena Walters – do you remember her? – she was restless; weeping and wailing...'

'Miss Walters suffers from brain congestion. She often weeps and wails.'

'But she was inconsolable. She said she'd been speaking with the spirit of a hanged man who had come to her to tell her she must warn us—'

'Maria...'

'No, listen, Nurse Everdeen, Miss Walters said the hanged man told her to warn us that a terrible malevolence is afoot. She used the word *evil*.'

Beneath the sleeves of her dress, the skin on Emma's arms prickled.

'Miss Walters is demented, Maria,' she said.

'She's been right about some things, though, hasn't she? She predicted Mrs Lovell's death.'

'Mrs Lovell was ninety-two.'

'But there's more.' Maria leaned forward and spoke in a soft voice. 'The inspector told Mr Pincher that there was a hanging yesterday at the prison. How can it be a coincidence, Nurse, that one day a man is hanged and that very same night an old lady is haunted by the ghost of a hanged man who warns her of terrible danger?'

'It's superstitious nonsense, Maria,' said Emma. 'Who told you this? One of the nurses? Dorothy Uxbridge? I thought you had more sense than to pay any heed to such gossip. And whoever the nurse was, she shouldn't have been spreading this kind of mischief either!'

'But something *is* wrong,' Maria insisted. 'Two women have been attacked – one murdered, the other left for dead – and Harriet is caught up in it too, a little, innocent child! If that's not evil at play, well, I don't know what is.'

Emma's mouth was dry. She reached for a cup and took a sip of water. Maria had her elbows on the table and was resting her head in her hands, her fingers tangled in her thick hair. Emma put a hand on her shoulder.

'The attacks took place on the coast,' she said gently. 'We are miles inland. And we live in a building surrounded by a great wall, with locks on the doors and dogs patrolling at night. We could not be any safer than we are here.'

Maria sniffed.

'And there have been no further attacks for some weeks now. If there is some madman at large, perhaps he has moved on.'

'No further attacks that we know of,' Maria said in an ominous tone.

Harriet skipped into the room. She looked from Emma to Maria and her joy faded.

Emma summoned a smile from somewhere. 'Hello, Harriet. Are you tired of your game?'

Harriet held up the knitted rabbit.

'Rabbit is hungry,' she said. 'He would like to know if Maria has any toffees in her pocket.'

Maria sighed and raised her head and turned to Emma. 'Well now, isn't that the strangest thing?'

'What is the strangest thing?' Emma asked.

'A few moments before I came up all those stairs from down below, I said to Mr Collins, "Samuel," I said, "there's a rabbit that lives in the room in the attic that is partial to a toffee or several." And do you know what Mr Collins said to me, Harriet?'

Solemnly, the child shook her head.

Maria put her hand into her apron pocket and withdrew a paper bag. 'He said: "Well, Miss Smith, you had better take these up for that poor hungry rabbit then!"'

Isak was sitting at the head end of his bed with the book of asylum photographs propped open on his knees.

'Lewis? What's the matter? What's happened?'

'I lost Mum's horse.'

'You lost it? How?'

'I dropped it down the space between the floorboards in Ward B. This is going to be the first night since Mum died that I haven't worn her pendant! What if that was the only thing keeping her close to me? What if she goes away now for ever, Isak, and I can't get her back?'

'Shhh,' said Isak. He put down his book, pulled me onto the bed beside him and put his arms around me. 'It's OK, Lewis. We'll get the horse back. I promise we will.'

I tried as hard as I could not to, but I couldn't help it. I began to cry.

'I'm not crying,' I said.

'Fuck's sake,' Isak said. 'It doesn't matter if you are.'

I wanted to ask Isak why he never cried. I wanted to tell him that I understood how sad and angry he must be feeling about what had happened to his family and that I didn't mind if he wanted to talk about it. It didn't seem fair that I was always telling him about my grief and he never said a word about his.

'I'm OK,' I said, hiccupping and wiping my face with my sleeve.

Isak held me until I had stopped sobbing, then he ruffled my hair and I ruffled his back and we had a little play fight.

'I need a smoke,' said Isak. 'Come out onto the ledge with me.'

'I can't.'

'Why not?'

'Heights are one of the things that make me faint. We were on holiday in Spain once and we went up a tower and I fainted at the top and it caused a queue right down the street because people couldn't get up until they could get me down. Some people were in the queue so long they missed the coach back to their resort and there was a big argument about who should pay their taxi fares.'

'But we're not in Spain.'

'It wasn't Spain that made me faint. It was looking down on the people in the square below. They were like ants. If there hadn't been a wall around the top of the tower I would have fallen to my death.'

'If you come out onto the ledge and faint, I'll catch you before you fall.'

'But you would say that, Isak, wouldn't you?'

'Not if I didn't mean it. I don't want to be responsible for you dying.'

In the end, I let him help me out of the window. I sat in front of the opening, so that if I fainted, I'd fall backwards into the room. Isak climbed further along the ledge and dangled his legs over the edge. He lit a cigarette and offered me a drag. I shook my head.

The moon was waning, only a sliver of crescent remained and that kept being sucked away behind great, amassing clouds. Below us the ghostly white barn owl moved through the grounds of All Hallows.

'What do you want to do?' I asked Isak. 'When we're out of here I mean.'

'Be a rock star. It would annoy my father if I was more famous than him.'

'And you'd get lots of sex,' I said.

'That, too.' He took a long drag and blew smoke up into the air. 'What about you?'

'I don't know. I used to want to be a detective but now I'm not sure.'

Isak flicked his cigarette butt over the edge. I wished he wouldn't do that in case it was sucked back in through an open window and set fire to the building. My mum's friend, Jemma, once flicked a cigarette out of her car front window and it went straight back in via the back window and burned a hole in the cushion that her mum had crocheted, which showed that such things could happen.

* * *

'Come and look at this,' said Isak, later.

I perched beside him on his bed and he picked up the book and showed me a photograph of a group of people standing outside All Hallows, arranged in a fan shape on the steps that led up to the front door.

'These are the asylum's staff at the end of the nineteenth century,' he said.

'There's a lot of them.'

'It was a big old asylum.'

The nurses were wearing white aprons over dark, long-sleeved dresses, and caps that covered most of their heads; dark stockings, robust shoes. The doctors were in three-piece suits with watch chains, hats and curly moustaches. There were other staff too: domestics, groundsmen and so on. One man, small and old, had a little Jack Russell at his feet. I guessed he was the ratter. Another, Mrs Goode's great grandfather, perhaps, was holding the reins of a handsome horse.

One of those nurses must be Nurse Everdeen.

'And here are some of their patients.' Isak turned the page to a photograph of three women enclosed in something the shape of a shoe box, but far larger and made of wood. Only the women's heads were visible through holes in the top of the box.

'"In early Victorian times, mental illness was regarded as a disease, which, logically, meant it could be cured,"' Isak read.

In some asylums, treatment took the form of punishment: beatings, starvation, cold water immersion, isolation and the letting of blood.

The more progressive institutions provided comfortable accommodation for the majority of patients, whilst segregating those with more severe conditions and those whose behaviour was unpredictable, violent, overtly sexual or difficult to control. Such patients were usually managed in dedicated wards and visitor access was strictly limited.

'Was All Hallows one of the progressive ones?'

'Who knows?'

He turned the next page and said: 'Recognise this?'

'What is it?'

He pushed the book towards me. It was an old photograph of Ward B. The partitions that separated the booths were there, as they were now, and the brackets on the walls. A warder stood at the far end, with a bunch of keys. In one of the booths, a patient was restrained by an arrangement of straps and buckles to a wooden chair with a bucket beneath it. In the next booth, the patient was attached to the wall bracket by chains, fastened to a metal collar around his or her neck. This patient was sitting on the floor, dressed in rags, shaven headed and dull-eyed. Both inmates looked as if they had lost the will to live.

'Are they men or women?' I asked.

'Can't tell.'

I didn't want to see any more.

I put the book down, stood up and picked up my towel and toothbrush.

I hesitated at the door. 'Isak,' I said.

'What?'

'Thanks. For being so nice to me earlier.'

'Fuck off,' said Isak, without looking up.

43

While Harriet slept that night, Emma remembered that she had forgotten to ask Maria if the new patient, Thalia Nunes, had arrived, and if she had, what kind of condition she was in.

No doubt she was a brave and headstrong woman but even the bravest would struggle to come to terms with being restrained in Ward B, everything about it being designed to humiliate and dehumanise.

Emma doubted a young lady raised in a household with all the comforts that money could buy would ever be able to comprehend the truth about life inside an asylum. The next weeks would be a shock to her. She hoped she would have the common sense to at least pretend to regret her actions, to apologise and be humble. That would be her best chance of being removed from Ward B and to have some privacy, and privileges, restored. She must remember to tell Maria to convey this advice to the new patient at her earliest opportunity.

To take her mind away from worrying about Miss Nunes, she opened the detective novel she was reading: *The Hound of the Baskervilles,* hoping to gain an insight into the rudiments of investigative work. The local police did not seem to be making a good fist of solving the puzzles relating to Mrs March and Harriet. If Emma set her mind to considering these mysteries herself, it might distract it from its dark meanderings.

Because Emma was afraid. When daylight was breaching through the window of the attic room, and Harriet was playing or singing, noisy and full of energy; when Maria brought up the trays and news from the asylum below, then it was easier to ignore the feelings that unsettled her. But when Harriet was sleeping, Emma was alone and darkness had fallen beyond the asylum walls; then the fear took hold.

She was having to take larger doses of the sleeping potion for it to have any effect. She needed more gin to feel the same sense of calm that a simple nip would have given her before.

She poured a little more gin into her glass now.

Emma had never judged those patients addicted to drink. After Herbert's death she might easily have gone the same way. It was Nurse Sawmills who taught her that hard work and the service of others were more reliable routes to a good night's sleep than the bottle and the dwelling on what-might-have-been. Nurse Sawmills had walked for hours with the young Emma through the grounds of All Hallows, encouraging her to talk about her loss, but Emma had struggled to do so. She had been brought up to suppress her feelings. Her father found any kind of emotional outburst tiresome. Her mother despised the 'silliness' of women who made a fuss about small things. The shame with which Emma had been filled when her parents had discovered she was with child lingered, even after that child's death; a shame so cloying, Emma had been unable to articulate it to Nurse Sawmills.

It was a shame that, fifty years later, lingered still.

Emma Everdeen was a vicar's daughter, from a good family, not from the working classes who (according to her father) 'fornicated and bred like animals'. When she was known to be in a delicate condition, the overriding priority was that nobody else – certainly none of the middle-class congregation – found out. Her parents' disgust and disappointment had been so bruising that Emma had been relieved when they employed the housekeeper of a neighbouring priest to bring her to the asylum and to leave her there amongst the lunatics and idiots, too many miles from home to attempt to make her own way back. In truth, Emma had felt more at home in the ward for fallen women than she had done when she was locked in the bedroom of the Surrey vicarage. The expectation was that the baby would be born and sold for adoption. But Herbert, when he came, with his miraculously deformed leg, could not be sold; nor was he the kind of child anybody would wish to adopt. So, the authorities had let Emma keep him, let her stay at the asylum, and to pay for her board and lodging, and Herbert's, Emma had worked. She had worked hard. She, with her clear skin, her manners, her nice way of speaking, her ability to read and write (the vicar had employed a governess to supply a rudimentary education to Emma and her sister), was useful to the asylum. And she liked being there. She had her own room, a room she shared with Herbert, and he had the grounds to play in and a host of doting aunties and uncles amongst the staff and patients, who loved him almost as much as she did. The five happiest years of Emma Everdeen's life had been the five years she lived at All Hallows with her darling Herbert.

And then he was taken from her.

The doctors said that nothing could have been done to prevent Herbert's death. They told Emma time and again that she had been an exemplary mother, but she did not believe them. Deep down within herself, she could not shake the belief that Herbert's death was punishment for her sin. She sat in the chapel every Sunday, and she listened to sermons that spoke of God's love, His benevolence, His willingness to forgive those who repented; and yet He must surely have a seam of spite as well to take away a little child who had not lived long enough to commit any sin; whose heart was as pure as love itself.

In the room in the attic, Emma sipped her drink, barely wetting her tongue; making it last. Having little Harriet with her reminded her of details about Herbert she had forgotten. It was how the child sat on her cushion at the table, her frown, her habit of throwing herself backwards onto the bed when she was frustrated; the way in which her lower lip trembled when she was about to cry; the ease with which she could be coaxed from ill humour to joy; her laughter – the most infectious sound that Emma remembered ever hearing – the tender way she came to sit upon Emma's lap when she was sleepy; the triangle formed by her lips when she was sleeping; picking up her cup with both hands; the concentration on her face when she knelt at the side of the bed to pray.

Herbert used to have exactly the same expressions.

Two five-year-olds, fifty years apart, who had no connection with one another save this woman, Emma Everdeen, who had promised to do the best by them.

She looked at Harriet, sleeping on the bed and she vowed, once again, that, although it could not be denied there were forces in the world that might hurt her, she would never let them close.

She would not fail Harriet as she had failed her flesh-and-blood child all those years before.

44

Up on the attic landing, I could hear the thump of the rocking chair runners behind the closed door of the fourth room. I did not have any intention of opening the door that evening; I didn't want to know any more about Emma Everdeen. I was a bit disgusted with myself for making such a big deal about the finding of the bones and for being so fascinated with her. How could anyone who worked at a place where they treated people like the people I'd seen in the photographs be a good person? Emma bloody Everdeen probably deserved everything she'd got. She was probably a piece of work, as Mum would say.

I went into the bathroom and pulled the cord to turn on the overhead lights. They flickered horribly before they finally burned, lighting up that big old bathroom, with its cracked tiles, its ancient bath and lavatory and basin.

I left the door open, put my towel on the chair, went to the basin and looked in the mirror. My face was swollen, blotchy from the crying and my skin was flushed. For an instant, I caught a glimpse of my mother's face in mine. I tried a smile, and from somewhere inside me, she smiled back.

'I'm sorry about losing the horse pendant,' I whispered.

It's only a thing. Things don't matter.

I ran the hot tap – it took ages for warm water to reach this distant part of the building – and when it was hot enough, put in the plug to fill the basin. I washed my face; and stood up straight. The mirror had steamed over now. I wiped away a circle of condensation with the back of my hand. My ears looked exactly like jug handles.

I sighed, put half an inch of toothpaste onto the brush, and began to brush my teeth.

And that's when it happened.

She came up behind me. She came so rapidly and aggressively that I did not have time to react before she shoved me between my shoulder blades and my head flew forward and banged onto the front of the mirror.

The pain on my forehead was intense. I bit my tongue and the toothbrush jabbed the back of my throat.

I turned to face my attacker, my hand to my face spitting toothpaste and blood.

Nobody was there.

Isak heard my scream and came running up the stairs. He found me huddled in the corner of the bathroom, holding my towel to the gash on my head. The water in the basin had overflowed and was making a puddle on the bathroom floor.

He pulled out the plug, and skidded across the room.

'Lewis! Are you OK, Lewis?'

I didn't know how to explain what had happened. I kept reliving the moment before the woman pushed me. I kept seeing her face zooming up behind mine in the mirror, but although it was clear in my mind, it was difficult to describe. I knew my attacker was a woman, and that she had long hair, because the hair had been flying, but otherwise... nothing. I could *see* her face in my mind's eye, but I could not have told anyone what she looked like.

Isak was staring at me, concerned.

'What happened?' he asked. 'Did you faint or something?'

'I think I might have seen her,' I whispered.

'Seen who?'

'*Her.* Emma Everdeen.'

Isak was silent for a moment, then he shook his head. 'You fainted,' he said. 'I'll go and fetch Matron.'

The thought of being left alone in the attic with the *thing,* whatever it was, was unbearable.

'No!' I cried, taking hold of his arm. 'No, it's OK. I'm OK. Let's go back to our room. I'll be fine.'

Emma collated some tips from the detective novels. First, she established the importance of breaking down the *bigger* question, which was: *What happened to Mrs March and Harriet?* into a number of smaller ones, and to look at these individually.

She did not have access to notepaper, but there were those useful blank pages at the back of her nursing manual, which she had been using to record Harriet's dreams. As Dr Milligan no longer appearing to be interested in these, she used this space instead to make a list of the questions to which answers were required.

Had the lugger's sails been raised when it was found?

How far was it from land?

Would an experienced seaman be able to say from whence it set out given the weather conditions on 2 October and he knowing the tide and the sea currents?

Mr Sherlock Holmes might have had access to the information necessary to work this out, but Emma would need specialist help.

Is it possible to sail from this part of England to France, if one knows what one is doing?

Emma had an inkling that it was possible; she'd overheard talk of a smuggling route, and if smugglers could cross in rowing boats, a lugger would surely be able to cope with the distance and the waves. Therefore...

Was crossing the Channel the intention?
    Would a woman of Mrs March's stature be capable of managing such a boat over the entire Channel on her own? (If that was the intention.)

She copied the questions onto a sheet of paper which she gave to Maria to put to Inspector Paul next time he visited All Hallows. Maria said she wasn't at all sure Inspector Paul would take kindly to Nurse Everdeen's 'help' but promised to approach him nevertheless.

As well as worrying about the mystery surrounding Mrs March and Harriet, Emma was worried about Miss Thalia Nunes, downstairs in Ward B.

Maria had reported that, since her arrival, Thalia had been so drugged she could barely speak, her words were slurred and she was confused about where she was. Her head had been shaved and her clothes taken from her and she was obliged to dress instead in one of the asylum's regulation coarse linen gowns and flannel underclothes.

'Her father has asked that she be treated harshly, in order to make her see the error of her ways,' Maria said. 'Mr Uxbridge is personally supervising her treatment and I don't like the way he is setting about it.'

'I wouldn't trust that dreadful man further than I could throw him.'

'Me neither. And Sam says he was only appointed in the first place because of his family's business connections. Did you know, Nurse Everdeen, that he was dismissed from his previous position for the telling of untruths?'

'It does not surprise me one bit. He and his niece are cut from the same cloth. Dishonesty and cruelty run through their veins.'

'What's the matter, Nurse?' Harriet asked, coming to her side and leaning against the nurse. Emma put an arm around the child.

'Nothing, my lamb,' she said.

'You look sad.'

'How could I be sad when I have you for company?'

'It's the weather, that's all,' said Maria.

'Maria's right,' said Emma.

And it was true. To add to Emma's woes, there had been a string of foggy days when it had been hard to see anything from the window; days when thick grey cloud had been pressed against the asylum like a pillow to a face. The walls of the room in the attic, already claustrophobic, had seemed to close in on themselves even more than before.

46

The next morning, we had the usual cross-country run through the rain. Running hurt. With every step my head bobbed up and down and with each bob, pain throbbed in the bruise that had developed on my forehead.

The soles of my trainers slapped the flat water lying in the grassy dips of the fields. Hundreds of feet following the same route every day had carved a muddy track. Isak, in an odd, distant mood, ran on ahead and I, feeling sorry for myself, dawdled behind. Once we were back in the classroom, I took out my books and sat waiting for the teacher, listening to the sound of the workmen sawing out rotten wood in the corridor above and wondering when I might have an opportunity to return to Ward B to look for my mother's pendant.

Eventually, the Latin teacher arrived. He was a fusty old man with a stoop, a pot belly and shaky hands. He shuffled to the podium and asked everyone to hand in their homework.

I'd forgotten to do the homework what with worrying about the pendant and then banging my head in the bathroom but fortunately Isak had let me copy his answers that morning, before breakfast.

I handed in my paper. The lid to Isak's desk was raised and he was rummaging inside.

'Mr Salèn, we're waiting,' the teacher said.

There was some nervous giggling.

'Mr Salèn!'

Slowly Isak closed the lid.

'I'm sorry, sir, I must've left my homework in the cloakroom, sir.'

Nobody else would have got away with it, but Isak was the teacher's unashamed favourite.

'You may go to the cloakroom, Mr Salèn,' he said. 'Fetch the homework. Hurry.'

'Mrs March gave Dorothy ever such a fright yesterday,' Maria told Emma. 'She suddenly, with no warning whatsoever, sat up straight in her bed with her eyes opened as if she was wide awake, but almost at once she slumped down onto the pillows again with a great sigh, and when Dorothy tried to rouse her, she couldn't.'

'I don't think it will be long until she is conscious.'

'Dorothy believes it will happen at any time.'

'Last time I checked Dorothy Uxbridge was not a qualified physician. Has Dr Milligan passed an opinion on the matter?'

Maria leaned closer and said in a conspiratorial voice: 'Indeed he has. He is considering an intravenous injection of a nerve tonic called cocaine to stimulate the brain.'

Emma raised an eyebrow.

'Nothing but the best for his favourite patient. He has had a desk brought in to her room and works there in the evenings so they can "keep one another company". I don't know which of them would be the least dull companion! The one who never says an interesting word or the comatose patient.'

The young woman cast a sly glance at Emma and continued:

'Dorothy says Dr Milligan stands by the window and describes the clouds blowing across the sky and their attendant shadows on the lawns beneath.' She sketched the scene with her hand. 'He goes all lyrical about the colours of the fallen leaves, the lapwings banking against a dark grey cloudscape. He says to Dorothy: "If Mrs March can hear me, I don't want to fill her mind with anything but pleasant thoughts and I trust that my language, the insertion of a line of poetry here and there, is appreciated by a woman so cultured."'

'How does he know she's cultured?'

'Because in his mind Mrs March is a perfect woman – a *queen*!'

Emma chuckled properly this time.

'Heaven help him,' she said, 'if she speaks in a common voice when she wakes.'

'Or turns out to be a fishwife,' said Maria, 'or worse!'

48

Isak was gone for longer than it would have taken to go to the cloakroom, pick up his homework and return. When he came back he apologised to the teacher, said he'd had trouble finding it. And he looked at me and he was frowning.

* * *

Later, he told me he hadn't been to the cloakroom at all.

'I went to Ward B,' he said. 'I went to look for your horse.'

I was so overwhelmed with gratitude, I could not speak.

'I found the marks on the floorboards where you said they were so I knew I was in the right place. I looked in all the cracks. Honestly, Lewis, I looked and it wasn't there.'

49

EMMA – 1903

At last the fog was gone but the weather that replaced it was scarcely less dreary.

Together, Emma and Harriet listened to the rain pattering against the window glass. They watched the autumn light, muted by shadows, moving around the room as the day progressed. The days each had the same shape: waking, washing, dressing, playing, eating. At intervals, Maria came, bringing food or books, or some other diversion in the form of news about Thalia Nunes or Mrs March. Sometimes she came with only a tray of tea and she and Emma talked or else the three of them would play a game together. Emma was teaching Maria and Harriet to play cards. Card lessons were Harriet's favourite pastime. Maria was a slow learner when it came to cards and Emma grew impatient with her and would pretend to be cross. Maria would lay down her cards and say: 'Rummy for three!' when she didn't have a single set in her hand and Emma would say: 'Oh, for heaven's sake, Maria!' and sometimes Harriet laughed so much she slid off her chair and curled on the floor holding her stomach and squealing with delight.

When they were alone, Harriet told Emma about the games she and Mama used to play. How they would race one another on the beach barefoot, Mama holding up her skirts as she ran and her hair flying behind her, both of them laughing, seagulls circling above. As Harriet described her memories in her childish way, Emma relived them with her. She almost felt, as if she were Harriet, the cold grittiness of the sand, Mama's strong hand holding hers, Mama hefting her up onto her hip and spinning her round; the glorious, dizzy feeling. Harriet pressing her face into Mama's neck; the warmth of her skin. Going home. Dipping their feet in the pail of water by the door to wash away the sand on their soles and between their toes and then going inside to warm up by the fire. Falling asleep on the chair beside Mama; Pippin the cat pawing at her skirt, fire crackling in the grate.

'Did you and Mama ever go to the abbey on the other side of the bay?' Emma asked.

'No. But on Sundays we went to the church of St Mary.'

'The church of St Mary?' the nurse asked.

'Yes.'

'Well, I never. What a clever child you are to remember that.'

That night, Emma wrote a second letter to Whitby. This time, she addressed it to the Reverend of St Mary's church. It was a similar letter to the first, except this time she mentioned that the two patients at All Hallows used to attend services at that very church and that they must be now absent from the congregation: a pretty woman in her early thirties and her little daughter, aged about five, a dear, clever child with dark hair and a birthmark on her wrist.

50

At the end of our last lesson of the day, one of the younger boys knocked on the door and came in with a slip of paper that he passed to the teacher. When the bell rang, the teacher asked Isak to come to the front of the class. They stood by the door, the teacher speaking to Isak; their heads close together. I felt a thrum of anxiety.

I put my books back in my desk and crossed the room.

'What is it?' I asked Isak when the teacher had left.

'Gotta go and see Crozier.'

'Why?'

'Something to do with my father.'

We walked along the corridor together, our footsteps in sync, but at the end of it, I turned one way and headed for the library; Isak went the other way, raising a hand like a rock star leaving the stage.

That afternoon, the sun was shining through the library windows; dust motes floating, the wood of the bookshelves polished to a mirror shine. Mrs Goode was in her office attending to some paperwork. She saw me through the window and raised a hand in greeting, and I waved back and then I hurried to the section on the history of All Hallows; our nook.

I sat at the table, opened my *Emma Everdeen* exercise book, tucked one leg beneath me and settled.

I wrote down the new things I knew about Emma in the book: about Herbert and Maria Smith, and Emma being a child murderer. At the bottom of the sheet I considered writing 'Died' or 'Executed', but both words made me uncomfortable. So instead I just wrote: 'Prison.' Then: 'Unmarked grave, Boxing Day 1903.'

I tapped the pen against my teeth. Where did I go from here?

Mrs Goode's face appeared.

'Oh, my goodness, Lewis, what have you done to your forehead?'

'I slipped.'

She frowned. 'Are you sure you simply *slipped,* dear, because if any of the other boys is picking on you then...'

'No.' I shook my head. 'Really, I just slipped.'

'OK,' she said. She peered a little more closely at my wound. '*Really?*'

'Honestly.'

'Right. Now there's a book here,' she put it on the table, 'which might be of interest. It contains case studies written by Dr Milton Milligan. His tenure at All Hallows overlapped for a short while with Nurse Everdeen's, and he mentions her several times in relation to the case of one of his first patients.'

'Thank you,' I said. 'That's amazing.'

'Is there anything else I can help you with?'

'Actually, I'm trying to find out about someone who was a patient in the asylum. Their initials were TN, and they were kept in Ward B.'

'TN?'

'Yes.'

'Male or female?'

'I don't know.'

'Could it be Thalia Nunes?'

Mrs Collins turned to the shelves and searched for a moment, then fished out a different book.

'Here you are,' she said. '*When I Was Mad* by Thalia Nunes. It's her autobiographical account of being forced into the asylum because she wouldn't behave as her parents wanted her to. She wanted to be a politician, to fight for justice and equality. They wanted her to settle down and make a good marriage.'

'At least she wrote a book,' I said.

'She had to pay to have it published abroad. Nobody in the UK dared publish her story because they were so afraid of being sued by her father or the company that owned the asylum. Here,' she passed it to me. 'I think you'll enjoy this. Thalia was quite a livewire.'

Maria had some news for Emma, but she was worried about how to break it. She began in a roundabout way, by telling the nurse that she was concerned about her.

'You don't need to be, Maria.'

'You don't seem well.'

'I'm tired, that's all.'

'Is the little one not sleeping?'

'She's good as gold.'

'What is it then?'

'It's the time of year. The short days and long nights. The darkness.'

'That's really all that troubles you? You have shadows around your eyes, Nurse, and... Oh, I might as well say it! I've noticed lately that there's a tremble in your fingers.'

The nurse moved her hands under the table.

'If I tell you something, Maria, promise me you won't say anything about it to anyone else, especially not to Dr Milligan.'

'I won't tell a soul.'

'Sometimes...'

'What, Nurse?'

'Sometimes I feel a presence in this room. It feels... horrid. And, of course there's nothing here, and nobody. It's my mind playing tricks on me. I know that's all it is, but I can't stop feeling it.'

'I'm sure anyone would be the same if they were locked up here for days on end,' Maria said. 'I don't know how you've put up with it for as long as you have! Should I ask Dr Milligan if I may bring you a tonic, Nurse Everdeen? Or perhaps even a little laudanum to help you sleep?'

'I have my own medicine for that. What I need is a change of scene and some fresh air. Perhaps you might ask Dr Milligan if an excursion into the grounds could be arranged. The air would put some roses into Harriet's cheeks and I'm certain it would give my heart a lift.'

'I'll ask him, of course. I'm sure he'll say "yes".'

Emma gave a weak smile. Maria was twitchy; fidgeting.

'What is it, Maria? Is there something you haven't told me? Oh goodness! Has it happened? Has Mrs March woken?'

A glance at Harriet to make sure she was not listening, then: 'She has! She's not *properly* awake, but she is opening her eyes and following movement around the room.'

'Does Dr Milligan know if she is going to be wholly recovered?'

'Not yet, but the signs are good. She has sensation in all her limbs and fingers. There's a definite intelligence; she pays attention to conversations. It will take a while yet, for her to regain her strength, but Dr Milligan is optimistic that she will soon be, if not exactly the woman she was before, then a very close replica.'

'Thank God,' said Emma, 'for all His mercy! Does this mean our little girl will soon be reunited with her mother?'

'Not for a while yet. Mrs March is still frail.'

'Then I shan't say anything to Harriet because she won't understand why she can't go to her mama immediately.'

'Meanwhile I'll talk to Dr Milligan and see if I can't arrange for you and Harriet to go out.'

'Thank you, Maria. It would make a world of difference to me.'

52

I did not see Isak alone again until supper time that evening.

I was sitting at one end of a table, by myself, when he came into the refectory. He walked with his usual arrogant stride, but his hands were in his pockets and something was clearly wrong. I raised my hand. He didn't acknowledge me, but a few minutes later he came over to the table and sat down with his tray of food. I had already finished mine so I had to wait while he ate. Isak never talked when he was eating.

When he was done, he pushed the tray away and I was a bit disappointed to see that nothing at all was left that I might scavenge.

Isak stacked his dishes on the tray. He looked at me for the first time.

'Let's go upstairs,' he said.

53

EMMA – 1903

Maria was so excited about her news that she left the breakfast tray at the foot of the stairs, hitched up her skirts and ran up two at a time, the tools attached to her chatelaine jangling at her hip. She unlocked the door at the top and, leaving it wide open with the key in the lock, she ran along the corridor to the fourth door; rapped with her knuckles and pushed it open without waiting to be invited in.

'Whatever is the matter?' Emma asked. She was alone in the room darning a stocking, one of several in a small heap beside her.

'Where is Harriet?'

'She's making a warren for the rabbit in the room next door. Why? What is it?'

'A gentleman has come forward,' Maria panted, 'who might be able to identify Mrs March! And it's all thanks to your letter, Nurse Everdeen! The vicar of St Mary's church in Whitby recognised your description of Mrs March and Harriet as regulars amongst his congregation until about one month ago, when they...' she made an exploding gesture with her hands, 'vanished!'

'My days!'

'It is exactly as you hoped! The reverend contacted the widow's landlord who contacted Mr Pincher. Obviously,' she added, 'it would have been more polite if he had responded to you directly but...'

'That doesn't matter. What did he say?'

'That his tenant is a widow. She is around thirty years old, a quiet and reserved woman who keeps herself and the child to herself but is well-liked by her neighbours, and good-hearted. Until now, she has been a model tenant, never falling behind with her rent and maintaining the cottage in excellent order, growing vegetables and keeping chickens. She has never given her landlord nor any of her neighbours a moment's trouble, and the child is quiet and polite but... a few weeks ago the woman went to a neighbour and said she and the child were obliged to go away for a short while because her father-in-law had passed on, and she would be grateful if the neighbour would take care of the hens and the cat, of which the child was very fond. The neighbour said she would be happy to do so and she saw the woman and child depart for the railway station. She did not worry until ten days had passed – the woman had said she would be back within the week or else she would be in touch, and she done neither, at which point the neighbour contacted the landlord and voiced her concern. Of course, neither of them thought of asking the police for help, no obvious crime or wrongdoing having been committed, but they did talk to the vicar, who advised them not to worry, and so they didn't and neither did the vicar until he received your letter.'

Emma lay down the needle and the stocking. She took off her spectacles and put them on the table. She rubbed her forehead with the tips of her fingers.

'How do you know all this, Maria?'

'I was there just now, in the boardroom, serving tea and toast and I heard Mr Pincher telling Dr Milligan. The landlord is coming to All Hallows to confirm whether or not the patient is his missing tenant. And it's all thanks to the initiative taken by you, Nurse Everdeen! You!'

'This is it, then,' said Emma. 'The mystery is solved.'

'Let's hope so! The superintendent is very excited about the possibility, that's for sure – although disappointed that Mrs March is not, apparently, the daughter of nobility!'

'What of Mrs March? Is she speaking yet?'

'A little. She remembers Harriet, indeed she has asked after her daughter, and if she is well. She wanted to know how much time had elapsed since she was brought here. Her memory is vague, she struggles to answer any questions about herself; does not even know her own name. Dr Milligan says amnesia is common in patients with head injuries.'

'Yet she remembers Harriet?'

'Oh yes. The maternal bond is a strong one.'

'Has she asked to see the child?'

'She is still too weak. Dr Milligan is afraid she might be overwhelmed by emotion. She is terrified, poor thing, of closing her eyes and falling back into the coma. Imagine that! Believing that each time you went to sleep you might not wake again.'

The tone of Maria's voice, when she spoke of Mrs March, was becoming softer. Emma realised that the lovely patient was casting a spell over Maria, in the same way that she, even unconscious, had entranced Dr Milligan. Although she was pleased, of course, that Mrs March was making such good progress, she felt a needle of jealousy.

Soon, I shall lose Harriet, she thought. Instantly ashamed of herself, she reframed the thought as: Soon, Harriet will be back where she belongs – a more positive way to look at the situation and the only way that was right and Christian. And, although pride was a sin, she couldn't help but take a little pleasure in the fact that it was her investigative work that might well have brought the mystery of Mrs March and Harriet's identity to a satisfactory conclusion.

54

It was a cold night but there was no wind or rain. Isak wanted to go outside. I was so worried about his state of mind that this time I followed him out of the window and then clung to the side of the building while he crept along the impossibly narrow ledge behind the ornamental, stone balustrades. The wall of All Hallows was to his right. To his left was a sheer drop of thirty feet. Or maybe forty. Fifty even. It was a bloody long way down.

'Come on, Lewis,' he called, 'it's a piece of cake.'

'I don't think this is a good idea.'

'I've done it loads of times.'

'Yeah, but, Isak, what if the window slams shut or—'

'Oh, for God's sake, stay there if you want to, Lewis. Be a wimp. Me, I'm going higher!'

He was my friend and he was unhappy and I didn't want to leave him out there alone. I gritted my teeth and held on to the wall, digging my fingers into the cracks between the stones and inched my way after him, trying my best not to think of the drop; trying not to think about fainting.

When we had gone roughly as far as the end of the landing,

we reached a turn in the wall. There was a passage at this level that stretched from our side of the wing to the other. I was relieved to reach the passage. Then I saw the narrow metal ladder fixed to the side of the wall. It climbed up past our storey, past the attic storey, to the roof.

Please don't climb the ladder, Isak, I prayed. Please, please, please, God, don't let Isak climb the ladder.

Isak climbed the ladder.

'Come on,' he called, leaning down from above. 'The view up here is amazing. There's a flat section in the middle of the roof; you'll be fine.'

The ladder was rickety and so narrow I could only put one hand or foot on each rung at a time. I felt awkward and clumsy and afraid. When my eyes were level with the top, I could see the ladder wasn't even bolted to the wall, it was simply hooked over the edge, the ends of the hooks sitting in a rusty old bracket. There was nothing to hold on to, only a flat, leaded roof about eight feet wide, with steeply sloping sides. Enormous chimney pots rose up at intervals. Isak reached for my hand and pulled me up onto the roof. Then he pushed himself to his feet and ran along the flat section, swinging around the chimney pots, leaping about like a goat, taking stupid risks. It was like he had a death wish. I lay on my stomach on the lead, feeling the world spinning below.

Isak went mad that night. He ran along that roof for ages. And when he finally grew tired, he had to help me down off the roof because I was too scared to move. He had to climb over me, onto the ladder and then coax me down, inch by inch, until we were back on the passageway. Then he had to help me along the ledge.

I literally dived through the window back into our room and then I lay on the floor shaking like a leaf and muttering: 'Thank you, thank you, thank you...' to God, the Universe, everything, because I was so grateful to still be alive.

And we'd been through all that together, but Isak still hadn't talked about his parents.

For the first time since she and Harriet had moved into the attic room, a visitor came who was neither Dr Milligan nor Maria.

It was Dorothy Uxbridge and Emma was not at all pleased to see her.

'What are you doing here?' she asked.

Dorothy smiled her sweet smile, blond curls straying from her cap and the uniform that was so unflattering on most girls somehow showing off her neat little figure to its best advantage.

'Good afternoon, Nurse Everdeen,' she said. 'Dr Milligan gave me his key and asked me to deliver this note to you. He said I was to wait while you read it in case there was any reply.'

Emma took the note. She did not invite the girl to sit. Dorothy stood, with her hands clasped in front of her, watching Harriet while Emma put on her spectacles and read the note.

Dear Nurse Everdeen,

Miss Maria Smith has conveyed to me your request for an excursion outside with your little ward. This is an excellent idea, and one which will enable us to kill two birds with one stone, so to speak.

I would like to propose this 'adventure' take place tomorrow. The weather is, I understand, set fair and both Maria and Mr Collins are available to chaperone and accompany you and Harriet.

Furthermore, we can use this opportunity to the benefit of your charge and mine. Mrs March, as I'm sure you are aware, has regained consciousness but remains weak and her memories have been compromised by the injury to her head.

Tomorrow afternoon, I will bring Mrs March to the window of her room and if you bring Harriet to the other side, the two may observe one another. This means Mrs March will have the delight of seeing for herself that her beloved daughter is doing well, without the exhaustion of having to deal with her in person. It should also provide some reassurance to the child that her mama is, indeed, on the road to recovery.

I trust these arrangements will be pleasing to you.

Yours, etc.

Emma laid the note down on the table and took off her spectacles.

'Thank you, Dorothy,' she said. 'Now go back downstairs and inform Dr Milligan that the arrangements he proposes are perfectly satisfactory. And please thank him for his trouble.'

'Very well, Nurse. Is there anything else?'

Emma hesitated. Something about the last part of Dr Milligan's message, the plan to let Mrs March and Harriet see one another through the window, felt *wrong*. But she couldn't think why, or see how any harm could come to either of them through that arrangement.

'No,' she said. 'That's all.'

* * *

When Dorothy was gone, the nurse took off her locket and showed Harriet how it could be opened by pressing a secret catch with a fingernail, and inside was the blurred photograph of Herbert, who couldn't sit still long enough for his likeness to be captured. Even so, you could see that he had been, at the time of the photograph, a solemn-faced little boy wearing a felt jacket and a cap.

'Was he a good boy?' Harriet asked.

'He was the best boy. As indeed you are the best girl.'

Harriet put the tip of her little finger into her mouth and smiled shyly.

'I am hoping Dr Milligan will let me have a copy of the photograph that he made of you, as he promised he would. I will put it in the other side of the locket, opposite Herbert.'

'So he and I can look at one another when the locket is closed?'

'So I can look at both you dear children at the same time.'

'But you can look at me whenever you wish, Nurse!'

Emma said: 'I know.' Then she straightened her back and said: 'Harriet, I have some very good news. Tomorrow, we are to go outside, you and I. You may play in the fresh air for as long as you wish.'

'And you will be with me, Nurse?'

'Of course, I'll be with you.'

'Will you play with me?'

'If you want me to.'

'I do,' said the child, and she threw her arms around Emma's waist and pressed her face against the woman's body.

Everything was happening as it was supposed to happen. Mrs

March was recovering, and Harriet had regained her confidence and would soon be returned to the care of her mother.

It was only right. But Emma knew tomorrow's tentative mother-child reunion would be the beginning of the end of her relationship with Harriet and that was a bitter pill to swallow indeed.

It wasn't until we were in bed that I plucked up the courage to ask Isak what had happened when he went to see Dr Crozier.

'Nothing important,' he said.

'What then?'

'Nothing!'

I lay on my back, staring at the ceiling, moonlight casting the shape of the window on the woodchip. I didn't say anything else, I waited, and waited, and in the end Isak said: 'My father's getting married to his girlfriend.'

'Oh,' I said.

There was a silence then Isak said: 'I know you know about my father. I went through your cabinet. I found the cutting your sister sent you. I kept waiting for you to say something but you never did.'

'Because you never said anything. I thought you didn't want to talk about it.'

'I didn't.'

I lay there, eyes wide open, feeling upset on Isak's behalf and anxious about how he might be feeling about the cutting in my cabinet.

'It's going to be in the papers,' said Isak, 'them getting married.'

'Not if they don't tell anyone.'

'They already found out. My father bought Phoebe an engagement ring, and some paparazzo took a picture of her wearing it and it's going to be in all the newspapers tomorrow.'

'Crozier told you that?'

'Yep.'

It was so careless and thoughtless of Isak's father, and the woman, to have allowed this to happen; to treat Isak like this. When my dad and soon-to-be-stepmother broke the news of their engagement to Isobel and me, at least they'd tried to treat us gently. At least we were the first to know.

'My father's political career has slipped since the scandal broke,' Isak said. 'His girlfriend has a new film coming out. He thinks the wedding will be a distraction from the other stuff that's going on in his life. It's what his career needs.'

What about what his son needs? my mother whispered.

Isak continued: 'He's marrying the woman he was having sex with in a hotel room the day my mother went into the forest and killed herself. Every time I think about them, that's what I think of. The hotel room. Him on top of her...'

'Don't think about them,' I said.

I turned over and reached my arm across the divide between our two beds. It wasn't long enough to touch Isak, but he dropped his arm and we held onto one another's wrists. I could feel his pulse beneath my fingertips.

'Fuck them,' I whispered. 'It doesn't matter about them. You're going to be a rock star. And then... then fuck them. You'll be the famous one and your mother, she'll be watching from wherever she is and she'll know, and she'll be so proud.'

Isak squeezed my wrist.

'It'll be OK,' I said. 'You'll be OK. You don't need him. In a few years you won't have to have anything to do with him. You can disown him. No, better than that, you can divorce him.'

Isak laughed. 'Yeah,' he said. 'That's what I'll do.'

And after that there was no sound around us, save that of each other's breathing.

'It's only me,' said Maria, breezing into the attic room, 'and I've come bearing gifts! These are for you, Harriet.'

'What have you brought, Maria? Oh! A coat! And a scarf!'

'And, Nurse Everdeen, I've brought up your shawls and boots from your room as you requested because...' she looked at Harriet.

Harriet jumped up and down and clapped her hands. 'We're going outside!' she sang. 'We're going outside! Hurray!'

They could hardly get ready quickly enough, Emma and the child, although the nurse's fingers trembled over buttons and boot-laces. Soon they were wrapped up, and for the first time in weeks they left the room in the attic and followed Maria's broad back down the narrow steps beyond the door. Emma was holding Harriet's hand and with the other she held tightly to the banister. Her legs seemed reluctant, not having encountered stairs for so long, to suddenly find themselves having to negotiate the steep steps. She did not entirely trust them, nor her own balance. She was afraid of falling and taking Harriet with her. She was worried about the world beyond the attic. What if it had changed in the time she'd been away? In these last weeks, the only people she'd spoken to were Harriet, Maria, occasionally Dr Milligan and yesterday, Dorothy Uxbridge. Would she be able to converse sensibly if they met anyone? Would she remember people's faces? Their names? The details of their families she normally recorded so fastidiously in the recesses of her mind so she could enquire about them? Would she know what to say?

They proceeded through the maze of corridors and down the staircases in the main building, Maria taking care to use the staff passageways. She did not want them to encounter any patients because she didn't want the child to be either smothered with an outpouring of inappropriate affection or alarmed by peculiar behaviour. The nurse gripped the child's hand tightly, ostensibly for Harriet's benefit, but really because she was afraid that if she let go, she herself might drift away, like a dandelion seed.

On the ground floor, they heard a fierce screech.

'What's that?' cried Harriet.

'Oh,' Maria laughed, 'that's only Prince Valliant, the parrot.'

The parrot! Of course! How could Emma so quickly have forgotten the parrot?

'May I see him?' Harriet asked.

'Not now,' said Maria. 'He's a bad-tempered old thing and he might bite your fingers. Come on, Harriet, hurry along. Mr Collins is waiting for us.'

At last, they reached the door, one of the side entrances down a dark interior alleyway used only by staff. Maria opened it and light spilled in. After the darkness of the asylum, it was glorious!

Emma would have liked to lean into that light like a bird, and let the wind carry her up and away. She closed her eyes and inhaled the smell of the moor; the wind, the heather, the dying bracken, the deer. She had not realised how badly she had missed it. She opened her eyes and the rooks were overhead, mobbing to drive away a buzzard. The larger bird flew gracefully amongst the rooks, mewing like a cat, and Emma's heart lifted like that buzzard as it flew.

They descended the steps and there was the groom, handsome Samuel Collins, waiting at the corner of the building, smoking a pipe, and his spaniel, Mac, was with him. He straightened when he saw them approach. His smile widened at the sight of Maria.

Harriet was delighted by Mac and the dog seemed pleased to have a companion who didn't scold him for sniffing through the fallen leaves. The two of them ran ahead together and the tails of the red scarf wrapped around Harriet's neck flew behind her. They passed the chapel and Emma glanced into the yard, to the small marker at the head of Herbert's grave. She saw that it was tidy; in her absence somebody had been keeping the graveyard free of weeds. She could have excused herself for a few minutes to visit her son but she did not wish to have to explain her situation to the groom or Maria. Herbert, his short life and death, although so much a part of Emma and her heart, and entirely pure when she kept her memories to herself, still prompted a twinge of hurt when she considered him as others saw him. Her little illegitimate son with his twisted leg. Her beautiful boy; her everything.

Once, Emma's mother came to visit her at the asylum. Only once she came, when Herbert was three months old. Emma did not know why she came. Perhaps she was prompted by some pang of conscience; perhaps it was because her husband's younger brother, who had been lodging at the vicarage the previous year, had been called before the magistrate accused of molesting the daughter of the friend in whose house he had been lodging since. Whatever it was, Mrs Everdeen came. Emma, her heart bursting with love, showed her baby to her mother. She could not see how her mother, the child's grandmother, could fail to fall in love with him too. She said her mother might hold him, if she wished. Mrs Everdeen did not wish. She took one look at her grandson's deformity and remarked that if the midwife had been doing her job properly, the newborn baby should have been put on the window ledge in a draught and left to die.

'It would've been kinder,' she said, 'for him and you both.'

Emma shook her head, to push the memory of her mother's cruel words away. Stupid woman, she thought, and immediately she felt a pang of pity for her mother, who had denied herself all the happiness she would have had, had she chosen to be part of Herbert's life.

'Nurse Everdeen! Watch me!' Harriet called.

Her laughter streamed behind her on the wind, like the tails of her scarf, and her cheeks were already rosy. Now they were outside Emma could see that the child had grown, even in the few weeks she'd been at the asylum. Harriet found a stick on the ground and threw it for the dog and clapped her hands when the dog brought it back to her, wagging his tail so fast it was a miracle it did not come off. Emma pulled the shawl tight about her and thought she had never seen anyone so uncomplicated, so inno-cent in their joy as that little girl and the spaniel dog.

That joy was infectious. Emma's heart had endured so much pain in its time that no doubt her mother would have said it would be kinder to let it atrophy. Instead, Harriet's happiness called to it, and Emma's heart responded.

It opened like a flower.

58

That night, I dreamed I was in a boat, out at sea. The boat was rocking madly and the sky above me was rocking too, big grey clouds in an angry sky. There was a woman with me; she had her arm around me. I thought it was my mother. I snuggled up to her for warmth, but she wasn't warm, and she didn't feel right and when I sat up and looked I saw that it wasn't my mother but the woman who had slammed my head into the mirror in the bathroom.

Isak was disturbed by my whimpering and threw his shoe at me to wake me up.

59

EMMA – 1903

Emma followed Harriet and Mac across the yellowing grass to the copse of beech trees at the furthest part of the grounds, so far away from the main buildings that it was almost as if the hospital didn't exist. Maria and Samuel Collins lagged behind, deep in conversation. The dog grabbed hold of the tail of Harriet's scarf and stole it from her, running off with the scarf trailing behind, and Harriet chased after him, laughing. In the joy of watching her, Emma forgot all her worries and sorrows; she forgot there was any bad in the world.

They stopped when they reached the beeches. Although the grass was littered with red and brown, the trees still held on to a few tenacious leaves. Emma remembered how she used to come to this very copse, at this time of year, with Herbert. She remembered the game they used to play. She had never, in all those fifty years since, thought she would have the opportunity to play that game again.

The dog abandoned the scarf and went off to flush out birds. Harriet looked up at Emma, her eyes shining brightly, her cheeks flushed, the residue of the laughter on her lips.

'Do you know what kind of tree this is, Harriet?' Emma asked, patting the nearest trunk.

'No.'

'This is a lucky tree. If we catch a falling leaf before it touches the ground, and we keep that leaf, it will bring us good luck. Understand?'

Harriet nodded enthusiastically.

'So, we wait for the wind. Are you ready?'

'Yes!' Harriet jumped up and down and clapped her hands.

'Good,' said Emma – severe, humourless, strict Nurse Everdeen – bending down and rubbing her hands together, 'because here it comes!'

They chased the leaves that autumn day, Harriet and Emma, for hours. The freedom was intoxicating. Each time a wave of cold air rolled in over the moor beyond the boundary wall the great beeches shook their branches as a dancer might shake her skirts, and the leaves that were left in the trees detached themselves and took flight, flying and spinning. The child and the old woman ran amongst them, arms outstretched, trying to catch just one and laughing because so often the one that was closest would lift away at the last second, skipping just out of reach. Sometimes the wind picked up the already-fallen leaves and tossed them playfully, and Harriet chased after those as well, Mac barking giddily around her.

Eventually, Harriet threw herself down in a pile of leaves raked by the gardener, and, although she knew the gardener would come after her to complain if he saw his work being undone in this fashion, Emma let her play; throwing the leaves into the air, laughing with delight.

It was the time of year for the sun to sink early below the horizon and the clouds were already low-hanging and dark. A mizzle began to fall and the air smelled wet and of the coal in the fires that were being lit in the rooms of All Hallows, smoke puffing out of its multitudinous chimneys. Maria and the groom had run out of conversation. Emma could tell they were ready to go back inside.

'We'd better go,' she said to Harriet.

'Oh! Must we?'

'We've been out here for so long, my lamb, it will soon be growing dark.'

Although Emma was weary herself, it was, for once, a good kind of tiredness; healthy and uncomplicated. She lifted the child onto her hip. Harriet was too heavy for her to carry far, but she relished the closeness. As they walked past the chapel graveyard, with this new child in her arms, Emma felt a pang of love so strong that it manifested as pain.

She did not want to lose this child yet she knew that the day was fast approaching when she would.

It is not a loss, she told herself, if you return Harriet to her mother safe and well. You will have done your job and the child will be happy.

* * *

Lamps had been lit inside All Hallows, a great dark slab of a building against which its windows glowed bright and golden, and beyond, the autumnal grey sky.

'I told Dr Milligan we would return this way,' said Maria, indicating the gravel path inside the ornamental wall that followed the line of the hospital on one side, and the long terrace where pelargoniums bloomed in old stone pots in the summer months outside the best and most expensive bedrooms.

They were diverting to go past Mrs March's window. Emma had not told Harriet about the plan. She could not say what, exactly, it was that had stopped her, but now the moment when Harriet would see her mother again was so close, she felt the beginnings of panic.

She put Harriet down, even though the child whined that she was tired.

'Don't complain, Harriet,' Maria said. 'Dr Milligan has arranged a special surprise for you. We are going to look through the window and wave to someone special.'

Maria smiled, and her expression said: *Isn't this lovely?* But her eyes betrayed sympathy for Emma.

'Who are we going to wave to?'

'You'll soon see.'

'Is it my mama?'

Emma gave the smallest nod. Harriet's eyes widened.

'Really my mama?'

'Yes.'

'Which window?'

'Over there.'

The stretch of terrace outside the window Maria indicated had been decorated with small topiary trees in pots, a pair of miniature holly bushes cut into the shape of ascending spirals. Harriet hared towards the window, which stretched from ground level a good eight feet upwards. The light shone gold inside and Emma could see the backs of the curtain swags. She had an impression of movement inside; an approach to the window. Harriet was there now, on the terrace, paralysed by a sudden attack of shyness. She turned back to look at Emma for reassurance.

'Go on, my lamb,' called Emma. 'Your mama will be so happy to see you.'

The child stepped forward and on the other side of the window, Emma's eyes made out the shape of a woman. She was being carried in the arms of a man: Dr Milligan. An armchair had been placed on the other side of the window and Dr Milligan lowered the bundle of satin and lace; the dark-haired, almond-eyed woman, into the chair. She looked at the glass and Harriet, on the outside, leaves caught in her hair, a tear in her stocking and the red scarf trailing, looked back through the glass at the woman. And then she turned and ran back towards Emma; running so fast that she tripped and fell, hitting the terrace stones hard. The nurse ran to pick her up. The palms of Harriet's hands were grazed and both knees were bleeding. The child let out a great cry of pain and Emma held her tight.

'There, there, my angel, it's all right, you are all right, Nurse has you safe...'

She could see the woman watching as she comforted the child and there was something about her face; a coldness... but the nurse must be imagining that. How distressing for Mrs March that her first sight of her daughter should be to see the child falling and...

The doctor's face, now, appeared beside Mrs March's. He was leaning behind her chair, talking into her ear.

Harriet screamed and writhed in pain although she was not really so badly hurt. It was unlike her to exaggerate like this.

'Harriet,' said the nurse, 'wave goodbye to Mama now and we'll go inside and clean the dirt from your knees.'

'That's not my mama.'

'It is, angel. You haven't seen her for a while and—'

'No!' the child screamed, and she began to kick her legs and beat the nurse's shoulders with her little fists. 'That's not my mama! She's not my mama, she's not, she's not, *she's not!*'

It was Saturday, which meant sports all morning and then lunch, and then we were 'free' in the afternoon. A film was being shown in the Great Hall, it was *The Elephant Man*. Posters had been put up on the notice boards. It was supposed to be a treat but the film didn't sound like a whole lot of fun to Isak and me.

We decided to skip it and went to the library instead, back to our nook where we wouldn't be disturbed by Alex Simmonds or any of his sort. Our stomachs were full of our Saturday lunchtime sausage and chip lunch, raspberry sponge and delicious pink custard that tasted like medicine for dessert. I sat at the table in the nook with Dr Milligan's *Case Studies*. Isak took the window seat, sitting sideways with his back against the wall, reading Thalia Nunes' autobiography. The light was falling onto one side of his face and although he was lost in the book, I could see the shadows around his eyes; he was still brooding over his father's betrayal.

I wished I had the Thalia book. I was struggling with Dr Milligan's flowery writing.

'Listen,' said Isak. 'Thalia literally fell asleep at home in her bed and woke up in the back of a carriage coming across the moor *in a strait jacket* so she couldn't move. Her father had had her drugged.'

'Her dad sounds even worse than yours.'

'Ha!' said Isak. 'And also, once she got here, she didn't think much of your Dr Milligan.'

'He's not *my* Dr Milligan! Why didn't she like him?'

'She said he was "wet behind the ears and completely incapable of standing up to the bully of a general manager."'

'Hold on...' I flicked through Dr Milligan's book until I found his account of Thalia Nunes' arriving at the asylum.

'He didn't like her much, either...'

She was unconscious when she was unloaded from the ambulance, her behaviour when she roused herself en route being so violent and aggressive that it necessitated the strongest sedation. No doubt, I said in a wry aside to Superintendent Pincher, she would be a harridan when awake; the kind of woman of whom both he and I and every decent, respectable man and woman of England despaired.

We both laughed at Dr Milligan's pompous way with words although at the same time they made me feel uncomfortable. Thalia hadn't done anything wrong, she hadn't hurt anyone, yet here she was being punished in the most terrible way simply because she wouldn't conform with what her father wanted and society expected.

The laughter died on my lips.

Isak had fallen silent too and now was gazing out of the window, a far-away look in his eyes that made me certain he was thinking about his mother.

I wanted to comfort him, but I couldn't think of anything that wouldn't sound stupid, so I said nothing at all.

61

EMMA – 1903

The child sat on a chair with her bare legs extended over Emma's lap while the nurse attended to the cuts and grazes on her knees with a bowl of warm water, a clean flannel and a bottle of inky iodine. Emma had given Harriet a toffee to suck, hoping it might help calm her. It wasn't working. Harriet was still sobbing and sniffing and wiping her eyes and nose with her arm, a dribble of toffee-coloured saliva at the corner of her lips.

'Why –' *sniff* – 'did you play that trick on me?' – *sniff,* she asked feebly.

'What trick, Harriet?'

'Saying that *she* was Mama! You said you'd never lie to me.'

'And I never have.'

'But you said Mama was at the window and it wasn't Mama!' A new rush of tears was bubbling up. 'I want Mama!' she cried. 'You said I could see Mama! You said she was here! *Where is she?*'

Harriet lashed out and tipped over the bowl. Dirty water spilled into the nurse's lap, soaking her apron and dress. Iodine stains bloomed like blood; they'd be the devil to scrub out.

Emma gathered the child into her arms and held her tightly.

'It's all right, angel,' she whispered. 'Everything will be all right.'

* * *

When Maria came up with the supper tray: bread, cheese, cold meat and potatoes, Harriet was sitting at the table with a scowl on her face and when Maria passed her bowl to her, she pushed it away and rested her cross face between her two fists, slumped so low her chin almost touched the table.

'Oh dear,' said Maria. 'Someone's in a temper. Which is disappointing, seeing as *someone* had a lovely treat today and made friends with a dog who would like one day to play with her again.'

Harriet's scowl deepened but she was listening.

It took a long time to persuade Harriet to eat any supper that night, and then she only obliged because of the promise of more outings with Sam Collins and his dog. The topic of Harriet's mother was not touched upon again.

At 7 p.m. Maria was obliged to go back downstairs to fulfil her other duties, although she touched Emma's arm on the way out and promised that she would be back 'with a bottle of something' later.

Emma eventually settled Harriet into bed. She read a chapter of *Treasure Island*. Harriet put her thumb in her mouth before the nurse had even got to the first chorus of the pirates' shanty, and was sound asleep by the end of the following page. Emma rested her back against the bedstead and massaged her temples. She closed her eyes and was about to nod off herself when Maria returned with a quarter pint of gin.

'Come on,' she said, 'let's have a game of rummy.'

Emma roused herself and sat at the table and shuffled the cards. By their third hand, and their third glass of gin, the conversation turned to the events of the afternoon and Harriet's reaction to the sight of Mrs March.

'Deep down, I think Harriet believes her mother is dead,' Maria said. 'She is so convinced of that fact that she cannot be persuaded otherwise even when she sees the evidence to the contrary with her own eyes.'

'Perhaps.' Emma picked up a card and added it to her hand. 'You don't believe there's the slightest possible chance that Mrs March is *not* Harriet's mother?'

'Oh, she's her mother all right,' said Maria. 'How could anyone doubt it? They're so similar in appearance and even their mannerisms are alike.' She put down the Jack of diamonds and picked up a card.

'I heard Harriet playing with her dolls the other day,' Emma said. 'She was showing them how she tried to wake her mother in the aftermath of the knife attack. She was shaking her shoulders, begging her to open her eyes.'

'That must have been a terrible thing for you to hear.'

'It was.'

Emma glanced towards the bed. Harriet was lying on her back, with one fist on either side of her head, her mouth slightly open, snoring like a kitten.

'She's been through so much,' said Maria. 'Maybe she is simply overwhelmed.'

'Maybe,' said Emma. But to herself she wondered if Harriet was right; that the woman downstairs was not her mother; if, perhaps, they had all made a dreadful mistake.

'Thalia *was* in Ward B,' Isak said. 'At least it sounds like Ward B.'
He read from Thalia Nunes' book.

> I was escorted to a long ward in the bowels of the
> establishment. The poor creatures already incarcerated there
> were huddled against the walls and in the corners. They
> looked thin and pale; barely human and the stench was
> disgusting.

Isak looked up and pulled a face.
'What else does she say?' I asked.

> The strait jacket was, thank God, removed, as were my
> clothes. I was given, instead, rags to wear. I was dressed by
> uncouth women who seemed to take pleasure in the shaming
> of the inmates supervised by a vile man called Mr Uxbridge.
> My hair was cut from my head and I was fastened to the wall
> by chains attached to a leather harness that I wore about my
> abdomen and my neck. There was no privacy; the wardens

were at liberty to come and stare at us whenever they wished;
sometimes they brought visitors who were curious to witness
the manifestation of lunacy.

'Grim,' I said.

We both read on in silence for a few minutes. Then Isak
suddenly sat upright.

'Shit,' he said quietly.

'What?'

'Lewis... *Shit!*'

'What?'

'Here in the book...

'*What?*'

He passed the book to me, pointed to the paragraph.

There were no books, no visitors, no change of scenery,
nothing to do, no distractions. I found a hairpin and used it to
make marks in the plaster of the wall to which I was chained
and to the floorboards beneath me. It must have been the
drugs, or else my mind, so altered by medicines that it was
playing tricks on me, but I became convinced that somebody
was responding to the marks I scratched into the wooden
floorboards. I called this person My Little Ghost.

63

EMMA – 1903

The Whitby landlord arrived at All Hallows Hospital in the fly, which had been sent to fetch him from Dartmouth. Superintendent Pincher invited him into the directors' dining room for a schooner of sherry to revive him after his long journey, followed by a good luncheon of chicken à la crème and stewed apple, before he was given a guided tour of the hospital.

It was a fine autumn day and from the small window in the attic Emma could see the Whitby landlord walking the grounds with Dr Milligan to one side and Mr Pincher on the other. He was taller than them both, broader of shoulder. Looking down on their three hats and three sets of shoulders was like watching gaming pieces being moved about a board.

They stopped at a certain spot and the landlord alone walked forward towards the terrace to look through the window of Mrs March's room as Harriet had done before. The landlord leaned forward, took off his hat, peered, turned back, looked again, stood up and shook his head. Emma's heart quickened. The landlord had not recognised Mrs March either! Despite everything pointing towards her being the missing Whitby woman, she was not.

Emma turned towards Harriet.

'Will you come here a minute, my lamb.'

The child slid off her chair and skipped the few paces across to the window. Emma reached down her arms and Harriet held hers up and Emma picked her up.

'Can you see those men down there?' she asked.

'Yes.'

'See the tallest of the men? He's wearing a hat but he might look up, you might see his face. Wait... here he comes, is he going to look up? Yes, I believe he is! There! Did you see him, Harriet?'

'Yes.'

'And did you know him? Have you seen him before?'

'I fink so.'

'Where have you seen him, my lamb? At home?'

'Yes.'

'With Mama?'

'Yes.'

'What did the man say to your mama?'

'He used to say: "How do, Madame," when he came to collect our rent money. And sometimes he brought flowers or some potatoes from his garden.'

Emma recalled then how she had once asked Harriet how people addressed her mother in an attempt to discover her surname. She had assumed, of course, that her mother was a 'Mrs'. Perhaps that assumption had been hasty.

'Harriet,' she asked gently, 'do all the ladies and gentlemen who visit call your mama "Madame"?'

'Yes.'

'Madame what?'

'Madame Ozanne.'

'Is your mama French?'

Harriet looked confused.

'Does she come from France?'

'No.'

'Then why do people call her Madame?'

'I don't know.'

Harriet looked anxious.

'It's all right, my angel, you've answered my questions very well.'

Emma held the child close. Her heart was pounding. She wanted to hold that dear child in her arms and never let her go.

* * *

Maria confirmed what Nurse Everdeen had guessed when she brought up the supper tray later. The landlord had been adamant that he'd never laid eyes on Mrs March before. Mrs March was not the missing tenant from the Whitby cottage.

'Has the landlord set off back to Whitby now, Maria?'

'Yes.'

'It's a shame nobody thought to ask him to look at the child.'

'If he didn't recognise Mrs March then he's hardly likely to recognise Harriet.'

'Harriet knew him,' Emma said, gripping Maria's arm. She leaned close and whispered in the younger woman's ear. 'She remembers him bringing small gifts to her mother; her *real* mother not that woman downstairs. And she's told me, at last, her mother's name: Madame Ozanne, but she says her mother is not French so I believe she must be an English woman who married a Frenchman and...'

'Nurse Everdeen. *Nurse Everdeen!* Your fingers are pinching me!'

'Oh! I'm sorry. Sorry, Maria. I...' the nurse trailed off. 'I'm afraid, Maria. I'm afraid of what will happen if that woman decides to take the child that is not hers.'

Harriet looked up, her eyes wide.

'Who is going to take me?'

'Nobody,' said Maria. 'Sit down, Nurse. Calm yourself. Have something to eat. Here, Harriet, you take some bread and butter. Good girl! And Nurse Everdeen, I shall put an extra lump of sugar in your tea and maybe a drop of gin for your nerves.'

'I'm not mistaken about this, Maria.'

'I never said that you were.'

'You are treating me as if I'm deluded.'

'I am not! I simply don't think we should be talking about this in front of you-know-who.'

'I am afraid for *her*, Maria. The little one. We need to think of a way to prevent that woman from—'

'Now is not the right time to discuss this matter,' Maria said firmly. 'Let me tell you instead about our favourite doctor, Milton Milligan's latest proposals. Dorothy says he's talking of the future now with Mrs March. Talking about returning to Vienna, one day, and taking her with him. He paints a picture of her wrapped in furs sitting beside him in a cab; a handsome white horse high-stepping through the streets, and he pointing out fountains and statues and the gates to gardens where they might later walk. He tells her they have an emotional and intellectual connection that transcends friendship, and is more spiritual than love. Dorothy is most taken with these plans. She believes Mrs March has become so fond of her that she might take her with her, as a lady's maid. As if she would!'

There's no child in that picture, thought Emma and she calmed a little. Perhaps Dr Milligan would take Mrs March and the dreadful Dorothy to Austria and Harriet would be left safely behind at All Hallows. With her.

'Who are you talking about?' Harriet asked.

Emma picked up a serviette and wiped a smear of strawberry jam from the child's chin.

'Dr Milligan,' she told her, 'and the pictures that he paints.'

'He never paints a picture for us.'

'You want to be thankful for small mercies, child,' said Maria.

As they did their chores in the small room in the attic the next morning, Emma tried, once again, to explain to Maria *why* she was so certain Mrs March was not Harriet's mother.

Emma was frustrated by Maria's reluctance to listen. She sensed that Maria thought she was becoming obsessed. Time and again Maria pointed out the physical similarities between Mrs March and Harriet. She said that when the woman frowned, she had the exact same line between her eyebrows that the child had.

'Will you at least ask Dorothy to ask Mrs March if the name "Ozanne" means anything to her?' Emma pleaded.

'Nurse Everdeen, I am tired of discussing this. Harriet and Mrs March have matching birthmarks!' Maria said, as if there could be no more definitive proof that the two were related, and then she changed the subject.

Emma had the distinct impression that Maria wasn't being completely open with her.

In this, she was right.

Maria did not want the nurse to know that Mrs March's strength was returning, along with her appetite. She did not want to have to tell Emma that Mrs March had, that very morning, requested that a bath be drawn for her. She was praying that Emma would not ask if Mrs March had asked after her daughter, because she had. She had specifically asked for Maria to come into her room so she could ask endless questions about the child, who was looking after her, where she was sleeping, who was with her at night and so on. She'd wanted to know every single detail about Harriet, showing the kind of thorough interest that only a caring mother would show. Who, other than a loving mama, would ask for a history of Nurse Everdeen's career; demand to know about her areas of expertise; her age, et cetera; *and* ask for the room in which Harriet was living to be described in detail, so concerned was she that her beloved daughter was being kept safe?

Because she could not talk about Mrs March's concern for Harriet, instead, Maria did her best to distract Emma with a topic that never failed to draw the nurse's interest: Thalia Nunes.

'I dressed her sores this morning,' she said.

'Sores?'

'Where she's been shackled. Mr Uxbridge had her bound up awfully tight. He has taken against her, Nurse Everdeen, and you know how mean he can be to patients he doesn't like.'

'Poor creature.'

'She is refusing drugs and food. He is threatening to force feed her.'

'Oh goodness!'

'Yet Miss Nunes is resilient. She fills her time plotting her escape. She says this experience will serve her well when she's in politics.'

'Politics?'

'Oh yes! She intends to represent all women one day by being elected to government at Westminster.'

'Really?'

'Really, Nurse Everdeen! She is magnificent!'

* * *

'Come now, Harriet, put the ball away, it's getting late,' called Emma.

'Must I stop?'

'You must. Nurse has a headache and it's late, my lamb. Time for bed.'

The sound of the ball bouncing stopped, but Harriet did not immediately appear around the door. Emma was darning the holes in the stockings that Harriet had torn when she fell outside Mrs March's window. She did not worry at first, but when the light had faded to a level where she had to get up to light the lamp, she went to the door and looked out. Harriet was in the corridor, sitting cross-legged on the floor, and her lips were moving. She was talking very quietly to herself.

Emma crossed her arms and waited. After a moment or two, Harriet became aware of the nurse's presence and she looked up and smiled.

'Who are you talking to?' Emma asked.

'Mama,' said Harriet. She stood up in that easy way she had and came to the nurse and put her arms around the nurse's waist. She pressed her face into Emma's stomach.

65

Next time me and Isak were in the library, Mrs Goode told us how All Hallows asylum had closed for good after the Second World War, and, she said it was a good job it had. She said there were other mental hospitals around Europe where thousands of people like Thalia, who had been admitted simply because they were an embarrassment to their families, had been left and forgotten. She said some of them were there for years and years and years until they became so institutionalised they were incapable of living in the outside world.

Imagine that.

Like being given a life sentence in prison even though you'd never done anything wrong.

'What happened to Thalia Nunes in the end?' I asked.

'She remained at All Hallows for another decade; and was released because of the intervention of her older sister after her father's death. She survived, but she was frail. She suffered from severe ill health, both mental and physical, for the rest of her life. The experience had broken her.'

'So she never got to fight for equal rights in parliament?'

'No,' said Mrs Goode. 'Sadly, she did not.'

66

That night, when Harriet was sleeping, the nurse went along the landing corridor to the bathroom to rinse out some underthings in the sink. While she was there, she heard footsteps on the stairs that led to the door at the end of the landing.

Assuming it would be Maria, who had forgotten something, she went into the corridor to meet her friend. The door at the top of the stairs was closed and nobody was there so she returned to her sink. Then she heard the rattling of the door knob.

'Maria?' she called. 'Is that you?'

There was no answer.

'Who is it? Who's there?' Emma called more sharply. She looked about her for some weapon. All she could see was the mop used to wash the bathroom floor and the metal bucket that housed it. She picked up the bucket – it was heavy enough to do damage to a person if swung with sufficient force – and crept out into the corridor. The door handle was no longer rattling, but she could see a line of lamplight beneath the door, interrupted by a pair of feet.

'Whoever you are, go away,' she called. 'Leave us alone!'

She took the bucket and the broom, blew out her candle and retreated into the bedroom.

'Harriet?' she whispered.

'Mmm?'

The child rolled over in the bed, one small hand above her head, the dear fingers curled towards the palm.

Oh, thank God, she is safe.

'It's all right,' Emma said. 'Go back to sleep.'

She moved the rocking chair across to the door and put the bucket on its seat to make a barricade. Then she picked up the fire poker and sat on the floor with her back against the opposite wall beneath the window and pulled a blanket around her shoulders. She would guard Harriet against harm. She would protect that child with her own life, if necessary.

To the left of her the flames of the fire flickered in the grate and the air in the chimney whistled as it was drawn up and out into the night. The wind gusted around the rooftops, and the rain threw itself against the window glass.

Emma did not sleep properly that night but once or twice she dozed and when she did her dreams were peppered with fear.

* * *

Strange how daylight, even half-formed, could make the terrors of the night seem ephemeral. So it was that Emma, shivering and stiff, felt her fear ease as the sky lightened. As the room took on the washed-out colour of the pale morning, and the outline of Harriet's dark little head became clear on the pillow, the nurse realised there were only two possible explanations for what had happened in the night. The first was that she had imagined someone on the other side of the door, although she was certain that she had not; and the second was that somebody was playing a trick on her. They wanted to frighten her for some reason; perhaps it was one of the other nurses who had seen her out in the grounds with Harriet and discovered that she was up here alone with the child. Perhaps that nurse, whoever she might be, was weary of cleaning up after the incontinent, being shouted at by the likes of Mr Uxbridge and told what to do by the likes of Mr Pincher, sick of the endless, boring, unpleasant work. Wouldn't such a nurse be jealous of Emma, living in a room in the attic; having her food brought up to her and nobody watching her every move? To a hard-working girl whose hands were red raw with cold, whose back ached, and who was sick of the smell of other people's bodies, Emma's current role must seem like a holiday. Yes, that was all it had been. Some disgruntled young woman teasing Nurse Everdeen.

Emma struggled to stand that morning. She did not want Harriet to witness her struggling so she was at pains not to grumble or groan as she straightened her aching joints and hobbled across the room to prod at the ashes of the fire, before she moved the bucket and chair from the door.

By the time the flames were burning brightly in the grate again, the sky beyond the window was glowing with a glorious winter sunrise and Harriet was stirring in the bed. Emma opened the door, pulled it wide and stepped out into the corridor. The chalk hopscotch squares she'd helped draw had all but rubbed away. The ball that Harriet had been playing with still lay on the floor. The corridor was empty as she had known it would be.

Everything was well.

Isak lay on his bed reading the Thalia Nunes book. I was fed up of Dr Milligan's writing and his pernickety ways and was sitting cross-legged on my bed, using his book as a base on which to write a letter to my sister. I was trying to condense Thalia's story and the scratches on the floorboards and the losing of Mum's pendant into a few sentences.

Isak interrupted me.

'I've got to the bit about Nurse Everdeen.'

'What about her?'

He passed the book to me. 'You read it.'

Dr Milligan did eventually pay his other patients – including me – more attention but only when his favourite patient, a woman known as Mrs March, was well enough to be released from All Hallows at the beginning of November 1903. Sadly, her release coincided with a dreadful tragedy. Emma Everdeen, the elderly nurse assigned to look after Mrs March's young daughter during her recuperation, had formed an unnaturally close attachment to the child and did not want to let her go back to her mother.

'Shit,' I whispered.
'Keep going.'

On November 1, the day the mother and daughter were due to be reunited, the apprentice nurse, Maria Smith, took up a breakfast tray for Nurse Everdeen and the child at 7 a.m., as was her routine. Usually, they were dressed and the fire was lit, the room ordered ready to greet her. That morning, the maid unlocked the door to the attic and reported that she felt a 'chill'. She went into the bedroom and realised at once that something was wrong. The curtains were drawn, the lamp unlit and the room was unnaturally cold. The maid could see that the child was in her bed although 'half out of it' and the nurse in the rocking chair in which she slept.

I looked at Isak over the top of the book.

'The rocking chair...' I whispered. 'Nurse Everdeen slept in the rocking chair.'

'I know.'

'Do you think it's...' I indicated upwards with my eyes, '*our* rocking chair?'

Isak moved closer to me. 'Keep reading.'

Reluctantly I let my eyes go back to the page.

The maid lit the lamp, all the while chatting to the nurse and the child to wake them up and to soothe herself, because she was beginning to feel very afraid. When the lamp burned bright, she hung it on the hook above the table and by its light she could see that the old nurse was fast asleep in her chair. Still believing the child to be sleeping, she went to the bed and crouched down, intending to wake the little girl gently and lead her from the room. It was only when she touched the child's hand that she realised that the child was dead. Her pillow was on the floor and there were bruises around her neck. She had been smothered.

I put the book down.

'Nurse Everdeen killed the little girl?'

'Sounds like it.'

I lowered my voice. 'In the room above ours?'

Isak nodded. His face was pale.

I reached my fingers up to the bruise on my forehead, recalled the violence with which I'd been thrown against the mirror. I thought of the times I'd been in that claustrophobic little room, of when I had sat in the chair and rocked it with my feet.

I literally felt my blood run cold.

Above us, there was a creaking noise.

The chair was rocking.

'Oh, no,' whispered Isak, 'not again.'

EMMA – SATURDAY OCTOBER 31 1903

Emma stood at the window. She was bone-tired but the winter sunshine and the white frost lifted her spirits. How beautiful the world looked on mornings like this, sunlight twinkling on the grass and the frozen seed-heads spiking like tiny white sentries. The lake water was black, reflecting the last hoorah of autumn colour amongst the baring branches of the trees; the birds were busy hunting for food, and fox and rabbit tracks wound through the grass.

She saw two people close together, puffs of exhaled breath and a dog sniffing around them. They came together and they kissed. Emma recognised Maria and Sam. The dog, Mac, was investigating the animal tracks. Maria and Sam kissed again, quickly and then Maria pulled away, but Sam was holding her hand, not wanting to let her go.

'Dear God,' Emma said to herself, 'I do hope they are being careful.' And she hoped nobody else was watching because romantic relationships amongst the staff at All Hallows were forbidden. They happened, of course, all the time. Where else were people to meet sweethearts on Dartmoor, if not at their place of work? The more religious amongst them, or those obliged by circumstance, were married, sometimes in the asylum chapel. But once married, that was the end of the woman's career. Marriage was the quickest way to lose an income, which was why so many couples kept their relationships secret; skulking between one another's beds and, like Maria and Sam, being out and about in the grounds at dawn, acting like criminals.

Emma's eyes followed Maria holding her shawl tight around her shoulders as she trotted back to the building, and then the nurse's attention was caught by the sight of a different couple. These two were older, more formal, he wearing a hat and coat, she, leaning on his arm, wearing a dark-coloured hat over her hair, a fur stole around her neck; a jacket, a heavy skirt. It was Dr Milligan and Mrs March, the two of them taking a morning walk across the lawn, their feet leaving dark prints on the icy grass, Mrs March's skirt swishing a trail, as a snake might make.

Emma had only seen Mrs March twice before; on the first occasion she had been lying on the stretcher, on the second seated in the armchair. She had not realised how tall the woman was, nor how regal her stature. Dr Milligan's regimen of exercising her limbs must have been effective. The speed of her recovery was remarkable and the sight of her, even at a distance, made Emma's blood run cold.

How could Emma allow that woman to take the child, knowing that she was not Harriet's mama, not the woman who took her little daughter paddling in the sea off Whitby beach, not the woman who was given flowers by the landlord of the cottage she rented, who kept chickens, who was liked by all her neighbours? How could she, in good faith, betray the child in that way?

Emma narrowed her eyes and watched. Her sight was not so good as it had been; the edges of her field of vision were blurred, but she could observe the couple well enough.

They were taking their time, seemingly deep in conversation. They wandered around the formal gardens; the doctor stopping to pick a dry hydrangea head and hand it to Mrs March. She held it to her nose to sniff it, as if it were a rose. The doctor laughed – *ha ha ha, how funny you are, Mrs March* – as if the woman had done something excessively witty. Then they continued towards the chapel where the chaplain was in the graveyard, rubbing his hands against the cold and talking to the gravedigger who was leaning on his shovel and smoking a clay pipe. The pile of soil to one side indicated that he was part-way through the digging of a hole. It would be hard work on a day like this, when the ground was frozen solid.

Emma watched and her mind turned over the information that she had, looking for something that she had missed, some way to prove that Harriet and Mrs March were not related. Nobody would take the child at her word, that much was certain. But also, it didn't make sense. If Mrs March was not Harriet's mother, why pretend that she was? For what purpose might she pursue this deception?

'Nurse?'

It was Harriet.

Emma jumped and turned. 'Hello, poppet!'

'What are you looking at?'

'The gardens, my lamb. There was a frost last night, everything is white.'

'Can I see?'

Emma looked across the lawn to the woman standing beside Dr Milligan. She felt an antipathy for that woman that was part fear, part distrust, part hatred. She didn't want Harriet to see her; didn't want her to be distressed again.

Dr Milligan and Mrs March were moving again; it looked as if they were going inside the chapel. Perhaps Mrs March wanted to pray.

'Can I?' Harriet pleaded.

'In a minute,' said Emma. 'For now, let's put some more coal on the fire, and then, when Maria comes with the tray, we shall make toast. It's going to be a cold day.'

At lunchtime the next day I went back to the library. I found Mrs Goode kneeling on the floor in the art section, surrounded by books that she was cataloguing. She looked up as I approached and smiled. The charm bracelet was gathered around her wrist.

'Hi,' she said. 'Just you this time?'

'Yeah, Isak was sent out of class and I couldn't find him.'

I moved a book about Frank Lloyd Wright to make space for me to sit down.

'Can I ask you something, please, Mrs Goode?'

'Of course.'

'Me and Isak were reading Thalia Nunes' book last night and we got to the bit about Nurse Everdeen killing the little girl.'

'It's a very sad story,' said Mrs Goode.

'Yes. We were wondering, why did Thalia call the child's mother "the woman known as Mrs March"?'

'Because they didn't know her real name. She'd suffered a head injury; had amnesia, I think.'

'Oh, I see.'

'Mmm.' Mrs Goode peeled a sticky label off a sheet and stuck it into the front of a book.

'Why do you think the nurse killed Harriet?'

'I don't think we'll ever know for sure. The poor woman had had a very hard life. She'd lost her own little child.'

'Herbert?'

'You've seen the gravestone? Yes. Herbert.'

I turned a page of the Frank Lloyd Wright book. There was a collage of buildings he had designed between 1900 and 1905. Funny to think that he was doing all that in America at the same time as Nurse Emma Everdeen was working at All Hallows and Thalia Nunes was a patient here.

'So, Herbert died,' I prompted, to make Mrs Goode carry on with the story.

'Yes, and Emma must have missed him terribly so when the little girl came along, she filled the hole in Emma's life made by Herbert. The theory is that she couldn't bear to be parted from her, so she killed her rather than give her back to her mother.'

'What happened to her afterwards?'

'She was arrested. She was held in the cells at the police station at Dartmouth and after her conviction, taken to Dartmoor Prison. She went to the gallows on Christmas Eve. The authorities did their best to keep it quiet. It wasn't a story that painted the asylum in a good light.'

'In Thalia's book it said there wasn't a post mortem because the woman known as Mrs March wanted to take the child's body home to her family.'

'That's right. I think after all she'd been through that was perfectly understandable. And there was no real doubt about who had killed the child.'

Mrs Goode sighed. She pushed back a strand of fringe that had come loose from her hairband. 'Nurse Everdeen was old and she drank too much. There were all kinds of rumours about things she'd done. Unfortunately, it was Maria who basically signed Nurse Everdeen's death warrant because shortly before the murder, she'd voiced her concerns about the nurse's mental state to the men in charge of the asylum. She never stopped feeling guilty about it.'

'It was the truth, wasn't it?'

'Yes.'

'So why would she feel guilty?'

'Because,' said Mrs Goode, 'in spite of all the evidence to the contrary, Maria never believed Emma Everdeen capable of harming a single hair on that little girl's head.'

70

Emma was sitting on the beach on Harriet's treasure island on the attic landing. She had removed her shoes so they would not get wet although she kept her stockings on because her feet were so knobbled and ugly she didn't want Harriet to see them. She was tending to the imaginary fire they had built so it would be hot enough to cook the fish that Harriet was currently attempting to catch along the landing. Harriet had tucked the hem of her dress into her underclothes and she was barelegged. She was wearing a hat that she'd found in one of the bedrooms to keep the searing sun from her face. Her fishing rod was an old walking stick, she had the cleaning bucket beside her, which contained the fish she'd already caught. It was such a vivid game that if Emma closed her eyes she almost could imagine herself to be sitting by the sea on some far-away island at sundown. Never even having been to a beach, she only had literary examples to go by, but she felt certain the picture in her mind was close to the real thing.

She wished that that desert island was where she and Harriet really were; far away from everyone else. She wished that more than anything in the world.

She was plagued by worry.

The main problem was that she did not know what she should do with the suspicions that she had about Mrs March. Her instinct was to insist on an interview with Mr Pincher and Dr Milligan so she could share her concerns, but she had to be cautious. Dr Milligan was in love with Mrs March, for one thing, and for another, Emma knew he regarded her as a silly old woman. He was unlikely to believe a word she said, and Mr Pincher, fool that he was, didn't know anything about anything and would certainly follow the doctor's lead. No, the telling-the-truth approach could easily backfire and even make Harriet's situation more precarious. If the authorities believed Emma Everdeen was losing her wits, they might take Harriet from her prematurely.

There was only one clear way forward that Emma could see and that was to find someone who knew Harriet's mother and who could confirm that Mrs March was not she. There wasn't the time to write another letter to Whitby, to start that whole process again. She needed a quicker route to the truth. Emma didn't know how much time there was, only that every hour that Mrs March's condition improved, the threat she posed to Harriet grew stronger.

Harriet came back to the beach, which was a moth-eaten yellow curtain spread over some cushions to make dunes, and threw herself down beside Emma.

'That was hard work!' she said.

'But you did it. How many fish did you catch in the end?'

'Umm...' Harriet looked into the bucket. 'One, two... ten!'

'Ten! My, we shall eat well tonight, Harriet.'

Looking pleased with herself, Harriet lay down and put her hands behind her head, crossing her feet at the ankles. Emma pretended to take a fish out of the bucket and put it into the imaginary frying pan, which she held over the flames of the imaginary fire. She shook the pan so the fish skin wouldn't stick.

'Smell that,' she said, wafting the pan in Harriet's direction.

'Mmm!' said Harriet.

'Harriet,' Emma said, continuing to cook the imaginary fish, and keeping the same light, playful voice, 'do you remember your papa?'

Harriet shook her head without raising it off the pillow of her hands.

'So you haven't seen him for a long time?'

'No.'

'I'll just turn this fishy over and cook the other side. There we go. Why haven't you seen him, my lamb?'

'He was a shoulder.'

'A shoulder? Do you mean a soldier?'

Harriet rolled over onto her stomach and picked at a thread in the old curtain. Emma had noted the 'was'. No doubt papa had been killed, probably in Africa. She thought briefly of Joan, the solemn girl with her big, gentle hands. She'd heard the battles in the Boer War were ferocious.

'What about your grandmama and grandpapa Ozanne?' she asked. 'Do you remember them?'

Harriet was silent.

'You see, I was wondering if Mama was planning to take you to France to see your grandparents if that was why you came to Dartmouth?'

The child picked at the curtain, pulling the thread, making a ladder in the fabric.

'Perhaps Mama told you not to tell anyone where you were going,' said Emma. 'Perhaps she wanted it to be a secret. If that's the case, then I would not want you to break your promise. But you can tell me if I am wrong, can't you?'

Harriet nodded.

Emma spoke very slowly. 'Am I wrong, Harriet, to believe that you and Mama had come to Dartmouth because you were going to meet someone who would take you to France in their boat?'

'Not France,' said Harriet.

'You weren't going to France?'

'No.'

'Where then, my lamb?'

'To Guernsey,' Harriet said quietly. 'Grandpapa Ozanne lived in Guernsey.'

71

I caught up with Isak in the cloakroom, getting changed for rugby. We sat side by side together, lacing our boots, amongst the bundle of other boys smacking one another with towels and chucking each other's clothes around. I told him I'd found out more information about the murder.

'Can we stop talking about this shit, please,' said Isak.

He stood up and pulled down the hem of his rugby shirt and then, without looking back at me, he pushed his way between the boys standing closest to us and disappeared into the crowd.

* * *

Later, in assembly, in the Great Hall, I sat between Mophead and Isak while the results of the week's sporting competitions were read out.

The Great Hall was big enough for all of All Hallows pupils to fit in at once, most of us sitting on chairs laid out in lines on the ground floor, with the Sixth Form taking the balcony. Dr Crozier and the teachers had seats on the stage at the front. They wore their gowns for assembly so they looked like a flock of crows.

We stood up for the hymn, which was 'Now thank we all our God' which was one of my least favourite hymns ever. Then there was the chaplain's sermon and prayers.

When the religious part of assembly was over, at Dr Crozier's invitation, the caretaker came up onto the stage to give us an update on the flood damage repair work. He kept repeating himself, but the long and short of it was that the workmen were pretty much finished. The dehumidifiers had done their work, all the rotten wood and furnishings had been removed and the electricians were now replacing the wiring. The decorators would come in over half-term to repaint the walls and woodwork. When school started up again after the break, we'd be able to return to the old dormitories, and the classrooms that had been out of action would come back into use.

Everything was about to change. Even if Isak and I were together in the same dorm after half-term, we wouldn't be free agents, like we were now. I couldn't imagine that we'd be able to climb out of the window and go up onto the roof or talk into the early hours. It would be hard for me, because I didn't know many people, but harder for Isak because he did, and they all hated him.

Maria brought unwelcome news when she came up with the supper tray that evening: that is to say, the news was unwelcome to Emma; Maria was positively bubbling with excitement. The news was that Mrs March had remembered who she was. Miraculously.

'And who does she say she is then?' Emma asked.

'Her name is Evelyn Rendall.'

'Not Madame Ozanne?'

'No.'

'Did you ask Dorothy to ask her about the name "Ozanne"?'

'I did and she did, and it was after this that Mrs March remembered she was really Mrs Rendall.'

'How convenient,' muttered Emma.

'She is the widow of a wealthy Scottish lawyer.'

'Well,' said Emma quietly. 'There's more proof that she's an imposter. Harriet's father was not a lawyer but a soldier and the family is not Scottish but comes from Guernsey.'

'Perhaps Harriet is mistaken,' Maria said in a conciliatory tone.

'Harriet is an honest child.'

'I'm not accusing her of lying. All I'm saying is that Harriet is hardly more than a baby herself, how can she know about her father's career? Perhaps he was a lawyer who became a soldier.'

'And she somehow or other confused a small island in the British Channel with the Highlands of Scotland did she?'

Harriet interrupted to ask: 'Please may I have a crumpet?'

'Yes, of course,' said Maria, rather crossly.

Emma helped Harriet up onto her chair. She hadn't wiped her hands but Emma didn't have the energy to insist on that now. She passed her a plate and a crumpet, then leaned across her to cut it in half and spread it with a pat of yellow butter.

* * *

Maria had not wanted to stay in the room in the attic to play cards that evening. She was in a prickly mood and Emma was glad that she was going so that she could be alone with her thoughts.

'I bought you another quarter of gin, Nurse Everdeen, as you requested!' Maria said as she left. 'Don't you go drinking too much of it now.'

This comment was both irritating and humiliating. Was Maria hinting that she believed the gin might be addling Emma's brain? Did the younger woman think Emma was drinking too much? Did she believe her a dipsomaniac?

That night, Emma was relieved to hear the landing door close, the turning of the key, the securing of the lock. She prayed that Maria wouldn't go telling tales to Dr Milligan or Mr Pincher, or say anything spiteful about her drinking to anyone.

Harriet took a long time to settle and by the time she did, it was late. It was a cold night, frost creeping over the window pane; but warm and cosy in the little room. Emma finished writing her notes about Mrs March and Harriet, in the back of her manual, the possible answers to some of her list of questions, and as she read back through the questions and answers, an awful possibility began to dawn on her.

No, she thought. Surely it cannot be.

She took off her spectacles and rubbed the bridge of her nose between her thumb and her finger.

Then she reached for the bottle of gin, took out the stopper and poured herself a nip. She read the questions she had asked, and the answers she had supplied, a second and then a third time and the conclusion to which her mind had turned seemed, with each time of reading, more likely.

Where were ~~Mrs March~~ Harriet's real mother and Harriet before they were in the boat?

   Answer: They had Travelled to Dartmouth from Whitby.

   Why were they in Dartmouth?

   Answer: To meet a man who was going to take them across the Channel to Guernsey in his boat.

   Who is Mrs March?

   Answer: Certainly not who she says she is.

   Why did Harriet end up in the boat with Mrs March, instead of her mother?

Why?

Could it be that there was a fight, a struggle, perhaps, over the child, and Harriet's mother was mortally wounded?

Was it possible that the body that had washed up was that of Madame Ozanne and that Mrs March, rather than being Harriet's mother, was in fact Harriet's mother's killer?

Nurse Everdeen's nursing manual was on the window ledge of the bedroom as Isak and I changed into our nightclothes. Isak must have brought it up from the library. I certainly hadn't. I didn't like the fact that it was in our room.

I was thinking about how all the strange things that had happened added up. The *thing* upstairs was Nurse Everdeen. She would never be able to rest in peace; never move on. She would be there for all eternity, trapped in that gloomy little space with her guilt. And the worst of it was that she had loved the little girl she'd murdered. She was condemned to spend forever trapped in a horror of her own making.

We ought to speak to the chaplain, I thought. Perhaps he would know how to rescue Emma Everdeen from her self-inflicted prison, carry out an exorcism or something. But I could not imagine him being sympathetic either to Nurse Everdeen or to my explanation of what had been going on.

Isak was still in his odd, quiet mood.

'Do you think we'll be in the same dorm together after half-term?' I asked him.

'How am I supposed to know?'

'Don't bite my head off, I was only trying to make conversation.'

'I'll be glad to be out of this room, that's for sure.'

I knew he was referring to the murder, etc., but I still felt a bit hurt by this comment.

There was a sound from the room above.

We both looked up.

'She heard you!' I hissed.

'No, she didn't. She can't have, because nothing is really there! It's just your imagination, Lewis, all this weird shit, and I'm getting tired of it.'

'You hear it too!'

There was another noise, as if something was being dragged across the floor of the room above.

'There! Don't tell me you didn't hear that!' I said triumphantly.

Then we heard a thump as if someone had jumped off the bed, and footsteps running around the room.

'The child is there too!' I whispered.

The footsteps moved out of the room into the corridor. They ran backwards and forwards and then there came a rhythmic thumping, like a ball being thrown against a wall.

'Jesus,' whispered Isak. 'Make it stop! Make them go away!'

'How?'

'I don't know! I can't bear it any longer!'

Isak stood up. He dragged my cabinet towards the door.

'What are you doing?'

'Making a barricade. In case any of those things come down and try to get in here.'

From the window ledge, there came a fluttering sound. Nurse

Everdeen's manual was open. The pages were turning by themselves.

EMMA – SATURDAY, OCTOBER 31 1903

Emma's eyes were tired and sore. Every bit of her body ached. One set of anxieties had been replaced by another and these she held now in her mind were worse than those she'd had before and those had been bad enough.

She poured herself another half inch of the gin.

Both Mrs March and the woman whose body had been found off the coast had been injured at about the same time, by the same weapon. Wasn't it likely they'd been injured in the same struggle? One of them died, the other, gravely injured, had taken refuge in the boat with the now motherless child she'd set out to kidnap.

The man commissioned to sail the lugger over the Channel had perhaps, arrived to find the wounded Mrs March and Harriet in the boat and panicked and pushed it out to sea. Maybe he was an insalubrious character himself; perhaps he believed, as the crew of the *March Winds* had, that Mrs March was already dead and feared he might be blamed for her murder.

Harriet's mother could only have organised the crossing by letter. The boatman would not have known what she looked like.

If he came to some prearranged meeting spot expecting to find a young mother and her small daughter, and found Mrs March and Harriet, of course he would assume that these were his passengers. Of course, he would panic. It was human nature. If Emma was right about events unfolding in this way then Harriet had been the witness to her mother's murder; she was a danger to Mrs March and Mrs March would want Harriet silenced. Yet the idiot doctor and superintendent were doing all they could to reunite the pair. They were literally going to hand the lamb to the slaughterer.

And Maria, Emma Everdeen's dear friend, Maria, had gone over to the side of that woman too.

Only Emma knew the truth. And Harriet. Emma needed to get Harriet out of All Hallows, out of harm's way. There wasn't time to try to track down family; no way to involve the police, who wouldn't listen to her anyway. She needed to physically remove the child from the danger that threatened her.

Emma took another drink and it dawned on her.

Oh dear God! The footsteps the other night! The rattling of the door handle! It hadn't been some silly young woman playing a trick, but Mrs March, testing the water! That woman had asked a hundred questions about where Harriet was being kept and about Emma Everdeen. It was obvious! Mrs March was planning to come up to the attic room and do some harm to Harriet here! She had decided to silence Harriet before she had the chance to speak out.

No. *No!* Emma Everdeen would not allow it.

She would take Harriet away.

She closed her eyes as she tried to think how this might be achieved. The window in the room was small, as were the windows in the other rooms on the attic level, and even if they could squeeze through, Harriet was too small to climb up onto the roof unaided, and Emma too frail, and in any case it would be madness to attempt it with that sheer drop below. The door was the only way out of this small prison and the only person who regularly came and who had a key was Maria.

Maybe she could persuade Maria to help her with the escape plan. But what if she asked Maria and Maria refused to co-operate? What then?

No, she couldn't involve Maria. It was too dangerous. Much as the thought appalled Emma, she would have to ambush Maria and tie her up so that she and Harriet could escape. Oh, dear God! The thought of hurting or even so much as frightening her dear friend was dreadful. But it was the only way she could see to save Harriet.

And after that initial struggle with Maria, when Maria was tied to the pipes in the bathroom, with a gag over her mouth so she could neither scream nor blow her whistle for help, Emma and Harriet would have to work their way down through the asylum without drawing attention to themselves. Emma had lived in All Hallows for so long that she knew all the back corridors and stairways, so that wouldn't be difficult. Once they were in the grounds, they would have to find a way through the boundary wall. Not the main entrance – that would be too risky – but one of the handful of gates in the wall that the gardeners used. They would have to trust to God and providence that one of the gates would be unlocked.

As she thought the plan through, Emma could see that there were a great many points at which everything could go wrong.

She took another drink.

Even if she and Harriet managed to make their way to one of the gates in the wall, and if, by some stroke of good fortune, it was unlocked, they still wouldn't be out of the woods. Assuming Maria hadn't yet been found tied up in the attic and a search party launched to track them down, she and Harriet would have to make their way across Dartmoor in the winter. Emma did not know the lanes and tracks beyond those in the immediate vicinity of All Hallows; she did not know in which direction she should turn to reach the nearest village. She was probably less familiar with the working of the world beyond All Hallows walls than little Harriet was. She had no money. She did not know anyone outside the asylum. She had never so much as visited a hotel or an inn for a dinner, let alone stayed in one. It seemed an almost impossible challenge. Yet she would rise to it; she would rise to it for Harriet's sake because she loved that child and she was not going to fail her the way she had failed Herbert. She had promised Harriet she would look after her and she would. She would not let that terrible woman harm so much as a hair on Harriet's head!

Emma finished her gin.

She needed to rest. They would leave tomorrow. She would need all her strength. All her strength and more.

She tried to stand up, but she could not move. Her limbs were too heavy. Something is wrong with me, she thought, and she wondered if she had taken too much gin, but she looked at the bottle and the level was only down an inch and a bit. It could only be some manifestation of her exhaustion that was paralysing her. She tried again but her legs might have been made of lead, they were so reluctant to move, and she had no energy. It was a struggle to stay conscious.

She could feel sleep tugging at her, pulling her down and the tiredness was irresistible; it was what she'd wanted for so long. Good sleep, deep sleep, had eluded her for days now, weeks even. She went to the edge of unconsciousness, stepped over the edge and began to slide down the slope and it was such a good feeling, the sinking into sleep, and she was almost there, she was so very close when she heard a shuffling, as if someone was outside the room, in the corridor.

Oh no, she thought, not now, because she was so close to sleep, she didn't know if she could fight it.

But someone was there, she was sure of it, and fear roused her, not completely, but it took her from the brink.

'Go away!' Emma whimpered. She tried to move, to push herself out of the chair but the muscles in her arms were useless, like lumps of dead meat. She tried to speak, to beg whoever it was to go away and leave Harriet alone, but her mouth was slack and her lips would not form the words; her throat was rigid.

She could not even open her eyes.

Not until morning. And by then, it was already growing light and the air in the little room was ice cold.

Maria was there, in the room in the attic.

And Maria was screaming.

On the window ledge, the pages of Nurse Everdeen's nursing manual turned by themselves.

'Stop it!' Isak yelled, his hands over his ears. 'Make the book stop, Lewis!'

I jumped over the end of my bed but didn't quite make it and ended up in a heap on the floor. I pushed myself up, grabbed the book and clamped its covers shut between the palms of my hands. I put it back on the window ledge. At once it fell open again and, once again, the pages began to turn. I looked for something to put on top of it, to weigh it down, and when I looked back, I saw that the book had fallen open towards the back. After the text, there were some blank pages, lined ready for the owner of the manual to make notes. These had been filled in by someone with small, neat, spidery writing that I recognised: Nurse Emma Everdeen's writing.

I was scared.

I did not trust her.

It's only a book, my mother said gently. *The book can't hurt you.*

I picked up the book gingerly, narrowing my eyes and struggling to decipher the handwriting.

Who is Mrs March?

Isak had pushed the bedside cabinets against the door to form a barricade. Now he turned.

'What are you doing?'

'I think the book might be trying to tell us something.'

Isak snatched it from me. 'Let's get rid of the stupid thing!'

'No!' I cried, 'Isak! Give it back!'

I scrambled after him, trying to grab the manual, but he was bigger than me and stronger. He kept his back to me as he opened the window.

'Isak, don't throw it out! It's ancient! You'll wreck it!'

'Why did you bring it here in the first place?'

'Me? I didn't bring it!'

'You liar!'

'Isak, it wasn't me! Stop it! Don't throw it out!'

But he didn't listen to me. He pulled back his arm and threw the book out into the night.

I pushed him to one side, leaned out over the ledge beside him, and watched as the book fell to the ground, the pages fluttering, like a bird that had been shot.

'Idiot!' I cried.

I leaned further but the book was falling close to the building and disappeared into the darkness.

I pushed Isak in the shoulder.

'What did you do that for?'

'It's gone,' he said. 'I got rid of it. That's all that matters.'

'What about Mrs Goode? What are we going to tell her?'

'I'll go and find it in the morning. I'll take it back to the library.'

'What if it's wrecked?'

'Then I'll fucking tell her it was my fault, OK? Stop fussing, Lewis! Stop acting like an idiot!'

I turned and sat down heavily on my bed. It was then that I noticed the button in the square of dusty carpet that had been hidden beneath one of the bedside cabinets.

I reached over to pick it up, held it in the palm of my hand. It was tortoiseshell.

'What's that?' Isak asked.

'Nothing.'

'Let me see!'

'No, it's nothing!'

I turned from him, holding the button in my fist. He leapt on me, pushing me back onto the bed, sat on top of me, grabbed my arm and prised open my fingers. I struggled but he was too big and strong and I couldn't stop him taking the button. In one move he had stood and thrown it through the window, lobbing it out so that it disappeared into the darkness.

It didn't matter.

I'd seen it. I knew who it belonged to.

I didn't know why the button was in our room, but I knew it shouldn't have been there.

EMMA – MONDAY, 2 NOVEMBER 1903

Emma had tried to make herself presentable but it was all but impossible in the poky cell at the back of the police station at Dartmouth, there being neither mirror nor access to washing facilities nor any clean clothing available to her. With trembling fingers, she had pulled back her hair into a tight bun and put on her nurse's bonnet and her shawl, hoping she would at least look respectable, but when she was shown into the small room where Maria was waiting, sitting on one of the wooden chairs on either side of a small table, she could tell by the shock on Maria's face that her efforts had been in vain.

'Sit down, Nurse Everdeen,' said Maria, indicating the opposite chair. 'I asked if we might have a cup of tea brought to us. The woman I spoke to was not polite but I dare say she might oblige.' There was something different about Maria. She looked the same but it was as if a shutter had come down around her. There was no warmth in her words. Her eyes were dull; her expression cold.

'Do you have any news of Harriet?' Emma asked.

Maria stiffened completely.

'What news would I have?'

'How is she? Is she going to be all right?'

'"How is she?" What do you mean?'

'I... I only wondered if...'

'Don't you remember, Nurse, how I came into your room and...'

'Tell me it was a mistake. Tell me she was only sleeping! Tell me that she is well, that she will recover, that she is happy! Please, Maria... *Please.*'

Maria exhaled slowly through her lips and shook her head.

'Please,' Emma whimpered. The older woman's face was crumpling, all pretext of strength and courage slipping. She reached her bony hands across the table to take hold of Maria's but Maria moved her hands away, slid them under the table, out of reach.

'I'm sorry, Nurse. I can't put your mind at rest. Nothing now can change what has happened; what you have done.'

She whispered these last words so quietly that they sounded almost like a prayer. They hung light in the air and Emma did not hear them, or if she did, she did not acknowledge them.

'That wicked woman!' she cried. 'I knew she was not Harriet's mother!'

'Nurse Everdeen—'

'I told you, Maria! I told you that Harriet was in danger but you would not listen. Nobody would listen to what the child had to say, yet they all listened to the woman, even though nobody had any proof that she was who she said she was, or—'

'Nurse Everdeen!'

'It's my fault that Harriet is dead. I know, Maria, that it is my fault.'

'I'm afraid it is. I am certain you didn't consciously intend to harm her but—'

'I did not hear her come in.'

'Who do you mean?'

'Mrs March! I didn't hear her come into the room. I knew somebody was in the attic, I could hear them beyond the door, and of course it was she, but nonetheless I fell asleep. I don't know why, I hardly drank a thing...'

'Nurse Everdeen, you drank the entire quarter-pint of gin.'

'I should have taken Harriet away. I should have left that evening. I could have pretended there was an emergency and summoned you, but I hesitated. I was worried about having to hit you over the head so you wouldn't stop me from taking her and I was worried about having to tie you up, Maria, but you wouldn't have stopped me, would you, you'd have helped me and—'

'Nurse—'

'I shall never forgive myself, Maria, for not taking Harriet away while I could. It is my fault that she is dead. I did not protect her. I should have stayed awake all night. I—'

She was interrupted by the opening of the door. The woman Maria had spoken to earlier, a stout woman with a dour face, wearing an ugly brown twill dress, held the door open with her hip. She had a cup of tea, without saucers, in either hand. Maria took them from her and set them on the table. The tea was a pale grey colour with an oily slick on its surface, and the rim of the cup was chipped and dirty. Beneath the table, Maria wiped the fingers that had touched the cup handles on her handkerchief.

'Did you hear me?' Emma asked Maria. 'Do you understand what I am saying?'

Maria gave the slightest nod and held the handkerchief to her nose. It smelled of Mr Collins' cologne. The scent masked the stink of drains that permeated this nasty little room. It helped hide her face. She kept her eyes lowered so that Emma would not see her disappointment; her absolute horror at the crime she had discovered, the revulsion she now felt for the woman who sat at the other side of the table.

'Where is Harriet now?' Emma asked. 'Is she in the chapel?'

'She has been laid out and tomorrow morning she will be gone.'

'Gone?'

'Her mother is taking her back to Scotland.'

'Her mother? You mean Mrs March?'

'Yes.'

'Maria, for goodness' sake, Mrs March is not Harriet's mother! How many times must I say it? It was Mrs March who came into the room in the attic and—'

Maria pushed back her chair. She stood up. 'I have to go, Nurse Everdeen,' she said. 'I cannot bear this any longer.'

She went.

The day before the end of my first half-term at All Hallows, we had a special assembly after lessons during which the chaplain told us that the chapel roof would be repaired by the time we returned to school after the break.

'Normal religious services will be resumed as soon as possible,' he said. 'Ha ha ha!' He clasped his hands in front of him and rocked on the soles of his feet.

As we filed out of the Great Hall, we passed the pigeonholes where our mail was left for collection. I had two items: a package from Isobel and a letter from my father. I picked them up and scooted off to our form room where I could look at them in private. Everyone else was going to the refectory.

I opened the package from Isobel first. There was a good selection of chocolate bars and a music magazine. No note, but two folded pages torn from the *Daily Telegraph* newspaper. An interview with Sweden's rising 'superstar of the right' Elias Salèn. There was a picture of Elias and his new bride taken on their wedding day. Elias, huge, blond, grinning, had one arm around his much younger, slimmer new wife. She was wearing flowers in her hair and holding a trailing bouquet of wildflowers. She was pretty and I guessed this must make things even worse for Isak. I couldn't imagine how hideous it would be to have someone who looked about the same age as my sister as my stepmother. But that wasn't all. It was obvious, even to the not-very-observant thirteen-year-old me, that Isak's new stepmother was pregnant.

I had been sitting on the radiator in front of the window. Now I slid down until I was sitting on the floor with my back against the heater. Isak hadn't said anything to me about his father expecting another child. He didn't know, I was sure of it.

My fingers went to my throat, to the empty space where my mother's pendant used to be.

What should I say to him?

Just be there for him, said Mum. *Be there when he needs you.*

Isak must never see this article. I tore the newspaper into strips, screwed them into a ball, and tossed the ball towards the waste-paper basket. I put my head on my knees and swallowed the urge to cry.

Things had been strained between Isak and me since he threw Nurse Everdeen's manual out of the window. He'd been good to his word, gone out to retrieve it the next morning, dried the pages on the radiator at the back of our classroom, the same radiator that was behind me now, and then taken it back to the library. We hadn't spoken about that evening since; not about the sounds we heard from the room above, nor about who had brought the manual into our room, nor the pages turning by themselves, nor the tortoiseshell button. All these things we couldn't talk about were like a wall between us. I didn't know how to get round the wall to reach Isak and I was pretty sure he felt the same.

I still had the letter from my father to read. I opened the envelope and unfolded the sheet of paper inside.

Dear Lewis,

I trust this missive finds you in good health. All is well here in Worthing.

I received an interim report from All Hallows last week. It was a mixed bag, which won't come as any surprise to you, I'm sure. We were disappointed to learn that you have already been put on report several times, but pleased that you have been knuckling down when it comes to English and Art. Dr Crozier mentioned that you have made some new friends, which is good.

Your stepmother and I will both be busy at a conference in Blackpool next week. For that reason, we have agreed with Dr Crozier that you will stay at All Hallows for the half-term week. In the meantime…

I screwed up the letter and threw it after the newspaper. I huddled down with my head on my knees and the tears came to my eyes. And it was stupid, because I didn't even want to go back to Worthing for half-term, didn't want to have to sit through interminable meals with my father and stepmother while they scrutinised me and asked questions about school. I'd rather be here, at All Hallows, with Isak, who had always known he wouldn't be going home for half term. But still, it hurt that my father, who hadn't seen me in weeks, would rather go to a conference about cardboard packaging than spend a few days with his son.

Tears ran down my cheeks. I wiped them away as fast as I could, telling myself not to be stupid. And then the door opened and somebody came into the room; two people.

I crouched lower. I didn't want anyone to find me crying. Looking between the legs of the desks, I could see two pairs of human legs, two pairs of feet: one wearing shoes with different coloured laces; the other wearing brown brogues with a nifty pattern of embossing.

Isak, then, and Mr Crouch. I wrapped my arms around my legs and pressed my face into my knees.

Mr Crouch perched on the side of one of the desks. Isak hesitated by the door.

'Come and sit beside me,' Mr Crouch said to Isak, and I heard the scuff of Isak's shoes on the floor as he did as he'd been told. Nothing more was said for a few moments. I raised my head and risked a peek. The pair were sitting close together, side by side, with their backs to me. Mr Crouch's arm was around Isak's body. Isak was sitting upright, straight and stiff. Mr Crouch was stroking Isak's back. From this angle I could see how the teacher's hair was thinning on top. I could see his neck bulging over his collar. It gave me an uncomfortable feeling in my stomach, the way the two of them sat so closely together, the man's big, baby-pink hand running up and down the boy's back, pausing every so often to squeeze the shoulder.

'Isak,' said Mr Crouch, 'the reason I asked you to meet me here today is because I have some news about your father.'

Isak said: 'I know already.'

'What do you know?'

'That he's married again. Dr Crozier told me.'

'And how does that make you feel?'

Isak didn't answer.

A silence followed, during which I imagined Mr Crouch's hand going up and down Isak's back. I pressed my forehead into my knees and wished the teacher would go away.

Mr Crouch spoke again.

'You know, if you want to talk about anything, I'm here for you, Isak. I'll always listen.'

The hairs on the back of my neck prickled. It wasn't what Mr

Crouch was saying, it was the way he was saying it. Teachers weren't supposed to talk to pupils like that.

I decided to stand up. I'd stand up and say: 'Excuse me,' and that would make Mr Crouch stop. I held my breath and counted back from five. Five; four; three...

'That's why it hurts me to have to say what I'm about to say, Isak, but you'll find out soon enough.'

'Find out what?' asked Isak.

'That your father and his new wife are expecting a baby.'

There was a rigid silence.

'It's in the newspapers,' Mr Crouch continued. 'The two of them, the parents-to-be, are posing proud and happy. They're talking about their new family and their future plans.'

'I don't believe you.'

'Dear boy, why would I lie about something like that?'

I stood up. I was a bit late, but I did it anyway. 'Excuse me,' I said.

Mr Crouch jumped off the desk and stared at me stupidly, smoothing back his hair with the flat of one hand. Isak glared at me from under his fringe.

'Isak...' I began.

'Shut up!' said Isak. 'Leave me alone.'

He opened the door and disappeared into the corridor.

Mr Crouch glared at me, flustered. 'Tyler, what are you doing? What did you—'

'Excuse me, sir,' I said, and I pushed past him and ran after Isak.

78

EMMA – 1903

Sam Collins had taken Maria to Dartmouth in the fly. He was waiting for her in the Pilot Inn and she had never been so glad to see him as she was that day. He stood as she entered the pub and Mac the dog came wagging over to the door, a smile on his big, soft face. Maria allowed Sam to take her in his arms and even let him guide her to their table. He had already paid for a schooner of sweet sherry for her and her fingers were shaky as she held the delicate glass.

'How was Nurse Everdeen?' he asked.

'Oh, Sam, she is denying everything. Not only to the police and to me, but to herself as well. She is adamant that Mrs March – Mrs Rendall, whatever-her-name-is – was responsible for the death of the little girl. But, of course it's nonsense. She's been obsessed with that woman for weeks: paranoid. I should have done something sooner. I should have told Dr Milligan how worried I was about the nurse's condition as soon as I noticed she was behaving oddly. Because she's mad, isn't she, Sam? It can't have been Mrs March. She had no means of getting into the attic and also why would she? Why would a mother kill her own daughter?'

Sam said: 'Hmm.'

They sat in silence for a few minutes. Then Sam said: 'What if Nurse Everdeen is right, and Mrs March is not Harriet's mother?'

'Don't be daft, Sam.'

'That afternoon when she and Harriet saw one another through the window...'

'And Harriet ran away? That was because she was still traumatised. When people have had a great shock, sometimes their minds don't work quite right for a while after. Of course, Mrs March is – *was* – Harriet's mother. What about the likeness between them? You cannot deny that! I never saw a mother and child who looked more like mother and child than Mrs March and Harriet do. They're two peas in a pod.'

The serving girl came to their table. 'Would you care for something to eat, miss?'

'What do you have?'

'Fish pie. It's very good.'

'No, I'm too distraught to eat,' said Maria. She sighed and pressed her hands into the table. 'Besides,' she said to Sam, 'even if Mrs March is not Harriet's mother, even then, why would she kill her? And, how could she? There are only two keys to the door at the top of the attic stairs and I had one about my person that night...' she gave Sam a knowing glance, 'and Dr Milligan had the other. And nobody, not even Nurse Everdeen, is suggesting that Dr Milligan might have crept into the room at night and drugged Nurse Everdeen and murdered the child.'

'Nurse Everdeen said she was drugged?'

'No, she didn't say that. She said she didn't understand how or why she slept so deeply when she'd only had a couple of glasses of gin. But I took her up a full quarter-pint that evening, Sam, and in the morning, the whole bottle was empty. She'd drunk the lot.'

'Or someone else had poured it away to make it look as if she had drunk it.'

'Don't, Sam.'

'Don't what?'

'Put doubts into my mind.'

'I thought Nurse Everdeen was your friend.'

'She is! I'm here, aren't I? I came all the way to Dartmouth to see her, even though being the friend of a child murderer is hardly a role I relish, thank you very much!' Her voice was becoming shrill. 'I always knew she was eccentric, Nurse Everdeen, but I never thought she'd... No! She never would have done it if she'd been in her right mind, but drink does terrible things to people, Sam. It addles their minds. She might have murdered poor little Harriet while in a drunken stupor and had a blackout and have no memory of it ever. That's what happens, you know. And I'm partly responsible. I took her the gin.'

'Now don't you start blaming yourself,' said Sam, but Maria was not listening.

'I still can't believe it of her,' she said. 'She loved that little girl, Sam. She loved the bones of her.'

'One minute you say she did, the next she didn't.'

'Don't mither me. I'm trying to have everything straight in my head. Two keys to the door. You and I both know that my key was kept safe that night. But what about Dr Milligan's?'

'What about it?'

'I shall have a word with Dorothy. I'll ask her if it's possible that the doctor fell asleep in Mrs March's room.'

Sam's eyes widened. 'Are they sleeping together?' he asked in a low voice. 'The doctor and Mrs March?'

'So Dorothy says.'

'My God!'

'You're not to tell anyone, Sam, not even your mother, for I haven't seen it with my own eyes. It's only what Dorothy has told me and you know as well as I how that girl likes to gossip. She has a malicious tongue on her.'

'But why would Dorothy—'

'Shh, Sam, I'm trying to think.'

Maria frowned. Then she asked: 'What if...'

'What?'

'What if Dr Milligan stayed that night in Mrs March's room? What if she slipped *him* something, some sleeping draught to make sure he did not wake during the night?'

'Yes...'

'What if she took the key while he was sleeping and went upstairs to the attic?'

'It would be possible.'

'And if Mrs March had drugged Dr Milligan, mightn't she also have drugged Nurse Everdeen? She couldn't have done it herself... But what if she paid Dorothy to put something in the gin bottle... some drug to make Nurse Everdeen sleep? I never thought to check if the seal was broken. And then when Mrs March went into the room in the attic, she could have emptied the contents of the bottle out of the window to make it look as if Nurse Everdeen had drunk the lot. What if that's what happened, Sam?'

'Well...'

'If that's the case, then everything Nurse Everdeen has claimed to be true *may* be true.' She paused and picked up her glass, saw it was empty, put it back on the table. 'Sam,' she said, 'I will have one more small glass of sherry for the benefit of my nerves and then you may take me back to the police station and I shall ask to speak with Inspector Paul.'

'Do you think he'll listen to you?' Samuel Collins asked.

'I shall do my utmost to ensure that he does.'

I searched everywhere, but I couldn't find Isak.

He wasn't in the bedroom, he wasn't in the refectory or the gym or the Great Hall. I bumped into Mr Crouch coming the other way down one of the corridors.

'Listen, Lewis,' he said, 'we need to have a little chat, you and I—'

'Not now, sir,' I said.

I headed towards the library and met Mrs Goode coming the other way.

'Lewis! I've been looking for you.'

'I can't find Isak,' I told her.

'He's at my house.'

'Is he OK?'

'He asked me to come and find you. Come on, I'll take you to him.'

We walked together to the old stable block. Mrs Goode rang the bell and the door was opened by a shaggy-headed man in a tracksuit who she introduced as her husband. The small dog was bouncing up and down yapping. The large black Labrador stood behind, wagging his tail at half-mast.

'Come through to the kitchen, Lewis.'

I followed her into a large, light room with a glass ceiling, like a conservatory. It was messy but in a nice way: colourful stuff lying around, coloured pencils in mugs and jam jars; sketches on scraps of paper, loads of plants, an open bottle of wine. The young girl was sitting sideways on a chair with a wicker frame, with her legs hooked over one of its arms and a cushion behind her back. She was twirling a hank of hair around a pen with a book propped open against her knees and headphones connected to a portable CD player. The smaller dog jumped onto her lap and made itself comfortable. Isak was sitting at the table by the window.

He had been crying. I'd never seen Isak cry. I didn't know what to do or say.

'Are you OK?' I asked.

He answered with a fierce scowl.

Mrs Goode beckoned me over to the table.

'I was showing Isak some old family photographs. Come and see what we've found.'

I went to sit beside Isak who wouldn't look at me. Mrs Goode was opposite.

'Guess who this is?' she passed a picture to me.

The image showed a young couple standing side by side – a wedding picture. The bride was short, dark-haired and pretty. Her husband was tall and broad-shouldered; good-looking by anyone's standards, his hair slicked down, his moustache shining. They stood close together, but neither was smiling. There was something sad about them both.

'Is that your great-grandmother?' I asked.

'Yes!' said Mrs Goode. 'That's Maria Smith and her husband,

Sam Collins, on their wedding day, April 1904. You can't tell, but she was pregnant there with my granny.'

Isak winced.

'They're standing outside the asylum chapel,' said Mrs Goode. 'You can just make it out behind. That must have been hard for Maria. It was she who campaigned for Nurse Everdeen's body to be brought back to All Hallows so she could be laid to rest close to her son.'

'But on the other side of the graveyard wall,' I said.

'Exactly. Here, this is a photograph of the woman known as Mrs March, taken in her hospital room a few days before the tragedy. You can see it was a grand room. Look at the swags of the curtains, the huge vases of flowers, the quality furniture. And she's had her hair done, and she's made up and goodness knows where that dress came from, but it looks as if it would have been expensive; all that lace and satin!'

Mrs March was beautiful – film-star beautiful. Her face reminded me of someone, or something, but I couldn't think what. Behind her stood a slight man, rather swamped by his clothes, with a droopy moustache. He was staring at Mrs March as if he'd never seen a woman before.

'Is that Dr Milligan?' asked Isak.

'It is,' said Mrs Goode. 'Don't you think it looks as if he had a bit of a crush on his patient? Which is both unethical and dangerous. People in positions of authority should never attempt to forge relationships with those over whom they have power.'

She knows about Mr Crouch and Isak, my mother whispered. *That's her way of letting you know she knows.*

'Is there a photograph of the little girl?' I asked.

'Only one.'

Mrs Goode sorted through the pictures until she found it. She lay it on the table so Isak and I could look at it together.

The child was dressed up, with a big bow in her hair. She was cute; like any other little kid, looking solemn for the photograph. She was standing with her heels together and her toes slightly apart, a stringy knitted rabbit tucked under her arm.

'That's the attic landing,' Isak said, 'she's standing outside the fourth door.'

I laid the photograph down. I was thinking about the footsteps we'd heard, the whispers; the little girl murdered in her bed; *this* little girl. Now I knew what she looked like, it made what had happened to her feel more real. The hairs on my arms stood on end. This child had been killed in the room above ours. My fingers went to the bruise on my forehead. I recalled the terror I'd felt when the woman had rushed towards me. I imagined how frightened the little girl must have been.

'You're welcome to look through the pictures, boys, and if there are any that particularly interest you, I can photocopy them for you in the library tomorrow. Would you like a cup of tea? Or some Coca-Cola?'

I hadn't had a Coke since the original trip down to All Hallows with Tracy, which felt like a million years earlier. Isak and I both asked for Cokes and Mrs Goode filled two glasses from a big bottle. Then she produced a metal tin that contained homemade fairy cakes in chocolate and lemon flavours.

'Georgia made them with her dad,' said Mrs Goode, with a nod towards the girl on the chair who ignored her. Isak and I helped ourselves.

'There's something else I really would like to show you,' said Mrs Goode. 'A few months before she died, Thalia Nunes wrote an extra chapter for *When I Was Mad*. It was never added to the book but she sent a copy to my great-grandmother for safe-keeping. I hadn't looked at it in years but I dug it out the other day and I think you'll find it of interest.'

EMMA – WEDNESDAY, 23 DECEMBER 1903

This was a different room, a different place.

It was a small cell in a big prison; a prison that stood stark on the moor, a great building, made of granite, six storeys high with rows of square windows, slick slate roofs; enormous chimneys. If All Hallows was overbearing in its Gothic architecture, this place was monstrous. With the hill behind it, the wall around it, the angled arch at the entrance like the mouth of some diabolical creature opened to consume any soul that passed through, the very approach to the prison was enough to strike fear into the heart.

Inside was no better.

There was no respite from the bleakness. No muting of the sounds of doors slamming, the clanking of locks, the rattling of bars or the desperate sounds made by men locked in cages.

Maria had to follow the guard past other cells, each occupied by a condemned prisoner, to reach the door to the room where Emma was imprisoned. The corridor was without ornament or window; a sheen of damp on the surface of the bricks. Maria knew the sound of her heels clicking along the flagstones would haunt her for the rest of her life.

In the cell, Maria removed her veil and bit her lip to stop herself from crying out in distress at her friend's appearance. Emma seemed smaller than she used to be, as if the shame and notoriety that had been heaped upon her since the death of the child known as Harriet March had sucked the juice out of her. She was diminished.

'Did you bring my manual?' was the first thing that Emma said.

Maria nodded, and passed the small book to the nurse, together with the fountain pen that Emma had requested. She watched as Emma opened the manual and wrote something in its first pages. Then she closed the book and lay it to one side.

'Will you come and sit beside me?' she asked.

Maria did not want to touch anything in that awful room, but she sat on the bunk beside her friend. She had fully intended to put on a brave face for Emma's sake but now it came to it, bravery eluded her. She took Emma's hand in hers. She could feel the nurse's pulse, the faint tremor like the heartbeat of a bird. Maria could imagine wrapping her in a handkerchief, putting her in her pocket and carrying her away. How she wished she could do that! How she wished she could spare the nurse from that which was coming to her.

'Tell me about All Hallows,' said Emma.

'It is busy,' said Maria. She cleared her throat. 'We've been preparing for Christmas. We are expecting some visitors, the weather being so mild this year.'

'Visitors?'

'Perhaps. A few. Those who feel guilty about not visiting for the rest of the year. A room has been prepared to receive them, to give a good impression. It's been decorated with holly and ivy. Apart from that room the place is as dreary as ever.'

'And the choir? Has the choir been practicing carols?'

'Not this year. The staff are too busy.'

The truth was that nobody was inclined to celebrate.

'I never could decide whether I liked Christmas, or not,' said Emma. 'All that fuss and work, and afterwards All Hallows always seemed a sadder place than it was before. It was only different when I had Herbert.'

'Yes.'

'He was my only family,' said the nurse. 'The only family that ever loved me for who I was.'

'There's me,' said Maria.

Emma took a handkerchief from up her sleeve and twisted it between her fingers.

'Did you do as I asked, Maria? Did you speak to the chaplain about me being buried in the same grave as Herbert?'

'I did.'

'So it's settled? I will be buried with my son?'

'It's settled.' Maria prayed God would forgive her for her lie, but she could see no virtue in honesty.

'That brings me more comfort than I can say.'

They were silent for a moment, each in her own way considering the prospect of Emma's internment. Then Emma asked: 'Is there any other news from All Hallows? What about Miss Nunes? Is she well?'

'Mr Uxbridge has had her moved her into a padded cell. She is given so many drugs now that conversation is impossible. Her arms are bound and she sits in the corner; her head lolls...'

'Why did they move her?'

'She would not eat. She is being force fed.'

Nurse Everdeen winced.

'Most of the nurses refuse to participate,' Maria said. 'They find it too distressing. Mr Uxbridge and Dorothy are managing it between them. Dorothy has been promoted. She is a matron now.'

'Dorothy,' whispered Nurse Everdeen. 'She always had a cruel heart.'

'Don't waste your time thinking of that girl,' said Maria. 'You are worth a million of her.'

For a while they sat in silence. It shouldn't be so difficult, Maria thought, to think of something to say. She was aware of the time passing and she both wanted the minutes to go more quickly, for this awful day to be over, and to slow, so Emma's time on this earth might be extended.

She asked in a small voice: 'Are you afraid, Nurse Everdeen?'

'I don't think I'd be human if I was not.'

'I don't know how you can bear it.'

'It will be over quickly.'

'How.... how will it happen?'

'Tomorrow morning, at dawn, they will come to fetch me. The priest will accompany me. They will take me outside, through the door at the end of this corridor. It's not a long journey, only a few steps...' she tailed off. Then added: 'The gallows is beyond.'

A gasp caught in Maria's throat. She had seen illustrations of hanging criminals; the bag over the head, the hands bound. She imagined the toes of Nurse Everdeen's worn old boots swinging beneath the hem of her skirt. She imagined how it would feel to stand on the gallows platform with the scratch of the noose about the neck, the knowing that your life could be measured in the seconds counted on the fingers.

She took the old woman's hand between hers.

'God knows the truth,' said Maria. 'He knows that you have done nothing wrong.'

'I didn't save Harriet.'

'But you tried!'

Maria's voice broke on the last words. 'Oh, I can't bear it,' she said, holding onto her friend as if she would never let her go. 'I can't bear to think of them killing you for a crime you did not commit! What they are doing to you is the worst kind of wickedness! Murdering an innocent woman who only tried to protect a child! Nurse Everdeen, if only someone had listened to you, believed you, then none of this would be happening now and...' she could not finish, overcome by grief, and although she had come to try to comfort the nurse it was Emma, now, who put her arms around Maria and said: 'There, there,' and, 'this will be over soon. It will be over.'

'If anyone is to blame it's me,' Maria sobbed. 'As God is my witness, I believed Harriet was mistaken about Mrs March. I thought she was so traumatised she did not recognise her own mother and you were so desperate to keep her that you would say and do anything... I trusted her word, that woman I did not know, over yours, Nurse Everdeen, you who I have known and respected for years! I am so sorry. I shall never be able to forgive myself! Never!'

'Now listen to me, Maria Smith,' said Emma. 'You losing yourself in regret and grief and sorrow will not do any good to anyone. It will only compound the sins already committed.'

She wiped away the tears that spilled from Maria's eyes.

'Nurse Everdeen...'

'If you really want to help me, you must promise me that you will be happy.'

'How can I...?'

'You must.'

The emotion of the exchange had exhausted Emma and she paused for a moment to gather her strength. In the meantime,

Maria composed herself somewhat also, her tears still falling, but her sobs brought under control.

'I know how hard you have tried to save me, Maria,' said Emma. 'You are a good girl, with a generous heart. And you have a quick mind. You will make a truly excellent nurse. I was wrong when I said Herbert was my only family and you were right. You are family to me too. I would like you to have this.'

She picked up the nursing manual and passed it back to Maria,

'I cannot take it, Nurse Everdeen. I know how much it means to you.'

'It's no use to me now, dear, and it would make me glad to think that you had it.'

She pressed the book into Maria's hands.

'I wrote an inscription to you.'

'Thank you,' said Maria. She leaned forward and touched her lips against Nurse Everdeen's cheek; the first and only time she ever would kiss her. 'I shall take good care of the manual.'

The prison guard opened the door and put his head round.

'Time is up,' he said to Maria. 'You must go now.'

'Oh, can't I stay just a little longer...'

He shook his head. 'Rules are rules, miss.'

Maria Smith looked at Nurse Everdeen.

'Nurse...' she whispered.

'Go,' said Emma.

'Nurse!'

'Go now,' said Emma. 'Let me be.'

'I shall never forget you.'

'I shall be with Herbert. I shall be content. Go. Live a good life, Maria. Be happy.'

Maria gave a small nod; gathered herself up, held the manual to her breast and turned and left.

The door closed behind her. The lock turned.

Emma held the locket with the picture of Herbert in the palm of her hand. She closed her fingers around it and she put it to her lips.

'Not long now, my darling,' she whispered. 'I'm on my way.'

.

The extra chapter for Thalia Nunes' book had been typed onto both sides of two sheets of paper that was old and yellowed. Mrs Goode unfolded the papers carefully. Georgia, on her chair, was pretending not to be interested, but she had slipped the headphones back round her neck so she could listen.

'Thalia wrote this many years after the events of 1903,' said Mrs Goode. 'The Harriet March murder case had never stopped bugging her, and she, being an invalid had plenty of time to think about it.' She turned the papers so the writing was facing us. 'Read it, Isak, so we can all hear.'

A few weeks after I was committed to All Hallows asylum, a terrible tragedy occurred. The child of one of the patients, a little girl of about five years old, known as Harriet March, was found smothered to death in bed. The child was being cared for by an elderly nurse in a locked attic room, and the nurse, who was supposedly addicted to drink and drugs, was accused of murder, found guilty, convicted and hanged.

Georgia swung her legs round and sat up properly in the chair, elbows on her knees, chin in her hands. The little dog jumped down and went to lie beside the big dog on the rug by the stove.

Isak read on:

The child had been brought to the asylum some weeks earlier with a woman assumed to be her mother. The woman, known as Mrs March, was badly injured and in a comatose state. Shortly before the child's murder, Mrs March had recovered and claimed to be Evelyn Rendall, a widowed Scotswoman. She said she and her daughter had been visiting relatives in Devon when their carriage was stopped by thieves and they dragged from it. She had no memory of how they came to be in the small boat in which they were found, but it was assumed she had fought off her attackers and tried to escape with the child. By some miracle, none of her jewellery had been lost during the attack.

Mrs Goode interrupted at this point. 'Obviously, amnesia is a useful condition to have if there are parts of your story you don't want to reveal and the asylum staff had no reason not to believe Mrs March. Everyone already believed she was the child's mother; they had nursed her back from the brink of death. They had a lot invested in the woman. So even though the attempted robbery story didn't quite add up, nobody questioned it.'

'Keep reading, Isak,' I said.

Isak cleared his throat. 'OK. So…

After the murder of the child, Mrs Rendall appeared inconsolable and the asylum staff, all of whom were greatly saddened by events, did all they could to assist her. She asked that the child's body be prepared for travel and placed in a shroud and she set off with it in a carriage, ostensibly en route for Scotland. Despite assurances that she would write, she was never heard from again. The doctor primarily responsible for her care, Dr Milton Milligan, Esq. spent all his savings trying to find her, but she had seemingly disappeared. Dr Milligan never married. He spent the rest of his life in the asylum.

'As a doctor, or a patient?' I asked.
'As a doctor,' Mrs Goode confirmed.
Isak continued reading:

With the benefit of up-to-date records, telephone directories and so on, I carried out my own research into Evelyn Rendall and, like Dr Milligan, could find no record of her. I contacted every Rendall family resident in Scotland and none had heard of this particular woman.

Isak paused. He reached out for his glass and drank some Coca-Cola.
'Are you following this?' Mrs Goode asked Georgia.
She nodded.
Isak picked up the story.

It was clear that Mrs March had been lying, and if she had lied about her identity to hide the truth, it was possible she had been lying about everything. Perhaps, as Nurse Everdeen had said at her trial, Mrs March was not the child's mother, despite the striking resemblance. Perhaps she had killed the child's real mother; perhaps, she was even responsible for the death of the child. But the question remained, why?

The only lead I had was what Maria Collins (née Smith) had told me: that Nurse Everdeen had established that the child and her real mother had been living in a rented cottage in the town of Whitby, on the North Yorkshire coast. I travelled to the town, booked a week in a small hotel close to the seafront, and asked around. I soon found people who remembered the woman and child who had 'disappeared'. The woman, whose birth name was Catharine Willowby, had been raised locally, but had married a man from Guernsey and moved to the island to live with his wealthy family, the Ozannes, until her husband's death. Then she and the child, Harriet, returned to Yorkshire because of 'difficulties' with her husband's sister, Jacqueline. The two women had not been friends, Catharine Ozanne reporting that Jacqueline was spiteful and jealous. These difficulties, she feared, would be compounded when Jacqueline realised that Harriet would inherit her grandfather's fortune on his death.

Isak paused to take another drink.
'Don't stop now!' said Georgia.

The old man died in September 1903. As soon as she discovered the terms of the will, Jacqueline paid an accomplice to track down her niece and sister-in-law. These are established facts. What follows is assumption but is the best way I can think of to finish the story.

Realising the danger they were in, I believe Catharine tried to make her way to Guernsey to claim Harriet's inheritance, hiring a small lugger to take her from Dartmouth across the Channel rather than using the ferry which she thought would be too obvious. Unfortunately, Jacqueline intercepted Catharine and Harriet while they were waiting on the beach to board the craft at high tide. Jacqueline stabbed Catharine to death, but she did not give in without a fight, and Jacqueline was injured. She managed to get herself and the child into the lugger which was later found drifting by the crew of the fishing boat, the March Winds... and that's when Jacqueline and Harriet were brought back to All Hallows. Catharine's body was washed away.

'So, Jacqueline killed Harriet so she would inherit the money instead of her?' Georgia asked.

'And, I imagine, because she was insecure and jealous,' said Mrs Goode. 'Because she hated her brother's wife for taking him from her; perhaps she held her responsible for her brother's death. She blamed her and the child for everything she had lost. The only way she could soothe her own hurt, was to get rid of them.'

'There speaks someone who's spent too much time reading psychology books,' said Mrs Goode's husband.

'Did Jacqueline get the inheritance?'

'Yes. She took the child's body back to Guernsey. Harriet was buried in the family crypt beside her grandparents. Jacqueline got everything. Every last penny.'

I left the others inside the house and went outside by myself. I thought of the ghosts trapped in the room above ours: Nurse Everdeen, the gentle woman in the chair, and the child we'd heard playing with her ball, and the other one; the one who had pushed me into the mirror. I knew who she was now. Jacqueline. The face in the photograph had seemed familiar because I'd seen it before; when it rushed up behind me. She was up there, still in the attic, guarding her secrets, scaring away anyone who came close to discovering the truth.

But we had discovered it.

I wandered around the Goodes' garden, part of All Hallows but separated from it by a wooden fence. A world within a world; like the room in the attic. I thought how sad the story of Emma Everdeen and Harriet Ozanne was. How different it could have been if only someone had made Emma aware of the danger that faced her earlier; if only she or Maria had known.

When I went back inside, Mr and Mrs Goode were in the kitchen and Isak and Georgia were at the table. Isak was telling Georgia about Thalia Nunes and the scratches on the floorboards. Georgia asked lots of questions and then she was quiet for a while, then she said.

'If you could get a message to Thalia Nunes to tell her to warn Maria about the murder, maybe it could be stopped.'

Isak said: 'But the murder has already happened. It happened ninety years ago.'

'We did time in physics last term,' said Georgia, 'and there's a theory that time isn't static, like a railway track, but that it's constantly in motion, like a train that can travel in either direction along the track.'

Isak and I looked at one another while we considered the implications of this.

'What is there to lose?' Georgia asked. 'If you scratch a warning on the floorboards and nothing changes, well, at least you tried.'

'You're right,' said Isak, looking brighter than he had done for days. 'We might as well give it a go.'

Most of the other boys left for half-term, picked up by their parents or taken by the school minibus to the station. Isak and I didn't watch them go, we were too caught up in our own plans.

The first night of half term, we didn't get into bed at all, but kept the window open so the fresh air came into our room, keeping us awake. We listened to the owls and the bats, the occasional bleat of a sheep, jumping every time we heard the slightest sound from above. We talked about the marks we should make on the floorboards, changing and refining the plan because we knew we would only have one chance to get this right.

When midnight came, we began to prepare.

We put sweaters and trousers over our pyjamas, picked up the penknife Georgia had given us, and crept out of our room and along the corridor. Isak was holding a torch, also provided by Georgia. She had been desperate to come with us, but it would have been impossible to break her into All Hallows at night. Still, it was good to think of her thinking of us.

The boards creaked beneath our feet. Above us, all was silent. I imagined Jacqueline Ozanne coming along the corridor from the other direction, on her way to suffocate little Harriet, walking along these exact same floorboards.

It gave me the creeps.

The only thing that was stopping us meeting her was time. And if time was flexible, like Georgia had said, then perhaps she was here; we couldn't see her, but it didn't mean she didn't exist.

Isak opened the door at the end of the corridor and shone the torch ahead. Its beam showed us that all was clear.

'You OK, Lewis?' he asked.

'All good,' I replied.

Be careful, my mother whispered in my ear.

We went quietly through All Hallows; through its dark corridors, the heating system gurgling and chuntering, stepping, from time to time into a patch of moonlight coming through a window. We went all the way down to Ward B and Isak opened the door.

It was dark and chilly. I could almost see the All Hallows inmates hunched in their stalls in the shadows; thin and ragged. I held out my hand to steady myself and my fingers touched the wall. It felt cold, and damp.

'Come on,' Isak called.

He was already in the stall where Thalia had been held and had moved the desk aside.

I crouched down beside him.

'Hold this.' He passed me the torch. I had supposed that I would be the one to write the message but Isak was so focused on what he was doing that I didn't argue. He unfolded the piece of paper that he had in his pocket and spread it out.

He began to copy the message into the floorboard.

MM WILL KILL HM 31/10

Almost all straight lines and the minimum number of marks

we could come up with to get the message across. I held tight to the torch, trying to keep the light steady while Isak carved. He was taking ages. I was worried, now, that the message wasn't clear enough. I tried to think of how it might be misinterpreted. I felt my mum close by.

It's all you can do, Lewis, she told me. *You can't do any more than this.*

Actually, I thought we could. If I had a knife too, I could write a separate message, be a bit more specific.

I jumped at a sound: a bell ringing the quarter-hour.

'What's that?'

'It sounds like the clock in the tower.'

'They must have fixed it,' murmured Isak.

He was chipping away with the knife, making marks that were larger than the old ones. They looked very obvious. *Too* obvious. If one of the cruel asylum wardens were to see them...

MM WILL KI

'Hurry up,' I told him.

'I can't go any faster.'

'Isak...'

MM WILL KILL H

'What?' He looked up. 'Are you scared?'

I nodded.

'Me too,' he said, 'but we have to do this.'

He kept carving.

I kept holding the torch.

MM WILL KILL HM

Then, suddenly, the door to Ward B opened and light fell into the corridor.

We slid back and pressed ourselves against the partition. I switched off the torch and held it close to my chest.

'Who's there?' a voice called. Mr Crouch. 'Who is it? I know someone's there.'

He stepped forward. We could hear his footsteps. Another step and he'd be around the partition and he'd see us. My heart pounded in my chest.

Keep quiet, my mum said. *Don't move.*

We kept quiet. Mr Crouch went away.

84

Maria brought the medicine trolley to a halt outside the door to Ward B, and kicked down the brake with the toe of her boot while she knocked on the barred window and waited for the door to be opened.

This was Maria's least favourite task at the best of times: bringing drugs to the patients kept in this awful ward that stank of shit and blood and despair. She did not relish walking amongst the most dangerous patients, those who were kept in chains because nobody knew what else to do with them. And also she hated to see the suffering endured by some perfectly sane woman, like Thalia Nunes, who had gone too far in provoking her parents.

She shouldn't even really be doing this job and had only agreed to help out because the asylum had so few nurses that the other staff were struggling to manage.

At least she now had a valid reason to talk to Miss Nunes. Nurse Everdeen would be sure to ask after her later and, besides, Maria liked talking to Thalia. Despite her horrendous predicament, Thalia had a spark about her, and Maria didn't want to see that spark extinguished.

The door swung open and Maria pushed the trolley into the ward, her senses at once assailed by the sounds and smells; the stink of peroxide in her nose. She set to work. She had a list of what drugs to give to whom. Mr Pincher insisted on a list so stock could easily be checked to ensure staff weren't pilfering drugs and selling them on. He didn't know that Mr Uxbridge had a separate system that he ran concurrently, selling drugs to line his own pocket. Patients with cash could buy whatever their hearts desired, in the pharmacological sense.

She progressed along the stalls, dispensing morphine and other sedatives to the first patients, stepping back when one woman jumped forward and spat at Maria, clawing with her fingers. Maria called for the warder, who came and beat the woman several times with his truncheon.

'That's enough!' cried Maria. 'Stop it!'

'It does no harm,' said the warder. 'Where there's no sense there's no feeling.'

The woman cowered, her hands over her head. While the warder was present, Maria stepped forward and administered her medicine via a syringe. She observed the scabs and blisters on the woman's skin, and the patchiness of her hair, as if hanks had been pulled out. Her breath smelled rank, her teeth were rotting in the gums. Not so long ago, this patient had been a respectable married woman. Maria didn't know her then, obviously, but probably she had a creamy complexion, thick, glossy hair, good strong teeth. Probably, she wore the latest fashions and lived a happy and fulfilled life. Nobody, especially not their husbands, ever discussed how women like this were contaminated with syphilis. Nobody even mentioned the disease by name: it was deemed too vulgar. Just as nobody, Maria imagined, in this poor creature's

former social circle would know the truth about what had
become of her.

'There,' she said, withdrawing the syringe. 'That'll make you
feel better.'

The woman shrank back and relaxed, slumped against the
wall.

'Sweet dreams,' Maria whispered.

The next stall contained Thalia Nunes. Thalia's clever brown
eyes looked up as Maria came around the partition.

'Good afternoon, Miss Nunes,' said Maria.

Thalia was restrained at the wrists and throat. She could only
move her arms as far as the harness allowed. The throat strap was
a terrible thing to endure, because any movement, for example, if
Thalia should fall asleep sitting up and her head were to nod
forward, would cause a most unpleasant feeling of suffocation.
Thalia's expression this afternoon was one of wide-eyed fury.

Maria said: 'Wait a moment, Miss Nunes, I need to measure
out a syringe for you,' in a voice loud enough for the warder to
hear. She parked the trolley beside the partition, in a way that
blocked them both from sight, then she held a finger to her lips
and came forward and loosened the strap around Thalia's neck.

'I'm sorry,' she whispered, trying not to jerk Thalia's neck as
she undid the buckle, 'I can't take it off altogether but I'll make it
more comfortable for you.' She examined the weals left by the
strap and went to the trolley, took out a jar of salve, and gently
applied it to Thalia's neck. The other woman winced. 'I'm sorry,'
Maria said again.

'You're kind to me, Nurse Smith,' Miss Nunes said as Maria
tended to her neck, making pads from pieces of lint to stop the
collar from rubbing.

'I'm not a real nurse yet, only a trainee. But, God knows, it's
my duty to help people,' muttered Maria. 'And I may not know

much but I know you shouldn't be on this ward. There's nothing wrong with you at all, as I can see.'

'There wasn't when I arrived,' said Miss Nunes. 'There might be by the time I leave. How much longer will they keep me in here?'

'I don't know.' Maria kept her voice low. 'I know it's not right, miss, but the quieter you are, the more obedient, the less trouble you cause, the more likely your father will receive a favourable report. It might be best to go along with it for the time being so as you can get out of here as quickly as possible.'

'I can't do that. I can't let them believe that they've won.'

'But they won't have won, will they? Can't you think of it as... as a battle strategy, perhaps? A means to an end?'

The expression on Thalia Nunes' face was one of rage. 'I feel like killing them all,' she said. 'My father, my mother, the people who keep me here...'

'I think you'd better not mention that to anyone else, miss, for the time being.'

From the corner of Maria's eye, she saw the warder step forward to see what she was doing.

'This is something to help you to sleep,' she said loudly and deliberately, holding up the syringe so the warder could see. 'You'll feel a sharp pain in the top of your leg...'

The warder turned away. Maria squirted the liquid onto the wooden floorboards and went to wipe it away with the toe of her foot.

'Has your little ghost been back,' she asked, 'making new marks for you.'

'You don't believe in my ghost, do you, Maria? Nonetheless, *someone* has been coming to visit while I'm sleeping.'

Maria laughed uneasily. She was convinced Thalia was subconsciously making the marks on the floorboards herself.

'He left me a little gift.'

She worked her fingers into the plaster behind the skirting board, picked at it with her nails and pulled out a token, a little metal horse. She showed it to Maria, it lying flat in the palm of her dirty hand.

'Well,' said Maria. 'I have never seen anything quite like that. Your ghost left it for you?'

'Nobody else has been here.'

The horse made Maria feel anxious. She wondered if it might be some kind of trap and whoever had put it there might return later and claim it had been stolen.

'Perhaps you should let me take the horse, Miss Nunes,' she said softly.

'No!' Thalia closed her fingers around it and snatched her hand back. 'It's all I have.'

'As you wish.'

Maria turned to the trolley. She dipped a flannel in the bucket of clean water at its base.

'Look at the new marks on the floorboards,' Thalia hissed.

Maria wrung out the flannel and crouched to look at the marks. 'These are new?'

'The light falls onto that patch of floor for a short time each afternoon. Before I slept those marks weren't there, but now they are.'

Maria took Thalia's hand, wiped the palm, between the fingers.

'"MM WILL KILL HM". What kind of horrid message is that?'

'A warning, perhaps.'

'A warning you need to stop scratching the floorboards. You're going to end up in all kinds of trouble if you're not careful.'

'Is everything well there, Nurse?' called the warder.

'I'm nearly done.'

Maria straightened herself and dusted down her skirt. She opened a jar, shook three medicinal lozenges into her hand and passed them to Thalia. 'The taste is vile but they will soothe your nerves and help the time pass more quickly.'

She turned and tidied the trolley, ready to move on.

'What is the day today?' Thalia asked.

Maria considered for a moment. Then she said: 'The last day of October.'

'All Hallows' Eve?'

'Yes.'

'Then someone with the initials HM has been murdered today. Or is about to be.'

Maria shuddered.

The warder's footsteps were approaching.

'You're taking your time with that one, Miss Smith!' he called.

'Goodbye, Miss Nunes,' said Maria.

She pushed the trolley away.

* * *

Maria finished her round and went to the cloakroom to wash her hands. Even so much as stepping foot in Ward B made her feel dirty. She took off her apron and put it in the laundry basket, took a clean one from the dresser and slipped it over her dress. She tied the belt and checked her appearance in the mirror. She looked tired. It was all this running up and down the stairs all the time. And having to keep her patience with that milksop, Dr Milton Milligan, and all his fussing over Mrs March.

Maria paused.

MM will kill HM.

Of course, it meant nothing. It was a subconscious ploy by Thalia Nunes to draw attention to herself. Thalia was obviously a highly intelligent woman who knew exactly how to manipulate others. Wasn't that exactly what Maria had overheard Thalia's father telling Mr Pincher on his very first visit to All Hallows?

'You can't trust a word that comes out of her mouth,' his lordship had said, and that was a father talking about his own daughter.

Obviously, his lordship was a fool but there was never smoke without fire, as Maria's mother liked to say.

Thalia *must* have made those marks herself. It couldn't have been anyone else.

Maria pinned some stray hairs under her cap and wished her shift were over and she could go and find Sam and the two of them could eat some supper together and then he could hold her hand while she told him about the trials of her day; all these matters that were bothering her.

She walked through the corridors, past the open doors of wards where those patients who were capable were being prepared to be escorted to the refectory for their supper. She took a right turn at the junction of the main wing with the west wing, and glimpsed the time on the clock above the archway. Every evening, she met Dr Milligan in Mrs March's room promptly at 6 p.m. Today she was a few minutes early.

She climbed three steep stairs and went through another door, this one leading to the grand and comfortable hallway outside the private rooms reserved for the wealthy female patients. The hallway was panelled, mirrored and carpeted. Bowls of scented greenhouse roses were displayed on tables polished to the finest of shines. It was like being in a different world, compared to the rest of the asylum. Mrs March was being treated in the first of these rooms. The one that All Hallows staff called 'The Royal Suite'.

Maria knocked twice with her knuckles, opened the door and went in.

Mrs March was standing by the window looking exquisite in a powder-blue day dress. Dorothy Uxbridge was with her. As Maria stepped into the room, she saw Dorothy put something into the pocket of her apron and Mrs March dusted her hands together. The actions of both seemed furtive.

'Good afternoon, Maria,' said Dorothy, regaining her composure more quickly than Mrs March. She smiled her dimpled smile, trying to look innocent as a baby with her pretty blue eyes, her skin all peaches-and-cream, uniform neat as a button.

'Good afternoon,' Maria said. 'I hope you are feeling well, Mrs March.'

'Very well, thank you,' said Mrs March. She turned to Dorothy. 'Thank you, Dorothy. Dr Milligan will be here shortly. You may go now.'

Dorothy Uxbridge bobbed a curtsey, turned, and left.

Mrs March turned her attention to Maria.

'Would you call for some tea,' she asked. 'Three cups and saucers. I'm sure Dr Milligan won't object to me inviting you to join us. We have a great deal of news to impart to you this evening.'

The message made, Isak and I returned to our room. Already that part of the school had a mournful feeling about it, as if it knew that, now the water damage had been repaired, it was going to be abandoned, its doors locked once again, its rooms and corridors left to the insects and the ghosts.

We were in a celebratory mood. Isak climbed out onto the ledge for a cigarette and I went with him. I was so pumped I hardly felt scared at all.

Above us, a moon that was almost full glowed bright in the sky; bright enough to cause moon shadows to fall from the trees and the chapel tower. I thought of Nurse Everdeen and the little girl in the room above ours, their window looking out in the exact same direction and I wondered what kind of moon rose in the sky on the last day of October ninety years ago and if they had looked out at it. And I wondered if the message had got back to Nurse Everdeen, that the child, Harriet, would be murdered that night and if it had, what precautions she was taking; whether she was afraid.

It was only when we climbed back into the room, and listened to the silence from the room above, that doubts began to prick at me.

'What do you think will happen now?' I asked Isak.

'How am I supposed to know?'

A while later, we heard the clock chime the hour.

'How will we know if we've saved them?' Isak asked.

'The books,' I said. 'The stories in the books will have changed.

EMMA – OCTOBER 31 1903

Maria came into the attic room with the supper tray, which she placed on the table as usual.

'I have some important news,' she said to Emma.

'Oh? What is it?'

'Mrs March has remembered who she is. Dr Milligan says it is a miracle.'

'And who is she, exactly, then?'

'Her name is Evelyn Rendall. She is the widow of a wealthy Scottish lawyer.'

'Well,' said Emma quietly, 'There's more proof that she's an imposter. Harriet's father was not a lawyer but a soldier and the family is not Scottish but comes from Guernsey.'

Maria did not answer. She was feeling unsettled.

Harriet came wandering into the room. She took her place at the table. 'Please may I have a crumpet?' she asked.

'Yes, of course, you may,' said Maria, 'seeing as how you ask so nicely.'

Emma helped Harriet up onto her chair. She hadn't wiped the child's hands. Maria noticed that they were grubby but decided not to say anything. She didn't want Emma to feel as if she was being criticised. She passed a plate and a crumpet to Harriet, then leaned across her to spread it with a pat of yellow butter.

'Is something troubling you?' Emma asked Maria.

'There is, but I don't wish to speak about it just now.' Maria made dramatic eye movements to show that she did not want Harriet to hear what was troubling her.

'As you wish.' Emma put on her spectacles and peered at the items on the tray.

'I asked for a quarter of gin,' she said, rather tetchily. 'Did it slip your mind?'

'No,' said Maria, 'no, it did not slip my mind, Nurse Everdeen, but I thought it best I didn't bring you any gin tonight. And also,' she reached for the morphine bottle on the shelf, 'I am taking this away as well.'

Emma watched her put the bottle in her pocket. Harriet, nibbling at the crust of her crumpet, watched too.

Maria was telling the truth. She had ordered a quarter bottle of gin for Nurse Everdeen and she had placed the unopened bottle on the supper tray, the tray labelled *Nurse Everdeen,* before she set off for Ward B with the medicine trolley. When she returned to the kitchens to collect the tray, worried now about the meaning of the message on the floorboards, and made fearful by Dorothy Uxbridge's shifty behaviour, she'd noticed that the wax seal around the stopper of the gin bottle had been broken. She had removed the stopper and sniffed. The contents of the bottle smelled like gin, but Maria did not trust them. She had poured the liquid down the sink and put the bottle back with the other empties ready for collection.

'What is it?' Emma asked Maria. 'Why are you taking my sleeping potion away?'

'Might we go into the corridor for a moment, Nurse...?'

'We might. We'll only be on the other side of the door, Harriet. You eat your supper like a good girl. You may lick the jam spoon, if you wish.'

Harriet nodded solemnly and the two women went into the corridor.

Maria leaned against the wall and tipped back her head, blowing air between her lips.

'What is it?' asked Emma. 'Tell me!'

Maria sighed. 'The main thing, is that she – Mrs March or Evelyn Rendall or whatever her name is – is recovered enough to return to Scotland. She is anxious to take Harriet away from All Hallows as soon as possible. Tomorrow, perhaps.'

'If we let that woman take her, Harriet will be in mortal danger.'

'Neither you nor I will have any say in the matter. We can't stop her.'

'If there is a risk Mrs March will take Harriet tomorrow, then I must remove her from All Hallows now. Tonight.'

Maria took Emma's hands. 'I understand your fear, but you can't take her away tonight. It's cold and dark – how would you find your way across the moor? Where would you shelter? The dogs would track you down in no time at all. You'd be in trouble and Harriet would be handed straight back to Mrs March and nobody would listen to you ever again.'

'I cannot let that woman have her.'

'I know. And we won't. But also we mustn't do anything foolish to jeopardise the situation and strengthen Mrs March's hand.'

Emma nodded.

'So let's stay calm, and in the morning I'll have Sam ride over to Dartmouth and make up some story to the police so that Mrs

March is obliged to stay here a few more days. We'll think of something.'

'Very well, Maria, if that's what you think is best.'

'It is. And in the meantime, tonight, please be vigilant, Nurse Everdeen. I have a feeling that something might happen. It is only a feeling but... here,' she pressed the key to the landing door into Emma's hand. 'When I'm gone, lock the door behind me from the inside and leave the key in the lock so no other key might be inserted into it. And...' she lowered her voice, 'it might be an idea also to put a chair, or some other furniture, against the door. Just in case. Better to be safe than sorry.'

How slowly the minutes go when you can't sleep.

I lay beside Isak, wide awake. My head was full of memories and thoughts and worries. What if our message wasn't clear enough? What if Thalia didn't see it, or did see it and didn't understand? What if she wasn't able to warn Maria or Maria didn't have a chance to warn Emma Everdeen? What if it was too late, and by the time Thalia saw the message, Harriet had already been murdered?

What if all this had been for nothing?

I'll still be proud of you, my mother told me. *You tried.*

The clock rang out again. It was half-past three. Wasn't that the danger hour? The time when people were most likely to die in their sleep, when their bodies were at their lowest ebb? I strained my ears. I heard footsteps on the floorboards of the corridor outside; the rustle of fabric. Through the crack in the door, I saw a flickering light; a candle flame.

'She's here,' whispered Isak. 'Mrs March has come.'

We lay, side by side, following the sound of the footsteps up the stairs. They stopped at the top step. The door handle rattled. We heard a murmur, a curse.

'She can't open the door,' Isak whispered. 'Something is stopping her.'

Above us we heard a creak. We heard the rocking chair runners rock once, and then a quiet footstep on the floorboards of the room above ours.

Nurse Everdeen was awake.

There was more rattling of the handle of the door at the top of the stairs, then the footsteps came back down, the other way. The steps were light. They ran past the closed door to our bedroom, and disappeared into the stillness of the night.

'She's given up,' Isak said. 'She's gone away!'

He slid out of bed and crept to the door. I watched him, in the moonlight, listening.

'She's definitely gone!'

I climbed out too and we bounced around our beds for a bit because we were so pleased with ourselves. The moon had disappeared behind a bank of pale grey cloud but the stars shone brightly in a velvet-black sky and we had saved Harriet March from murder.

88

At first I thought it was cigarette smoke that I was smelling; I thought Isak had lit a cigarette. I turned over and pressed my face into the pillow, but that smelled of smoke too. I opened my eyes and I saw something drifting through the cracks at the edges of the door. It took a moment to understand what was happening.

'Isak!'

I jumped out of bed and grabbed his shoulders. I shook him.

'Smoke!' I cried. 'There's smoke on the landing.'

Emma had not slept. She had been awake when the footsteps came up the stairs, she'd heard Mrs March struggling to insert the key in the door at the top, heard her rattling the handle. She had never, in all her life, been so afraid. This was the evil she had sensed, this was her nemesis: that woman; that beautiful stranger, who had fooled them all; who had killed Harriet's mother and who was determined, now, to have the child as well.

She did not call out to Mrs March. She thought it best if Mrs March did not know that she was awake listening for her. However, she remained on her guard even after Mrs March's footsteps had receded down the staircase. She did not believe that the woman would give up so easily.

She did not know what Mrs March would do next. There was no other way into the attic. She sat in her rocking chair, facing the door to the bedroom, with the poker on her lap. The remains of the small fire that she had lit had burned low in the grate; only the glowing ash remained.

It was a quiet night, the weather still for once. These hours before dawn were always the quietest. These were the hours when the sick and the old tended to slip off their mortal coil. Emma did not mind these dying hours. She found them peaceful and unworldly. If a person knew they were dying, but was clinging on to life, the nurse understood why they would uncurl their fingers in these quiet moments, why they would choose then to let go and drift away.

The window pane rattled; a gust of wind.

Emma looked across at Harriet. She'd kept the lamp burning very low so that she could check on the child, who was sleeping peacefully, one hand beside her cheek, the little fingers curled.

The nurse pulled her shawl around her shoulders. It was cold in the room. She stood up to poke the ashes in the grate, trying to draw out the last dregs of heat from them when the first fingers of smoke seeped under the bedroom door. Emma thought what she was smelling was the smoke from the fireplace. It wasn't until her eyes began to sting too that she understood what was happening.

Isak put his hand on the door handle.

'Don't!' I said. 'You're not supposed to open doors when there's a fire.'

He opened it anyway and he whispered: 'Oh Jesus!'

The wooden staircase that led up to the attic landing was blazing. Flames were licking up the stairs; the black paint on the door at the top was bubbling.

It was not real. It could not be. In 1993, there was no locked door at the top of the stairs. And yet we could feel the heat, we could smell the smoke as the old wood burned, and the old paint boiled, and the ancient animal hair in the plaster caught and singed; and we could hear the roar of the flames. The dry wood burned ferociously. As we watched, a segment of the stairs collapsed and fell away. Nurse Everdeen and Harriet were trapped in their little room at the top of those stairs. The fire, surely, would already be making its way along the attic landing; their room would be filling with smoke. They wouldn't be able to escape down the stairs. Even if the alarm was raised now, it would be too late. Nobody would be able to get up the stairs to save them. And there was no other way in.

Isak shut the door and put his trainers on.

'We'll have to get in from above,' he said.

He went to the window, pushed it open and hopped up and out. I followed him, out into the night air, cold and clear as water, and we began to make our way along the ledge.

I clung to the stonework, my pyjamas flapping about my ankles and waist.

Isak looked back at me over his shoulder. 'You OK, Lewis?'

'I can't do this.'

'You *are* doing it.'

Above us a reedy voice cried: 'Help! Help us, please!'

I thought: Oh God, they're going to burn to death, which was worse, in some ways than what had happened before. Smoke was gusting around us, being drawn out through the open window of the room above. The moonlight was all but extinguished behind the cloud.

We reached the passageway between the two sides of the building. Isak climbed the ladder. I followed.

On the top, Isak was already on the other side of the chimney, pulling at the lead on the roof. He was trying to make a hole, to burrow down through the roof but there wasn't enough time for that.

I took a deep breath – winter air, dusty with the taste of smoke – and crawled along the roof, trying not to think about the drop below. Wisps of smoke were puffing up through the chimney pot, disappearing into the night. Slowly, holding onto it with both hands, I pulled myself upright. The pot was huge, far, far bigger than it looked from ground level. It was at least as tall as I was and so wide that I certainly could not reach around it. The scrappy remains of a wire bird guard were silhouetted against the night sky.

Gripping the top of the pot with both hands, I stood on tiptoe and peered down.

Something moved. Something was down there, in the room below.

91

EMMA – 1903

Emma put the chair by the window and told Harriet to stand on it.

'You stand there and breathe the fresh air, my lamb, while Nurse thinks of a plan.'

Harriet stood on the chair, shivering in her nightdress, clutching the knitted rabbit. Emma crossed the room, went to the door and touched the wood. It was hot. The furniture she'd stacked in the corridor was providing the flames with fuel. There was no escape that way.

She sloshed the water from the jug along the base of the door. There was a dreadful hiss and the flames were extinguished, but only for a moment.

Then she lit a candle, went to the fireplace and she crouched down on her hands and knees beside the grate, put her head inside and looked up.

92

As I looked down, the face of an old woman, lit by the candle-light, looked back up at me. Together we observed how the chimney narrowed to accommodate the slope of the roof just before it opened into the pot. The nurse must have been hoping she and the child might be able to escape up the chimney but it was too narrow. They'd never make it.

93

The gap was too small. Even Harriet, tiny as she was, could not fit into that space. And the thought of her trying to climb the chimney, and becoming stuck, was too hideous to contemplate.

'Nurse, what can you see?'

Harriet was beside her. Nurse Everdeen moved away and let Harriet look up the chimney.

'There's someone up there,' Harriet said.

'No, angel, no, there's only smoke.'

94

I could see flickering shadows. The flames must be licking under the door, coming into the room above ours. Isak was grunting as he tugged at the roof leading, but it wasn't shifting. Shadows crowded the fireplace. I saw a small child far below me, her face pale, crouching to look up the chimney. I recognised her from the photograph.

She didn't look like a child from almost a century ago. She looked like the kind of child who would ride her scooter up and down the pavement outside our house; like an ordinary, living, frightened little girl.

'It's OK,' I called to her, 'we'll find a way to get you out.'

She didn't hear me. She looked past me as if I wasn't there.

Isak came over. 'I can't shift it.'

'They can't get out this way either. The only way is through the window.'

We were silent for the length of one heartbeat. We already knew it would be impossible for them to come out of the window. Neither Harriet nor the nurse were tall enough for their feet to reach the ledge below, or the roof above. They weren't strong enough to hold onto the wall to await rescue. They would either fall to their deaths, or die of smoke inhalation.

We lay on our bellies and looked down, over the edge of the flat roof. Smoke was pouring from the window now and they were leaning out of it, no more than four feet below us, Nurse Everdeen holding the child forward so Harriet could breathe the fresher air. Smoke had already filled the room; it billowed around them. The little girl was crying, calling: 'Mama! Mama!'

'If we could drop something down to them,' Isak said, 'give them a way to climb up.'

We looked about. There was nothing around us, save the chimney pots and the lead that Isak had dislodged.

'What about the ladder?'

We went back to it, dropped to our hands and knees. The hooks had rusted into the bracket but by moving it about, we managed to dislodge it. We heaved it up onto the roof and then manhandled it past the chimney pots, stopping at the point above the window of the room above ours. Slowly, carefully, we manoeuvred the ladder down until it hung in front of the window. We watched as Harriet reached out a small hand; touched it, saw that it existed, in her time as well as ours.

'One of us needs to be on the ledge,' said Isak, 'to keep it steady at the bottom.'

He was heavier and stronger than me. He needed to be here, holding the top of the ladder, taking the weight. We didn't discuss it. I scrambled to the roof edge, turned round, wriggled over as far as I could, then dropped down onto the passageway. I landed in one piece. Uninjured. Fine.

I went to the side of the building, took a deep breath, stepped onto the ledge, and clinging to the stonework, inched my way along. Smoke was gushing from the window now: clouds of it.

I made my way along until I was directly below the window of the room above ours. The ladder was hovering. The faces of the nurse and the child were close together, both gasping for breath. I took hold of the bottom of the ladder and held it steady.

'Come on, Harriet,' I said. 'Come now.'

Nurse Everdeen said to the child: 'Look. This is how we will escape. We will climb the ladder, you first and then me.'

She lifted Harriet up to the window. She was just above me. I reached out for her, but I couldn't touch her; I couldn't help, I could only watch as the nurse encouraged the child to take hold of the sides of the ladder with her little hands, told her to move her legs, lift her feet; go up.

The child did as she was told, but when her foot was on the third step, she looked back down at Nurse Everdeen.

'What about you?' she asked.

'I'll be coming right behind you.'

'Right behind?' Harriet asked.

'Right behind,' the nurse repeated. 'Hurry now. Don't look down.'

I held the bottom of that ladder and Isak held the top. Between us, we held it steady while the little girl, barefoot and wearing a flouncy nightdress that was too big for her, bravely climbed up to the roof. Isak tried to help her but it was as if, for her, we didn't exist.

Emma Everdeen had been looking up, through the small window. She saw that Harriet was up on the roof, out of reach of the fire. I couldn't see, but I imagined the flames must be creeping across the floorboards now, swallowing the rug. The rocking chair would be beginning to burn.

Down below, distantly, I heard a scream. Somebody in the grounds had noticed the flames.

I knew she couldn't hear me, or see me, but I stared at Nurse

Everdeen's face, at her eyes, and although she was trapped in a burning building, she did not look afraid; rather her expression was peaceful.

She stepped back into the room and she disappeared into the light.

95

Maria had not slept. She was in the groom's quarters behind the stable block with Sam Collins and she got up to pour herself a cup of water and looked out of the window and that's when she saw the flames leaping out of the window of the room on the attic floor, and smoke pouring from its chimney.

She dropped the cup and Sam came stumbling from the bedroom in his undergarments.

'What is it, my love?'

She turned, ashen-faced, and pointed.

Sam cried: 'Come on!' and he hopped into his trousers while Maria pulled her dress over her head and then the two of them put on their boots and ran out onto the courtyard. Maria grabbed Sam's shoulder.

'What is it?'

'Up there, Sam, on the roof. Someone is on the roof by the chimney. I think it might be Harriet.'

'I can't see anything.'

'Please, Sam. Please go up there and check. I'll raise the alarm.'

Sam headed off into the asylum, and Maria followed. She went first to wake Mr Pincher, who was sleeping in his bed in the grand apartment in the main building, and he telephoned the fire brigade to come and help, although they told him it would take at least an hour and a half to get there. Then he sounded the main alarm and the staff emerged from their quarters and began to evacuate the west wing, moving the patients out of danger.

Maria stood for a moment, in the midst of the people moving around her, and her instinct was to go up through the west wing, up to the top to see if there was anything she might do to help Nurse Everdeen, but common sense told her she could do more good here.

She went to Ward B. She helped the warder release the patients from their shackles. When all were free, and he was herding them through the door, they cowering from his truncheon, Maria took Thalia Nunes by the arm.

'Where are we going?' Thalia asked, woozy.

'We're getting you away from here,' replied Maria.

96

LEWIS – 1903 AND 1993

Harriet was shivering. She was covered in soot from head to toe. But she was a brave little kid. She sat with her back against the chimney pot and her arms wrapped around herself, clutching the toy rabbit that had been tucked into the neck of her nightdress, and she waited. It was not a good place to sit, right above where the fire was blazing, but we had no means of moving her.

'Come on, Nurse Everdeen,' she whispered into the night air. 'Hurry, please.'

She wasn't alone but she didn't know that. We sat close to her, waiting with her. Mostly the smoke was snatched away by the wind, but sometimes it surrounded her and she would disappear into it and each time I thought she wouldn't come back; each time she did.

From our vantage point, we could see the masses of activity down below. It hadn't taken long for the alarm to be raised about the fire, and already patients were being led out of the asylum, some traipsing out obediently in lines with blankets around their shoulders, others limping, or being carried or pushed. They were assembling at the front of the building, staff in their nightclothes trying to keep them together. One man came out carrying a large parrot cage. Behind him a woman emerged helping another, stooped and stumbling. They turned away from the other patients and disappeared into the shadows.

The flames were breaking out of the windows now; we could hear pops and cracks as structures inside the building gave way.

'We ought to move,' Isak said.

'We can't leave Harriet.'

And we couldn't, although the roof beneath our legs was growing warm now and I was worrying about it giving way and us falling into the fire.

Five more minutes, I told myself, and my mother, although she didn't say anything, took hold of my hand and let me know that she was there.

I started counting to measure the seconds: *One elephant, two elephants,* and when I got to ninety-nine elephants, the shape of a man appeared through the smoke. He was running towards us across the roof of the west wing, from the opposite direction. He was shaggy haired, strong, big-built. He loped over to us, ignored Isak and me, and reached his arms down to Harriet.

'Oh, thank God,' he said, crouching down to be on the level with her, 'thank God you're safe.'

'Hello, Mr Collins,' she said, although her teeth were chattering. 'Where's Mac?'

The man picked her up and held her close to him, as if she were his own daughter.

'Are you hurt, Harriet?'

'No.'

'How did you get up here, little one?'

'Nurse Everdeen said I should climb out of the window and up the ladder.'

Sam Collins looked around. He couldn't see any ladder.
'And where's Nurse Everdeen now?' he asked Harriet.
Harriet took a big gulp. She clutched the rabbit tight.
'She said she would be right behind.'

97

Isak and I followed Sam Collins to the other end of the west wing. We followed him through a service hatch that dropped us down into a different part of the All Hallows building, a cavity in the roof that was pitch-black. We lost sight of him and struggled to find a way out of the cavity. By the time we emerged via a narrow set of stairs, the modern-day fire alarm was ringing. We could tell we were back in the present day by the emergency lighting and the carpet on the floor.

Isak and I spent the rest of that night in the refectory, far away from the fire that was ravaging the west wing. The few other pupils who had stayed for half-term had been evacuated to the refectory too. We were supposed to sleep on PE mats but everyone was too excited to sleep. This was the most dramatic thing that had ever happened to us.

Matron, still in her dressing gown, cooked bacon for sandwiches, and there was as much hot chocolate as we could drink.

We were tired, Isak and I, and our moods went up and down. One minute we were elated at having saved Harriet, the next despondent because we hadn't managed to rescue Nurse Everdeen; that she'd been left in the room above ours to die.

We heard snippets from the staff, and the firefighters when they came in to the refectory to rest. We heard that the fire in the west wing was burning so fiercely now that that part of All Hallows was beyond saving. They had decided to let it burn, and concentrate on saving the rest of it.

* * *

In the morning, a coach came and took Isak and me and the other pupils to the hospital in Plymouth. We were checked over and Isak and I were declared to have suffered smoke inhalation, but nothing too serious. We were sent to a Travelodge to bathe and rest. Matron came with us and stayed in a separate room.

Dr Crozier came to see us. He must have been worried about our safety, we being billeted in the room closest to the seat of the fire. He said the blaze had most probably been caused by an electrical fault: the contractors had been finishing off the repairs to the wiring. He said he would be writing to our fathers to explain. He gave us each a chocolate bar. He did not go so far as to say he was sorry.

* * *

Isak and I were happy in the Travelodge. We had twin beds, an en suite bathroom with lots of little toiletries, a safe in the wardrobe, which was pretty neat, even though we had nothing to put in it, and a television. Food was brought to us regularly. We spent most of our time propped up against our pillows, eating and watching TV.

We mainly watched the kids' programmes for the nostalgia, but one afternoon the news came on and there was Isak's dad shaking hands with other top politicians from different countries. I had the remote control. Isak, without looking up, said: 'Please will you turn that crap off?'

I switched channels to *Teenage Mutant Ninja Turtles*, and Isak cheered and jumped up onto his bed and pretended to be a rock guitarist playing the theme tune. At the end, he leapt off the chair and smashed his imaginary guitar against the wall.

* * *

That same day a call was put through to the telephone in our room. I answered. It was Dad. He asked how I was.

'I'm fine,' I said.

My father cleared his throat. 'Matron says that you'll be well enough to come home tomorrow. Your stepmother and I will come and pick you up.'

I glanced towards Isak, who was pretending not to be listening.

'Actually, Dad,' I said, 'if it's all right with you, I'd rather stay here.'

* * *

After half-term, when school restarted, Isak and I were moved into a dormitory; not in the west wing, which was uninhabitable after the fire, but in the east wing. Isak's bed was three beds away from mine. Our beds were comfortable and the room was lighter, brighter and more modern than our old room. In spite of myself, I found I slept better there. I got to know the boys on either side of me and made friends with them, and Isak seemed to get on with his neighbours too – at least he spoke to them and there were no fights.

Lessons resumed.

Ward B had been destroyed. Detentions, we were told, would take place in our form rooms from now on.

The fire in the west wing was supposed to have been put out but sometimes, when we were outside, doing cross-country, I swear I saw grey wisps of smoke rising up from the ashes. And at night, if I woke up, I could still smell burning. A safety fence was erected around the lake after one of the smaller boys fell in and almost drowned. He said someone had come out of the water and grabbed his ankle to pull him in, but his friend, who was with him, said nobody else was there.

* * *

Isak and I went to the library at the first opportunity. A young man with a beard and plum-coloured corduroy trousers was sitting behind Mrs Goode's desk. We asked about her and he said he didn't know who she was. Isak and I followed the route to the nook where the books about All Hallows history used to be, but it was no longer there either. In its place were lines of shelves containing European language texts. The new librarian said he didn't know anything about All Hallows' history, but when we asked for the books we'd looked at before, he did manage to find Thalia Nunes' *When I Was Mad*, listed in the directory, although the book itself appeared to be missing. Isak and I couldn't remember if it had been up in our room on the night of the fire. Probably it had.

We asked the librarian if he could order another copy. He said that it was not on the curriculum or on any of the recommended reading lists and therefore no, he could not. Isak asked who the book had been published by, and the librarian said Macmillan, one of the biggest publishers ever.

We searched for Nurse Everdeen's nursing manual, but that was not there either.

* * *

As soon as we could get away, Isak and I went outside to the converted stable block. It didn't look the same as it had before; it was shabby and unkempt. We rang the bell and the door was opened by a sour-faced woman. Inside was dark; a fug of cigarette smoke.

'Yes?' the woman said.

'We're looking for Mrs Goode,' said Isak.

'Never heard of her.'

'Whose home is this?' asked Isak.

'It belongs to the Uxbridges,' said the woman. 'It has been passed down through our family for generations.'

One fine winter's day, Isak and I walked across the grounds to the chapel. I vaulted the wall around the graveyard and made it over in one piece this time. I must have grown a few inches over the course of the term. We approached the part of the graveyard where Herbert Everdeen's little gravestone stood. The grave was still there, but now it was tidy. The weeds, dead nettles and brambles that had been there before were gone and in their place were some brightly coloured pansies.

At the top of the headstone were the same words as before, devoted to Herbert Everdeen, aged five years and two months. Below them was a new inscription:

Also, Nurse Emma Everdeen, his adoring mother, who departed this life 1 November 1903.

    A courageous and kind woman who did not know how greatly she was loved, reunited with Herbert and both safe in the hands of God.

The chapel was open now; the roof had been repaired. Isak and I went inside to check the burial records, just to make sure. The entry in the records pertaining to Emma Everdeen confirmed that she had died of suffocation by smoke in the early hours of the morning of November 1st 1903 and that when her body was recovered, a pendant that contained the picture of her son was clasped in her hand. It was buried inside the coffin with her.

We noticed something else. There was a memorial stone fixed to the inside of the chapel wall, commemorating the good work of one of the asylum's early benefactors: Mrs Evelyn Rendall. That must have been where Jacqueline Ozanne found the inspiration for her fake name.

99

I left All Hallows at the end of that term and never returned because the school never reopened. There was some problem with the insurance. Perhaps the company thought All Hallows too big a risk after first the flood and then the fire, and refused to give cover – I don't know. I transferred to a different boarding school, on the South Downs. It was more progressive than All Hallows, less conventional. Punishments consisted of litter picking in the community or clearing graffiti from sports centre walls. After A levels, I went to Bristol University to study architecture and I spent a lot of time with Isobel and Bini, in their flat. Occasionally we had dinner with my father and stepmother and we were all polite to one another. My father did not directly criticise my appearance or my friends or my work, and although he and my stepmother still could not resist the odd small jibe, I did not let them get to me. I had learned that I was all right. I did not need to change or to pretend to be anyone else. I was in love by then, and my girlfriend liked me as I was, and so did my friends.

I could accept that I was not the son my father wanted me to be, and never would be. Nor was he the perfect father. That was fine. We could live with who we were.

Isak returned to Sweden and was expelled from two schools before he was packed off to America, where he finally received some counselling to help him cope with his father's behaviour and the loss of his mother. He also told the counsellor about Mr Crouch and was encouraged to report the teacher to the relevant authorities, which he did. I do not know what happened to Mr Crouch.

Isak fell in love with a boy called Grant, with whom he had been writing songs. Somebody gave them a camper van and they toured the world, performing together at music festivals. Isak was not a reliable correspondent, but he stayed in touch. I wouldn't hear anything for six months, and then a package would arrive for me, care of the university, and it would contain a pair of lanyards holding badges granting backstage access to the VIP areas at Glastonbury, or wherever. My girlfriend and I would go to see them perform, and we'd have the happiest of times with Isak and Grant, wherever they were. We'd laugh and drink, dance at the front of the audience as the night settled over the festival, and listen to their music. I'd watch Isak on the stage, and I was so proud of him.

So proud and full of love.

We're older now, and Isak and Grant aren't together any longer. Isak is now something of a hero of the green movement. He's always busy and I am no less proud. He spends a great deal of time with his and Grant's two daughters and their love for him, and patience with him, is extraordinary.

A few days ago, Isak called me to let me know that his father was dying.

'His new girlfriend messaged me,' said Isak. 'She says he's told her not to say a word to anyone but she thought I should know.

So, do I go and see him and pretend I don't know? Or do I go and tell him the truth? Or do I simply not bother?'

I didn't know what to say. 'I'm sorry,' didn't seem enough, although I *was* sorry. I was desperately sorry for Isak, sorry for all the sadnesses of his past and all that he'd endured.

For Isak, the division between him and his father was, I was certain, the rottenness at the core of all his unhappiness. When you're younger, you tend to think your parents are gods, and that everything they say is right. You think that they will live for ever.

But now the clock was ticking and there were only a few weeks for Isak and his father to mend what was broken. I didn't know if it was even possible.

* * *

My wife's name is Georgia Goode and we've been together since university. We met in the library. She did not recognise me and I did not want to take advantage of having prior knowledge of her – I felt it would be dishonest – so I didn't do or say anything until she spoke to me. Things happened slowly; we were friends for a long time before we were lovers. She invited me to her parents' silver wedding anniversary party. The Goodes lived in a house in the Somerset countryside, on a hill overlooking a reservoir. They had two dogs, a small terrier and a large old Labrador, and the house was untidy and colourful and joyous.

Mrs Goode greeted me warmly: 'It's wonderful to meet you, Lewis. Come in, please; make yourself at home.' And then she stepped back and said: 'Have we met before? Do I know you from somewhere?'

The party, that night, took place in a marquee erected in an orchard, with lights strung through the branches of the apple trees, and moths and bats flitting about. We danced barefoot until the early hours. And afterwards, when the other guests were gone and Georgia, her brothers and I were clearing up, Georgia took off her bracelet and put it to one side where it would be safe. It was the same charm bracelet that I once saw her mother wear.

I picked it up and looked through the charms. Amongst them I found a small, galloping horse, exactly the same as the one my mother used to wear on a cord around her neck; the same as the one I lost all those years earlier in Ward B, only older, and worn smooth. The next morning, at breakfast, I asked Mrs Goode where the charm had come from.

'My great-grandmother gave it to me,' she said. 'It was given to her by a friend of hers called... oh, what was her name? Anyway, she used to be a patient at the asylum where my great-grandmother worked. She found the charm between the floorboards of her cell. Always claimed it had been given to her by a little ghost.'

Later, a different time – I don't recall exactly when – Mrs Goode told me in more detail about her great-grandmother, Maria Smith, and how she used to work at 'some awful great rambling asylum in Devon', how she'd married the groom, Sam Collins, so they could adopt a child orphaned in a fire. The child, on her twenty-first birthday, had access to a large sum of money she'd inherited, which she'd used to build a hospital for women. Maria had been the medical director and run the hospital with enormous success until her death.

'What happened to the child?' I asked.

'She followed in Maria's footsteps: studied medicine at university, went to America, became one of the world's leading paediatric doctors. There's a statue in her honour at Harvard. She set up a charitable foundation. She's done untold good.'

* * *

While I was growing up, I often thought about All Hallows, and the events that took place there, and sometimes I wondered if I had imagined most of it; if my mind, so traumatised by my mother's death, had invented a complex story, one in which I could become a kind of hero; one where I could change the past to produce the outcome I desired. I wondered if it was a way of helping myself to heal and come to terms with what had happened.

Isak and I never spoke of that time. I didn't want to remind him of the pain he was enduring and, I suppose, part of me was afraid that he might tell me my memories were wrong. But occasionally, in the middle of the night, he'd call me.

'I can't sleep, Lewis,' he'd say. 'Come out on the ledge with me while I have a smoke.'

And I would climb out of bed and go to sit by the window, wherever I was, while Isak smoked a cigarette, wherever he was, and we rarely said very much, but even if we were continents apart, we were connected.

It was for the same reason – fear that the whole sequence of events would turn out to be false memories – that I refrained from researching Thalia Nunes' story until I came across a copy of *When I Was Mad* one day in a second-hand bookshop in Brighton. I bought it, obviously, bought myself a coffee, and went to sit on a bench on the seafront to read it. It was evening and I was close to the burned pier, which seemed apt. The starlings were murmurating.

The first part of the book was as I remembered it. But in this version, in the second part, there was a fire in the asylum. The supervising warden in Ward B panicked and unlocked the shackles that bound the inmates. Maria came looking for Thalia and helped her escape. She and Sam hid her in the hayloft above the stables and Maria nursed her back to health. Thalia was assumed lost in the fire by the authorities. When she was well enough, she travelled to London, told her story and joined the suffragette movement. She became a leading light of the campaign, and eventually took up a career in politics, working closely with Nancy Astor and winning a seat in the 1923 general election.

* * *

Georgia and I have three teenage sons and a four-year-old daughter, Maisie, who was a surprise arrival and a delightful one. We are a close family. I try, and have always tried, to be a good father. It's not easy. It is particularly difficult when one of the children says or does something that goes against everything that we, as parents and human beings, believe in and the values we've tried to instil in them.

I understand why my father struggled with me.

I wish my mother had lived to see her grandchildren. I know how much she would have loved them. When we are altogether, our family and Isobel's family, and the kids, and their partners, I sometimes have to wander away, on my own, because I am filled with so much love that I can hardly bear the weight of it. I know that it frustrates Georgia when I do one of my 'disappearing acts' but she understands why I must.

My father and stepmother are both still alive. When we see them, it's usually in a restaurant of their choosing, neutral territory; the kind of place where children aren't encouraged. We choose from a traditional menu and the waiter asks my father, as the senior male, if he'd like to taste the wine. Dad always insists on paying, which is kind. Once, I tried to tell him that I was sorry... I don't know what for exactly, but anyway, he brushed me away.

'There's no need for that kind of conversation, Lewis,' he said.

So, we will never have one of those father-son-making-peace-with-one-another chats that you see in films and read about in books. That's OK, I guess. Not everything in life has to be resolved.

* * *

My mother still talks to me. Less frequently now, or perhaps it's just that I don't always hear her, my life being so full and my mind so busy.

Whenever I see a dappled horse with a long mane, I think of her and Zephyr. Several times a year, Georgia and I put on hi-vis tabards and go out with our local community group to litter pick along the verges of the lanes and country roads and with each fast-food wrapper I pull from the hedgerows I imagine a horse not being startled, a life saved.

Maisie is only four but already she's pony-mad. Some passions run in the blood.

Once, I started to tell her that horses were dangerous creatures.

Don't put fear into the child's head, my mother said. *Don't hold her back. Let her follow her dreams.*

Maisie likes to play with Georgia's charm bracelet. One day she will inherit it. For now, she spends ages examining the charms to decide which ones she likes best. Her favourite, obviously, is the galloping horse.

* * *

Before I returned to All Hallows that last time, I took out Thalia Nunes' book, and I turned to the section about the fire. Thalia had recorded Harriet's escape and praised Nurse Emma Everdeen for her courage and selflessness in saving the child.

She went on to write about the fate of Mrs March.

Several witnesses reported seeing Mrs March, as she was known, amongst the other patients assembled outside the building as the fire took hold. Dr Milligan, who was, that night, suffering from a mystery malaise that caused great inertia, himself observed that she was safe. But later, when she saw Harriet being carried safely from the blaze, Mrs March seemed to break down. She snatched the child from the arms of her rescuer and tried to run with her back into the blazing building, but was stopped before any harm came to Harriet. Later, one of the nursing staff swore she had seen Mrs March gathering stones from the garden. And later still, the chaplain, who had been approaching from the other direction, said he had seen a woman fitting Mrs March's description walking into the lake. It seemed the stones were intended to weigh her down.

Her body, if it was in the lake, was never recovered.

EPILOGUE

At the services, on the way back from All Hallows, I bought a coffee and a sandwich and remembered Tracy and thought what an odd couple we must have been; the long-suffering cleaning woman and the skinny Goth kid with the weird hair and make-up.

And then I remembered the woman coming out of the lake and the smile died on my lips.

When I returned to the office, I'd recommend that Redcliffe Architects didn't tender for the design work for the redevelopment of All Hallows. I'd say the building was unsuitable for conversion to residential use; that its condition was poor, the fire damage too great. All of this was true, but the real reason was that something dreadful lingered in that place, something that should be left well alone.

Some wrongs can never be put right. Not all pain can be alleviated. Human beings are an optimistic bunch, but it's disingenuous to think there will always be a happy ending; that that which we believe to be right will always triumph.

I finished my snack, picked up the catalogue and I went

outside into the fresh air. I felt terribly lonely; as if the world was carrying on, spinning around me, and I was by myself; trapped by memories I could not share, truths I could never tell.

But I wasn't entirely alone.

I took my phone out of my pocket, a photograph of my wife and children as the screensaver, and I called Isak. He picked up on the third ring.

'Hey,' I said.

'Hey. You OK?'

'Yeah. I was just wondering if you had decided what to do about visiting your father?'

'No,' said Isak. 'I mean, I know I should go but...'

'I'll come with you,' I said. 'We'll go together.'

'Seriously?'

'Yeah. I can fly to Stockholm from Bristol. I'll be there first thing tomorrow. I'll drive you. And afterwards, if you want to, we can get drunk and, you know, hang out.'

Isak was quiet for a moment. 'You'd do that for me?'

I stood and watched the traffic roaring by. I felt the world moving about me.

'It's no big deal,' I said.

And on the other side of Europe, my best friend said: 'OK!' and in Somerset my mother whispered in my ear: *Well done, Lewis. Good work!*

ACKNOWLEDGMENTS

Thank you to my truly wonderful agent, Marianne Gunn O'Connor, Pat Lynch, Alison Walsh and Vikki Satlow. I know how lucky I am to have you on my side. Sincere and heartfelt thanks to the brilliant Boldwood Books team, especially my amazing editor Sarah Ritherdon, but also to Nia Beynon, Claire Fenby, Amanda Ridout, Rose Fox, Yvonne Holland, Alice Moore who designed the cover and everyone else at #TeamBoldwood. You are the best. Thank you to everyone involved in printing, producing, designing, recording the audio version, marketing, selling and in other ways working for the benefit of this book.

Thank you to everyone who supports me and my books in my real and virtual life; family, friends, booksellers, bloggers, authors, librarians, readers and the fantastic Romantic Novelists' Association. You are so important to me and I really do appreciate you all.

The Room in the Attic was written in the South West of England during the 2020 and 2021 lockdowns, a time when we were all, to some extent, confined to our rooms. Because I wasn't able to visit Dartmoor, or any of the other locations in this book, the descriptions are from memory and imagination and I apologise for any errors. All Hallows and its inhabitants are entirely fictional. Dartmoor Prison is still a working gaol but is due to close in 2023. As far as I know, no real woman has ever been put to death within its walls.

Phyllis Chesler's classic feminist work Women and Madness was immensely helpful during the writing of this book. All the 'treatments' and punishments mentioned in The Room in the Attic were used at some time in asylums within Britain, North America and Australia. Thalia Nunes is not based on any real woman, but many real women suffered similar fates.

Finally, from the bottom of my heart, I'd like to thank the National Health Service and all the brave, committed and incredible people who work for it. This book was born from a desire to say 'thank you' to you all for everything you have done to help us through the pandemic and specifically for the care given to members of my own family.

READING GROUP QUESTIONS

1. There are two stories in this book, the turn-of-the-century story of Harriet and Emma Everdeen and the later account of Lewis and Isak's friendship. Which do you feel is the stronger storyline? And why?

2. Are there any themes in the 1903 story about All Hallows asylum that are relevant today? What about the 1993 story?

3. The author has stated that one of the strongest themes of The Room in the Attic is 'Motherhood' even though most of the mothers are missing. Do you agree? Why/why not?

4. What is your opinion of Nurse Emma Everdeen? Would you trust her to look after your child?

5. How much is Emma a victim of her time? Would her life have been very different if she'd been born in 1960? Or 1990?

6. Is the room in the attic a safe haven for Emma and Harriet, or is it a prison?

7. The Thalia Nunes character represents the many real
    women who were consigned, without recourse, to
    asylums by their husbands and parents over the
    centuries. Would you have liked to read more about
    this, or less, or is the balance about right?

8. In what ways is All Hallows itself a character in this
    book?

9. Did you spot the ways in which The Room in the Attic
    pays homage to Gothic classics such as Jane Eyre, The
    Turn of the Screw, Rebecca and Wuthering Heights?

10. How do you feel about Lewis's father? Is he a good
    man or not?

11. How important is friendship to this story?

12. Both Isak and Lewis have lost their mothers. How is
    grief affecting each boy differently?

13. Are the ghosts real? Or did Lewis, with his
    imagination, create a fantasy story in which he could
    be a hero and save a life in order to come to terms with
    his mother's death?

14. In what ways (if any) might The Room in the Attic be
    described as a feminist book?

MORE FROM LOUISE DOUGLAS

We hope you enjoyed reading *The Room in the Attic*. If you did, please leave a review.

If you'd like to gift a copy, this book is also available as an ebook, digital audio download and audiobook CD.

Sign up to Louise Douglas' mailing list for news, competitions and updates on future books.

http://bit.ly/LouiseDouglasNewsletter

The House By The Sea another chilling and captivating novel from Louise Douglas is available now.

ABOUT THE AUTHOR

Louise Douglas is the bestselling and brilliantly reviewed author of 6 novels including *The Love of my Life* and *Missing You* - a RNA award winner. *The Secrets Between Us* was a Richard and Judy Book Club pick. She lives in the West Country.

Follow Louise on social media:

facebook.com/Louise-Douglas-Author-340228039335215

twitter.com/louisedouglas3

bookbub.com/authors/louise-douglas

ABOUT BOLDWOOD BOOKS

Boldwood Books is a fiction publishing company seeking out the best stories from around the world.

Find out more at www.boldwoodbooks.com

Sign up to the Book and Tonic newsletter for news, offers and competitions from Boldwood Books!

http://www.bit.ly/bookandtonic

We'd love to hear from you, follow us on social media:

facebook.com/BookandTonic

twitter.com/BoldwoodBooks

instagram.com/BookandTonic

Printed in Great Britain
by Amazon

86415344R00224